The Capricorn Affair

By

Tim Dale

To my wife Pat.

ISBN-13: 978-1981937790
ISBN-10: 198193779X

Prologue

Johannesburg – Thursday 9th June 1977

The motorcycle weaved through the Johannesburg traffic. The rider was clearly enjoying himself. But he was minutes from death. A black Mercedes van approached from behind. The rider was thrown into the air and came down directly in the path of a lorry. People rushed to the prostrate figure. A horrified crowd gathered. A man went into a nearby shop to call the emergency services. When he came out the crowd had grown but most people were standing a little apart from the tragic scene. He suddenly became aware that the van that had caused the accident was nowhere to be seen.

It was several blocks away. The driver was concentrating on getting through the traffic as quickly as he could without drawing attention to himself. In the passenger seat a fair-haired young man was examining the package that had been strapped to the pillion seat of the motorcycle. He had snatched it while everyone had been focusing on the injured rider. He looked at the label. It was addressed to 'Dr Lothar Neethling, Chief Deputy Commissioner, South African Police – Forensics Unit'.

"What have you got there?" asked the driver.

"Nothing to interest you; just drive, man."

They lapsed into silence.

Sometime later the van pulled into a deserted area on

an industrial site. A faded sign was visible over one of the derelict buildings. It read 'South African Breweries'.

The passenger got out of the vehicle.

"On your way," he said to the driver. The van drove off.

He took the parcel into the building. The first area he entered was a warehouse. Small red lights gave away the presence of CCTV cameras. At the far end was a heavy roller door. Two armed guards waited for the fair-haired man to produce an identity card. They waved him on. The card was inserted into a reader and the door rolled upwards. He went through into a second similar area. In the far corner was a spacious cubicle. It was hermetically sealed off from the rest of the building. The ventilation system had been designed with 'negative pressure' – a system whereby the air pressure was kept at a slightly lower level than that outside. If any air from the cubicle was inadvertently allowed to escape it was immediately drawn back.

He punched in an eight digit number and entered an inner chamber. Through a small window he could see a figure encased from head to toe in protective clothing. Only the eyes were visible and they were totally sealed within the garment. He placed the package on a small shelf and activated a glass partition sealing it from the outside. The figure opened a similar partition on the inside and took the package. The fair-haired man exited.

A little while later a woman emerged. She had changed into normal clothes after showering in a chamber within the sealed unit.

"Everything OK?" he asked.

"Yes," replied the woman. "I have stored it in liquid nitrogen at minus eighty. It should be alright there for the time being – as long as nobody finds it and tries to mess with it."

"Don't worry on that score. Nobody will get near it,

trust me."

"I see it was addressed to Lothar Neethling; who is he exactly?" she asked.

"Quite an interesting guy. He came to South Africa from Germany after the war. Some Afrikaners sympathetic to the Nazis had set up something called the German Children's Fund. The idea was to adopt a number of German orphans. A boy of thirteen, Lothar Tietz, was adopted by the chairman of that organization, Dr Neethling. The boy took his name and became a South African. They say he is a brilliant scientist, very much part of the apartheid establishment. He set up the forensics unit of the South African police."

The woman looked towards the sealed unit.

"We badly need someone to deal with this who has expert knowledge," she said. "I do not have the background to analyse this sample properly. You need an experienced microbiologist to take it on."

"Leave it to me," he said.

He got into a car that was parked outside the building and drove away.

Sometime later he pulled into the car park of a sports club in Vereeniging, south Johannesburg.

He was met in the foyer by a young woman. She was striking in appearance; dark hair, brown eyes, deeply tanned skin, an athletic female figure. She was from Cuba.

"Everything OK?" she enquired.

"Yes. The motorcycle rider was almost certainly killed but we got away quickly without being challenged."

"Good." Clearly she was indifferent to the motorcycle rider's fate.

"What's the panic about?" he asked.

"Sorry it was all so rushed," she replied. "We only got wind of it a few days ago."

"Got wind of what?"

"That the package was on its way."

"What exactly is in it?" he asked. "I know it is a blood sample but it must be a bit special for us to want it so much."

The young woman paused, deciding how to answer the question.

"Last year an epidemic broke out at a mission in Zaire. The doctor at the mission could not identify the illness. He sent a blood sample of a sick nun back to Europe. He asked for help in analysing the sample. The Belgian scientist who dealt with it, a man called Peter Piot, has subsequently gone to Zaire."

"What happened to the nun?"

"She died – like everyone who contracts this illness. They get a fever which gradually worsens and then they start bleeding – internally and sometimes from the mouth, ears and eyes; they bleed to death."

"How horrible. Do they know what the illness is yet?"

"Only that it is a new virus. Originally they thought it might be Lassa fever or Marburg virus but it is different to both."

"Has the virus got a name yet?"

"Not that I know of," replied the Cuban. "They'll probably call it something like Yambuku virus. The mission is at a place called Yambuku – about a thousand kilometres north of Kinshasa. It's at the most northerly point of the River Congo where a tributary, the River Ebola, runs into it."

"How did we get on to this?"

"A subordinate of Neethling got to hear of it through a South African doctor working near the mission. He asked to have a similar sample sent to the SA police forensics unit. That is what you have just intercepted."

"Why do they want it?"

"The government is alleged to be thinking of starting up a section of the South African Defence Force provisionally codenamed 'Project Coast'. It is very much in an embryo stage at the moment."

"What is its purpose?"

"To develop a South African chemical and biological warfare capability."

"Bastards." He spat the word out. "Well, they may get a dose of their own medicine if we can find out what this stuff is and what it can be used for."

"That's where you come in," she said. "Your job is to come up with someone who has enough expertise in this field to analyse what is in this blood sample and take the work forward. Do you know of anyone suitable?"

"I met a guy at university – Stuart Holder – he was a leading biologist – went to work at the UK's top microbiological research place on Dartmoor."

"Is he up to it?"

"I can find out. If he is, I think I know a way to persuade him to come."

"OK, do it."

Chapter One

London – Monday 12th September 1977

"Got a moment, Mark?" The voice of Geoffrey Pritchard, predictably known to his subordinates as 'Pritch', was at once courteous yet authoritative.

"I'm on my way," said Harvey. He walked out of his office putting on his jacket.

Harvey sat down opposite Pritchard and looked at the older man; not that he was that old, he thought – fifties maybe. He just looked as if he had seen quite a few sobering sights; that nothing much would surprise him anymore. The greying hair at his temples and the scar that ran from his left eye to the corner of his mouth were testimony to the action they had been through together. Harvey could never look at that scar without remembering a foul winter's night in the Falls Road, at the height of the Troubles. He had saved Pritchard's life that night; a favour Pritchard had returned on two subsequent occasions.

Geoffrey Pritchard was the commander of an elite squad formed specifically to fight the growing threat of terrorism – both within the country and internationally. Mark Harvey had worked on his team for three years. He respected the older man greatly. Pritchard, in turn, had a high opinion of Harvey. He assessed him as mentally strong, quick to react, possessed of sound judgement, cool under fire; in fact the only thing wrong with him was his obsession with golf – bloody stupid game, thought Pritchard. As far as he was concerned real men played rugby.

"Good morning, Mark; how's the golf?" Pritchard began with the regular banter.

"I'm thinking of changing from overlapping to interlocking." Harvey played along.

"I was talking about your golf not your sex life." Prichard was pleased at winning the exchange. "Right. Business. I have fixed you up with a date tonight; very nice looking girl by all accounts. I wish I was free to go myself. She will be at the British Airways Victoria terminal at 6 p.m. tonight, in the lounge on the first floor. She is twenty-eight years old, blonde, about five-foot-eight with green eyes; she will be wearing a navy skirt and white blouse."

"Sounds very nice; who is she?"

"Susan Bennett. In her own right she wouldn't normally be of interest to us but she has an unsavoury friend. Do you remember Neil Jardine?"

Harvey was silent for a few moments. He certainly did remember Neil Jardine. In his previous job, in Special Branch, he had the task of going through the television footage of the October 1968 anti-Vietnam war demonstration in Grosvenor Square. It was the second such demonstration. The first one in March had been particularly unpleasant. This one was smaller. Nevertheless, there had been a very nasty moment when a group of demonstrators charged the police cordon. Right at the front had been a fair-haired young man. Harvey had never forgotten that face contorted with hate. He had ultimately identified the man as Neil Jardine.

"Yes I do; what is he up to now?" he replied.

"We are not sure. This girl – Susan Bennett – went to South Africa recently. She is a salesgirl at Harrods – works in the Skirts and Blouses department. It seems she was legitimately on holiday and there was no reason why we would have been interested in that. But on the way out she spent time talking to Neil Jardine in the departure lounge – presumably on the plane as well, although we have no certain knowledge of that. Anyway, she obviously knew him. The South African authorities keep a watch on Jardine's movements. When he was at the University of Kent he was very much involved in the 'Stop The Seventy Tour' – you remember, the campaign to prevent the South African cricket team touring England in 1970. As a result he is not top of their Christmas card list. However, he seems harmless enough these days; runs a recruitment agency for secretarial temps in Johannesburg."

"So what is the problem?" asked Harvey.

"There may not be one; but Bennett was also involved in the Stop The Seventy Tour. She was at Kent University at the same time as Jardine. The guys in the Bureau of State Security – BOSS – South Africa's security service, are always bloody paranoid as you know. They see plots and treachery everywhere – but it does seem a little odd that Jardine and Bennett are getting together again. I'd like you to meet her and find out what, if anything, is going on."

Pritchard looked at his watch.

"I must go now, Mark. I'm meeting Gordon Peters from Boughton. I don't want to be late."

Harvey strolled pensively back to his office. He felt ill at ease but whether it was Jardine that was troubling him was doubtful. More likely it was the mention of Boughton. He knew of Peters, the head of security at Boughton Microbiological Research Centre on Dartmoor. The suspicion of what went on inside that fortress never failed to appal him. However, that was not his responsibility. Jardine was. He turned his mind to the matter in hand.

Once in his office, he locked the door and went over to the wall safe. Inside were a number of computer diskettes, arranged in alphabetical order. He took out the ones marked 'J' and 'BE', relocked the safe and went over to the mini-computer in the corner of his office. He loaded the 'BE' diskette and opened the file with his access password.

The computer was a novelty. It had been installed only recently; the first one Harvey and Pritchard had ever had in the department. The programmer had shown him how to key-in a password. It had been impressed on him that he should not share this word with anyone. The only person he would have been tempted to share it with was Pritchard, but that worthy regarded the computer with great suspicion as a new-fangled gadget. He refused to have anything to do with it; hence it was in Harvey's office.

He realized his password was a mistake. 'Kate1971' brought it all back too painfully. They had been on the point of getting married when MI6 had sent her to East Pakistan in 1971. She had never come back. Six years later he still had no idea what had happened to her. He had not had a meaningful relationship since. He told himself he must get hold of that damn programmer and get the word changed.

There was very little about Susan Bennett.

Name: Susan Bridget Bennett

Date of Birth: 25.2.1949

Father: Edward Bennett – farmer in Woodchurch, Kent

Mother: Mary Dorothy Bennett, née Painter

School: St Mary's Convent – St Leonards-on-Sea,

Sussex. Left July 1967

University: Kent University 1967 to 1970, Lower Second in Sociology

Political Action: Passing acquaintance of Neil Phillip Jardine
Involved in 'Stop The Seventy Tour' campaign
No recorded political activity since

Children: Boy, David, born 28.2.1971. Father unknown

Employment: Harrods Ltd, Knightsbridge – started October 1972

File closed: 31.12.1973

Hardly the stuff of revolution, mused Harvey. Many young people got involved in some cause or another at university. Most of them settled down into a conventional lifestyle in due course. Susan Bennett was probably destined for that.

Harvey switched the diskettes. There was a very much larger file on Jardine. Shortly the printer beside the IBM began to chatter. Harvey locked the diskettes away in the safe again. He gathered up the sheets from the printer, sat down at his desk, and began to read.

The British Airways terminal at Victoria was not crowded. As Harvey made his way up the stairs to the first floor he recognized Susan at once.

"Susan Bennett?" he enquired, smiling.

"Yes, you must be Mark Harvey." She realized she had expected an older man in a raincoat; overweight, thin on top and a bit pompous. That was how she imagined detectives to be. Instead the man who stood before her was over six feet tall with dark hair and the hard muscular build of an athlete. She judged him to be in his mid-thirties. She was well aware that his blue eyes were taking in her face and figure with a healthy interest. She did not mind or feel embarrassed. Good-looking, masculine men seemed to Susan to be an endangered species. She was pleasantly surprised to be meeting one.

His handshake was firm but considerate. He didn't crush her hand. She noticed his Sidi suit and thought that he looked like a successful young lawyer or stockbroker. She was not to know that the deep lines at the corner of his eyes were not the result of the 5.45 Waterloo to Woking but a legacy of Shankill Road.

"I've got my car outside," he said. "Let's go somewhere where we can talk in peace and quiet."

He drove up Sloane Street, under Bowater House, into Hyde Park and parked beside Rotten Row. The area around the Serpentine was crowded with tourists and students. They walked over to some benches next to a deserted bandstand.

"You must be wondering what this is all about," he began.

"Very much so; all I know is that Mr Jefferson, our Chief of Security at Harrods, called me down to his office this morning and told me the police wanted me to help with an enquiry. He gave me the date and time of this meeting. I didn't see any reason to refuse so here I am."

"You've just been to South Africa haven't you?"

"Yes."

"Would you mind telling me why you went there?"

The girl was silent for a moment. Harvey could see she was calculating how much to tell him.

"I can't believe this can be of interest to the police," she said. "It's not a crime to feel out the lie of the land about moving jobs is it? I know I haven't said anything about it to Harrods, but even if they have found out, they can't be referring it to the police surely?"

"Is that why you went there?"

"Yes. I'd rather Harrods didn't know but I went to have an interview for a job at Stuttafords in Adderley Street, Cape Town. You may wonder, Mr Harvey, why a graduate of twenty-eight is still a salesgirl. The reason is I have a little boy of six. Harrods has been flexible in helping me at half-term and school holiday times but it is preventing my career going anywhere. I have an aunt and uncle in Cape Town. They have offered to ferry David – that's my son – to and from school. I could then work full-time and build a career at Stuttafords.

"How well do you know Neil Jardine?" asked Harvey.

Susan blinked wide in surprise. Harvey thought she had beautiful green eyes.

"That's a bit of a change of tack," she said. "I used to know him in my university days at Kent. The last I saw of him was in the summer of 1970 – that is until my recent flight out to South Africa. By an amazing coincidence he was on the same flight."

Harvey looked closely at the girl but she gave no sign that she was not telling the truth.

"The thing is, Miss Bennett, in my line of work we don't like amazing coincidences. Did you know he was going to be on the plane?"

"Absolutely not. If I had I would have taken a different flight."

"You don't like him?"

"No I don't."

"Why not?"

"Well if you must know he was a nuisance at university. He had a thing about me. I found him repulsive. Eventually I had to have a showdown and tell him to stop pestering me."

"When exactly was the last time you saw him before this recent meeting?"

Susan hesitated. He could see that there was something she did not want to tell him.

A golden retriever suddenly bounded up to them and insisted on giving Harvey a boisterous welcome.

"Friend of yours?" asked Susan.

"Never seen him in my life before; nice dog though."

A harassed middle-aged woman appeared. "Humphrey, come here, you naughty boy! I do hope he hasn't been a nuisance."

"No problem; he's a great dog." Harvey was indulgent.

"Wretched hound." The woman attached a lead and was whisked off by the dog on some new adventure.

"Sorry about that; go on." Harvey sought to get the conversation back on track. He was frustrated that the dog had given Susan time to think.

"Do people really call dogs Humphrey?" she giggled.

Harvey remained silent; he required an answer to his question.

"We were both involved in The Stop The Seventy Tour campaign. It was ultimately successful and the tour was called off. The last time I saw him was just after that. That was when I told him to leave me alone."

Harvey sensed a change of nuance; her tone was defensive. She was keeping something back. What was she hiding?

"How was it between you on the flight?"

"Pretty ordinary really. I only met him quite by chance in duty-free when we were waiting for the flight to be called."

"And on the plane?"

"Once when we were queuing for the loo. He may have engineered that."

"Any idea why?"

Susan Bennett looked at Mark Harvey, raised one eyebrow, crossed her legs and smiled demurely.

"Yes, OK; point taken." He smiled back. "What did he talk about?"

"We just chatted generally. He asked me about my trip. I told him I was going on holiday. He wanted to get into the business of whether I supported apartheid. I told him I did not but that was not a reason why I should not visit the place."

"I suppose there could be a conflict there – I mean between your joining the Stop The Seventy Tour campaign in 1970 and going for a job interview in South Africa now?"

"I was twenty-one then. I'm twenty-eight now. You see things differently. I do not support apartheid in any sense at all; but then I don't support the government here – cow-towing to the unions and bringing the country to its knees."

"Did you get the job? Are you going to go there?"

"I don't know. They said they'd write to me. I'm still waiting to hear."

"Have you had any further contact with Neil Jardine?"

"No."

There was silence between them. Susan seemed at a loss to know why the police should be so interested in her trip to South Africa. Harvey was trying to gauge her truthfulness.

He stirred himself.

"Can you think of anything, however seemingly inconsequential, that you haven't told me; particularly anything that might indicate whether Jardine's presence on the plane was a coincidence or planned?"

She looked taken aback

"Do you think he had planned it then? That would actually quite frighten me."

"Why frighten?"

"Well I always thought he was a bit unstable. At university we were all on a mission against apartheid but it was more than that with him. He was filled with a terrible hatred. He was quite a frightening person. The thought that he might have kept track of my movements for the last seven years… that really would be creepy."

"But he was OK this time?"

"Yes, he seemed pretty ordinary."

"How did you part?"

"I had to change planes at Johannesburg. He got off there."

Harvey decided he could get no further. The best thing would be to sleep on it and have a talk with Pritchard in the morning.

He looked at the girl beside him. She was wary and looked somewhat strained. Even so, he had to admit she was a very attractive young woman. He had become only too conscious of her physical presence beside him. Come to think of it, he was supposed to be finding out all he could about her, wasn't he?

"Look, I don't know about you but I'm feeling decidedly peckish; can I buy you a bite to eat?"

Susan was programmed to block that sort of approach. For six years she had had to be at home every night to look after David. Even now her first thought was to get back to him. He should be in bed soon. Neighbours on the floor above her flat were looking after him until she returned. But she was drawn to Harvey. She was unsettled at being summoned by the police and felt tense. He seemed reassuring and in control.

A number of young men had offered to take her out since she came to London. She had accepted one or two invitations. They had drifted away when they realized the good looks and stunning figure were not on offer for them. They had been boys. Mark Harvey was clearly a man; a strong man; a thoughtful man; a passably good-looking man – even bloody dogs liked him for God's sake; what was she waiting for?

"I must go home and look after David," she said, "but if you can survive until 7.30 he will be in bed and I might be able to stretch the spaghetti bolognese to two."

"OK done," he replied. "I'll drive you home and while you attend to David I'll go and buy a bottle of wine to go with the meal."

They stood up and began to walk back to his car. An elderly lady sitting on an adjacent bench watched them go past. They made a fine couple, she thought; young and good-looking. She wished she were their age again.

Chapter Two

London – The Next Morning

Geoffrey Pritchard looked as if he had been up all night. His face was tired and drawn. His tone was peremptory when he summoned Harvey to his office.

"Sit down, Mark," he said curtly.

Harvey took a seat. He noticed there was no golf banter today.

"I'm afraid we have got ourselves a serious problem," began Pritchard. "As you know I had a meeting yesterday with Gordon Peters, the chief of security at Boughton."

Harvey had not seen the boss looking so worried for some time.

"Not to beat about the bush we have a man missing from Boughton. Not just any man; the top scientist working on virus research. We have to face the possibility that he may have taken a highly toxic virus with him as well."

The room was very quiet. Biological warfare was something few people knew much about. Anybody with any imagination at all found it very frightening.

"If he has taken something, the problem could be more than serious. Apparently it is possible to multiply a virus from pretty small amounts. If you know what you are doing it is not that difficult. It only requires access to a lot of eggs and some chemicals that are pretty widely available. It could be done undercover in something like a pharmaceutical plant. The missing person, a man called Stuart Holder, most definitely does know what he is doing; he is the best we have."

"How would he get a virus out of Boughton?" asked Harvey.

"Well, there's the rub," responded Pritchard. "Peters is adamant that he could not have done so. The security protocols at Boughton are very strict. The virus Holder was working on is a category four pathogen. To you and me that means it's bloody dangerous. No one can go near it without proper authority being signed off. Anybody working on this stuff would have to be in complete protective clothing. There would be no way they could smuggle anything in or out. Peters says it's impossible."

Harvey looked at Pritchard unconvinced.

"Lots of things are impossible until someone figures out a way to do it," he said.

"Precisely." After a pause, Pritchard continued, "They only realized something was up when Holder failed to come to work yesterday. It is taking time to double-check if anything is missing. Our task is to get everything back – and Holder alive preferably."

"Have we any idea where he is now?" asked Harvey.

"South Africa we think."

"Why there?"

"Not certain, but we do know that Holder and Jardine both flew out to South Africa the night before last. Due to the nature of his job, security around Holder, while low key, is present. We like to know where he is. When he didn't show for work yesterday, without notifying Boughton, Peters checked every possible avenue; found him and Jardine on a British Airways passenger list to

Johannesburg. Unless he has gone on to somewhere else he must still be in South Africa. Peters is working on that as we speak."

"Have we any idea as to why he has suddenly disappeared?" asked Harvey.

"No, not at the moment. It is right out of character. We suspect Jardine may be behind it. He knew Holder. They were at Kent University at the same time and went around together. We are guessing that Holder is acting under duress. What Jardine might have on him we don't know. Peters and I are working on that as well."

Harvey was thoughtful. "We seem to be building up quite a little party of ex Kent University people," he said. "Counting Susan Bennett we are now up to three. What makes you think they are in cahoots?"

"We don't know that they are. What did you think of Bennett?"

"She seemed pretty normal. Says she went to South Africa for a job interview. I checked that this morning and it's correct. Says she had no idea Jardine would be on the plane. In fact the idea that it might not have been a coincidence definitely seemed to scare her. My judgement is that everything she actually told me was the truth. I did feel that she was holding something back about the end of her time with Jardine on the Stop The Seventy Tour campaign. Nothing I could put my finger on – just a feeling."

"Anything else?"

"I didn't get round to asking her about her boy. Probably nothing of consequence but there doesn't seem to be a father about."

"Do you need more time with her?"

"Certainly wouldn't be a hardship."

"Oh I see; getting the testosterone swishing around is she? Let's hope to God she doesn't play golf. I'd never see either of you again."

Harvey felt unaccountably defensive and changed the subject.

"What's Holder's security record like?"

"Hitherto excellent; no reason to suspect him of foul play. This is entirely out of character which is why we presume duress from Jardine. The only possible factor suggesting he could have gone voluntarily is that he has a black wife. He will presumably be no friend of apartheid South Africa."

"What was he working on? Anthrax? That's the usual thing isn't it?"

"No, Mark, not anthrax; much worse than that."

"Worse? What can possibly be worse?"

"Something you have probably never heard of – Ebola."

"What the hell is Ebola?"

"It's a tributary of the River Congo in Zaire." Pritchard paused.

"And…?" prompted Harvey.

"You are probably more familiar with the place under its old name of The Belgian Congo. The River Congo runs right through the country and one of its tributaries is the River Ebola. In that area a new virus was discovered last year. It was slow to be recognized as a separate illness because it starts off very much like malaria – fever, headache, sickness, diarrhoea, muscle pain. However, it soon takes on other really horrible symptoms. An infected person might start bleeding; internally and from the mouth, ears and eyes."

"For crying out loud!" exclaimed Harvey. "What the hell are we doing messing about with stuff like this? I thought there had been a convention banning it."

"You are quite right," answered Pritchard. "The Biological and Toxin Weapons Convention came into full effect two years ago. Biological research with a view to offensive military capability is halted…"

The telephone on Pritchard's desk suddenly erupted into life.

"I said no calls, Lesley." Pritchard was clearly impatient; there was a pause while a voice could be heard on the line.

Harvey had a lot of time for Pritchard's PA, Lesley Joyce. She was efficient, cheerful and easy to look at. He had taken her out once or twice. They had got on well on a just-friends basis.

"Alright, put him through." Pritchard put his hand over the mouth-piece and whispered to Harvey, "Peters."

"Good morning, Gordon. What can I do for you?"

The conversation proceeded with Peters doing most of the talking. Eventually Pritchard wound it up.

"Thank you for updating me. I'll get back to you when we have decided our next move."

He put the phone back on its cradle.

"I'll put you in the picture in a moment… So, where were we? Oh yes the 1972 agreement. Actually I ought to go back to 1969. Richard Nixon ordered a halt to all offensive biological research. America then pressed hard for a universal embargo. The result was the 1972 agreement."

"Why did he do that?" asked Harvey. "I thought the UK and the States were leaders in the field."

"He claimed it was for humanitarian reasons. That was garbage. The real reason was that biological weapons are cheaper and easier to conceal than nuclear ones. America is the richest country in the world. It's in their interest to make war as expensive as possible. If they stick to nuclear weapons – which are cripplingly expensive – they can out-spend the Soviets. Once they go to biological weapons they do not have that edge."

"Yes, I see," said Harvey.

"Anyway the upshot was the 1972 agreement. It is more than doubtful that the Soviets are honouring it.

Satellite surveillance shows continued activity at their plant at Zagorsk, outside Moscow. However, we are still active in this sphere as well. Our interest is supposedly directed towards finding vaccines and a viable defence against a germ warfare attack."

"I don't like the word 'supposedly' in there." Harvey was suspicious.

"Let's not get into that." Pritchard was dismissive.

Harvey knew when not to press.

"OK but why Ebola? As I said, I thought a more usual agent was something like anthrax?

"You will have to bear with me here. I am not an expert in this field and only know what Peters has told me – and he is a security man not a scientist. He explained that things have moved on from germs and bacteria which is what anthrax is. Efforts are concentrated on virus research these days. Apparently a virus is much smaller than a germ and infiltrates the human body more easily. Also, bacteria can be countered by antibiotics whereas viruses are immune to them. Ebola is a virus not a germ. Once the disease has taken hold there is no known treatment. It is usually fatal." Pritchard paused; he had been forced to learn a great deal about the subject of biological warfare in a short space of time. He was resolved to pass it on as accurately as he could to Harvey.

"Apparently the goal is not necessarily to wipe out the enemy with a deadly disease; that is science fiction stuff. The current thinking is what they call 'controlled incapacitation'. The idea is to have large numbers of the enemy languishing in their sick beds; that ties up more resources than if they are just killed off."

He cleared his throat to continue.

"Any chance of a cup of coffee?" interrupted Harvey.

Pritchard rolled his eyes skyward.

"Lesley!" he called. "Jack Nicklaus here wants his caddy to bring him some coffee!"

Lesley appeared shortly with coffee.

Harvey looked at the girl as she entered; just a run-of-the-mill, good-looking secretary in a short skirt, you'd think. You would be wrong. Harvey was one of the few people who knew – he was one of the few men who had bothered to ask her about her life – that she coped with tragedy every single day. She had a little boy with cerebral palsy. The father had taken off when he learned how much dedication was going to be involved in looking after his son. She smiled at Harvey when she gave him his coffee.

Back to business. Pritchard was speaking again.

"Anyway our job is to find Holder and any substance or substances he is working on. We are talking about small quantities so it will be like looking for a needle in a haystack the size of Western Europe."

"Sounds like a walk in the park," said Harvey ruefully.

"It gets worse. The problem with Ebola as a biological weapon is getting it started. As far as we know it is not airborne. It is contracted through contact with an infected person's bodily fluids. Once started it spreads like wild-fire but you have to get it started first. The idea is that, if they can blend it with something else more infectious, it would become easier to spread in the first place. For that reason Holder was also working on two other viruses – myxomatosis and smallpox."

Harvey was appalled. "An Ebola myxomatosis mixture – sounds like a prescription from hell. Incidentally, what did Peters have to say just now?"

"He is certain, in fact adamant, that nothing is missing from Boughton."

Harvey was thoughtful.

"The problem is we have to assume that there is something missing," he said. "If there is and we don't get on to it… all those bloody people who love to bash the service will have a field day with us."

"Yes, Mark; that's as near to a hole-in-one as you are likely to get today," said Pritchard dryly.

"How do you disseminate a virus?" asked Harvey.

"Most likely by a spray from an aerosol type container."

"How deadly is it?"

"No one really knows the answer to that yet – except possibly Holder. As far as we are concerned we have to start from the assumption that Holder has the ability to start a full scale Ebola epidemic."

Harvey sat quietly for a moment, reflecting on what he had been told. "What sort of defences do we have?"

"NATO forces are in possession of P2S pralidoxime mesylate pills which give increased resistance to nerve gases and of course they have nuclear, biological and chemical warfare suits."

Pritchard looked at his watch. Harvey realized the explanations were over.

"So what do we do next?" He had moved into action mode.

I want you to get in touch with Russell Friedland at BOSS to see if they have a line on Jardine. I have some more questions for Gordon Peters. I'd like to meet back here at twelve midday."

"See you then," said Harvey.

Chapter Three

South Africa – 21st March 1960

It started as an ordinary day. The ten-year-old boy ran out of the side door of the clubhouse, that was his home, in the Johannesburg suburb of Vereeniging. He ran across the golf course and down towards the river in the valley. He was bored with the interminable talk on the radio. The Pan Africanist Congress and its campaign against the pass laws meant nothing to him. He took the first opportunity to escape and be on his own.

He had taken to sitting by the river during his Christmas holidays. At first it was the seclusion, the peace and the coolness that attracted him. Sometimes that peace was disturbed by the African women who came to wash clothes in the river. They called raucously to each other, chattering loudly and laughing. Or they sang while they beat the clothes against the rocks in the stream. It was very shallow at this time of year and, while the women worked, a little girl hopped from one rock to another. She started crossing the stream and setting foot on club property. She was blissfully unaware of the implications of what she was doing and her mother was preoccupied with her work. So it was that the little black girl stumbled on to the white boy's patch.

Soon young Sara was stealing away from her mother whenever she could, to go and play with the fair-haired 'young master' from the country club. On this morning Sara's time was limited. Everyone from her area was going on some kind of walk to the south; to a police station in the township of Sharpeville. Her mother told her they would have to leave early. When they had left home, her father had shouted at them angrily not to be late back. Sara was about to set off when the white boy told her that he did not wish her to go. He was stubborn and threatening and demanded obedience. Sara had not seen his anger rise before. What she now saw frightened her. In the end she did not know whether she was more terrified of her father or the white boy. In desperation she ran.

The boy was incandescent with rage at being thwarted. He chased after her. At first he kept his distance because he knew, if he was seen, Sara's mother would insist that he went home. But Sharpeville police station was a great deal further than he had expected. As five kilometres became ten his anger subsided and was replaced by fear. After a further five or six kilometres – it seemed longer – more people joined the crowd. It became impossible for him to stay out of sight. More and more people saw him but they did not know what to do about it. An unaccompanied white child just did not go into that area.

The crowd grew larger and larger and he became more and more frightened. His rage had evaporated and his defiance with it; he knew only fear. He stumbled on. Finally he caught up with Sara and her mother. Sara's mother was horrified when she realized what had happened. She was fearful of what his parents would do if they ever found out; and she was terrified of her husband's anger.

She need not have worried about her husband. Johannes Zandukwe was in a trance of fervour and excitement. This day was the culmination of months of planning and weeks of build-up. Today his congress would defy the white oppressors of his people. Today they would stand before the police station without their hated passbooks. Today the world would learn of their defiance.

The crowd had grown to thousands. The women and children were thoroughly frightened. The boy took little Sara's hand while her mother tried to comfort and protect them. They seemed to have stopped. Gradually the crowd began to clamour and roar. The children were pushed and jostled. In panic they moved forward through the jungle of legs.

Suddenly there were no more legs. They could see they were standing in front of the police station. A white policeman raised a megaphone to his mouth and began to try to quieten the thousands in front of him. At that moment three South African Air Force Sabre jets screamed over the crowd drowning his words. In seconds the situation was out of control. The mass of people began to roar and stamp their feet. And it began…

Chaos. Terrifying chaos. The crowd of thousands surging forward. The two children at the front. Policemen shooting. People screaming and shouting; running in all directions – some of them falling suddenly and not getting up again. The boy knew they were in mortal danger. And for the first, last and only time in his life, Neil Jardine, aged ten, fell in love. Only one thing mattered to him; to get Sara, the little black girl, away from this scene of slaughter. But he was much too late and pitifully helpless in the face of such carnage. Even as he grasped her hand, she was shot through the heart by a bullet fired at random into the crowd. With a scream he leapt upon her to cover her body with his own, refusing to accept that she was dead. The superhuman strength of terror possessed him. He hung on as he had never clung to anyone in his life.

He never knew how long he lay there. After what seemed an eternity, the uproar began to die away. It was followed by a silence that was almost as frightening. They found him lying over the pathetic, mutilated body that had once been Sara.

"What the hell are you doing here?" came an amazed exclamation.

Slowly the little boy turned to gaze up at the policeman who had found him. And that tough Afrikaner stood transfixed. The stare of implacable hatred on that young face and the malevolent, insane fury burning in those young eyes was seared into his brain forever.

Chapter Four

Kent, England – 1968–1971

The University of Kent is situated on a hill overlooking the historic city of Canterbury. It has a beautiful view dominated by the mighty cathedral. The sight must have brought joy to the heart of many a pilgrim as he journeyed along the Pilgrims' Way close by. It would have been his first sight of the holy place to which he had come to pay homage.

Neil Jardine first saw it on a dull October afternoon in 1968 when he arrived to take up his place at the university. What struck him was not the difference in temperature between Kent and his native South Africa; nor the fact of the constant drizzle. It was the difference in the light. He felt starved of colour in this grey climate.

He recalled the vivid colours of the tibouchina and bougainvillea on the club golf course which had been his home until now. He thought back to the day which was emblazoned in his memory for all time – 21st March 1960 – Sharpeville. He shuddered at the memory.

The years after Sharpeville had not been easy. Although academically bright, he was not popular at school. He was not keen on sport and his smouldering temper made him a favourite prey of teasers and bullies. His life at home was equally unsatisfactory. His father refused to acknowledge the inevitability of adolescence and did not permit him to 'fool around' with the few white girls that showed an interest in him.

For all of those reasons the young Jardine spent long days on his own wandering in the club grounds. He became steadily more introverted.

19th August 1967 was a Saturday and Jardine sat, as he invariably did at dusk, on the edge of a quiet stretch of the river. He thought about the good times that other seventeen-year-old boys enjoyed on Saturday nights.

Suddenly there was a rustling in the thicket behind him. He leapt up and turned round. Standing there was a young black girl. It was difficult to judge her age precisely but he could see she was roughly the same age as himself. She was a fine looking young woman with a striking face and eye-catching figure. She was dressed in a vivid cerise skirt and a white blouse.

"Good evening, master," she said respectfully.

"What are you doing here?" he demanded.

"I am Mary, Sara's sister," she replied.

He looked at her and knew she was telling the truth. The resemblance was marked once his attention had been drawn to it. He had not seen any of Sara's family since the nightmare of Sharpeville. They had all melted away into the township. When the police found him he had steadfastly refused to utter one word to anybody in explanation of how or why he had been there. They had threatened him, bribed him and pleaded with him but to no avail. Their only reward was that sullen unremitting stare of hate that disturbed them all. Eventually they just gave up.

Mary stayed about ten minutes that evening; a little longer on subsequent evenings. It became a habit for them to meet whenever they could. Jardine became progressively more attracted to her on a physical level. He didn't dwell on the fact that her home may well have been some fifteen kilometres away from the club at

Vereeniging. She had to walk there and back every time they met. As far as Jardine was concerned that was the sort of thing Africans did all the time. It did not occur to him, in his arrogance, that she might be doing it for a reason – or that someone might be helping her with transport.

One evening she arrived having apparently fallen into the river. He could hardly believe his eyes. Her clothes were entirely transparent and, in a move that took his breath away, she removed them slowly and deliberately one by one. In the end she stood before him completely naked. With fumbling inexperience he grasped her and they made love. After that day he stopped envying other seventeen-year-olds their Saturday nights.

Eventually he had to go back to school for his final year. He gave her the date of his next holiday. When he returned they met again in their secret place. The connection between them was not lost…

But here he was now, eight thousand miles away in England. Jardine settled in to Kent University well enough. He found it less irksome than school in South Africa. He was not forced to take part in sporting activities. He was more in tune with the mood of his British contemporaries. Their anti-establishment views chimed with him better than the obsession with rugby of his countrymen at home. The whole culture of Britain was quite different to that in South Africa. He fitted in much better. He made no close friends but became accepted in the 'left' political set.

Within three weeks of arriving he was involved in the anti-Vietnam war protest in Grosvenor Square on Sunday 27th October. It was not as dramatic as had been the one in March. Nevertheless there was a nasty moment when a group of protesters formed a human chain and charged at the police cordon. Jardine was at the forefront of the chain. He was noted by a young Special Branch officer,

Mark Harvey. Harvey was particularly concerned at the manner in which the young man attempted to rouse his fellow protesters to acts of violence. He never forgot that face, contorted in hate.

Marianna Webster was a Jamaican girl at Kent University. She was chiefly remarkable for her ability to sing more loudly than anyone Jardine had ever heard. She made pocket money by working on a semi-professional basis as a singer. She operated in the pubs and clubs of the Kent coast towns such as Margate and Ramsgate. Apart from having a very loud voice she was full of energy and personality. She was black and beautiful in a wild kind of way. Tragically she had become involved with the dope peddlers of her home district of Brixton in South London.

Jardine was fascinated by her and started to attend her shows whenever he could. He was sitting in Gideon's nightclub in Herne Bay one night when he noticed, at the next table, someone he vaguely recognized from the university.

"She is quite something hey?" he said

"Yes she is; I reckon she could give Shirley Bassey a run for her money," replied the other.

"Don't I recognize you from Kent?" enquired Jardine.

"Yes, you do. I started in October '66 but I have seen you around."

"May I join you? My name is Neil Jardine."

"Certainly," replied the other man holding out his hand in a quaintly formal way. "Stuart Holder," he said.

They lapsed into silence listening to the girl's singing. At the end of the evening they went their separate ways. But the acquaintance had been made and was not lost.

It transpired that Holder had a car, a Mini Cooper. It was not long before he was giving Marianna and Jardine lifts to and from the girl's gigs. It was in the back of that Mini that Marianna introduced Jardine to cannabis. Holder disapproved. He was a serious young man who stuck to the rules. He found it profoundly disturbing that he was so hooked on Marianna. He followed her around like a faithful dog. She used him unmercifully. She seemed to enjoy demonstrating her power by humiliating him on a regular basis. She would take a delight in flirting with Jardine in Holder's presence. She knew that it hurt him but that he was too decent to take it out on Jardine and too scared to react. The wonder of it was that it did not affect his work. When he worked Holder became a different man; confident, assertive, decisive. He was a quite brilliant biologist.

The summer of 1969 wore on and Marianna and Jardine became lovers. Soon it was more than cannabis changing hands in the back seat of the Mini. Jardine never knew where she got the cocaine from but get it she did. Inexorably it began to work its deadly destruction on them both. It all came to a head one sweltering night in June just before the end of the summer term.

The three of them were returning from Ramsgate where Marianna had been singing. It was her last gig of the academic year. They had celebrated the occasion with a heavier than usual alcoholic intake. In addition to that Marianna and Jardine were more than a little high on cocaine. Disaster was inevitable.

Once out of Ramsgate, Holder stopped the car and got out to relieve himself of an excess of beer.

"I'm going to drive," announced Marianna and leapt out of the back of the Mini.

"No, you certainly are not," retorted Holder from behind the hedge. He was not a habitual drinker and his head was beginning to swim. He felt sick.

"Yes I am," she cried and slipping into the driving seat began to rev the engine wildly.

"Come on, Marianna, stop fooling about and let me back in." Holder was beginning to become alarmed.

"Get in the other side!" she yelled and let out the

clutch.

The Mini lurched forward and Holder started to stumble along behind. She had not gathered speed yet and reached across to open the passenger door. It began to swing to and fro with the uneven progress of the car. Holder managed to heave himself in with nothing worse than a twisted ankle. He made a desperate attempt to turn off the ignition but found his hand held in a vice-like grip. He turned to be met with the glittering eyes of Jardine.

"Just leave her, man. We are going for a joy ride. Let her rip, sweetheart!"

Marianna knew how to drive but the effect of the drink and the drugs dulled her senses. Her reflexes were numbed and her judgement distorted. The little car began to scream along the straight road towards Canterbury. Holder seemed paralysed with fear and sat motionless, staring through the windscreen, his face ashen. Jardine was shouting and laughing, urging Marianna on to go even faster.

By the time they reached Canterbury she was driving the Mini to its very limit. They jinked through the back streets. She nearly lost control as they jolted across the level crossing above the West Gate to the city. Then Marianna took the wrong road. Instead of going straight up the hill to the university she became confused and followed the wider road to the left and set off towards London. It was only a matter of time before disaster struck. It came on the hill leading down into Harbledown.

Fred Bostock was trudging up the hill with several pints of Shepherd and Neame's beer in his belly; just as he had done every Saturday night for the past forty years. He was on his way home and took no notice of the howling car that came bearing down on him. He could have done nothing anyway. At the crucial moment Marianna lost control and swerved. The Mini slammed into the old man sending him flying.

"Christ Almighty, what have you done?" screamed Holder, galvanized back into life.

At the foot of the hill Marianna managed to get control of the car and stopped. They sat in silence for some moments. The last drop of euphoria had been knocked out of her. She sat in the half light of the car's interior panel illumination; her face was a ghastly grey colour and a deep horrendous dread gnawed at her stomach.

Jardine was the first to pull himself together.

"Get in the back, Marianna," he instructed jumping out and taking the driver's seat himself.

"Now listen, you two – get a hold of yourselves. Nobody witnessed the accident and there is nothing any of us can do for that poor sod up there. No way did he survive that. So let's just get out of here…"

"No." The one word was spoken with total authority. It stopped Jardine in his tracks.

"First we will see whether there is anything we can do for that man." Holder was quite clearly not to be denied. He got out of the car and jogged back up the hill.

Neither Jardine nor Marianna moved.

He was gone about ten minutes and Jardine was getting very restless in case another motorist appeared. But none did and Holder returned. His face told all. He shook his head. "He's dead," was all he said. He got back into the car.

Jardine took over again.

"OK so we were returning from Ramsgate to Canterbury, remember? We had no reason to be out here and there is no reason for anyone to connect us with it. I am going to drive back in a wide circle via Chilham. I will approach the university through the town just as if we were returning from Ramsgate. We will park the car out of sight and clean up the wing as best we can. Tomorrow we will take off early and get it patched up miles from here."

And that is how it was. With a mixture of luck and

cunning they avoided suspicion being aroused about the damage to the car.

Marianna and Holder were due to leave Kent at the end of the month. The girl had turned to the upright figure of Holder for support. Her dalliance with Jardine was discarded forthwith. Their shared ordeal bound Holder and Marianna together and he arranged for her to have treatment for her drug problem. Fortunately it was early enough to be effective and she never returned to drugs. A few months later, much to the well disguised horror of Colonel and Mrs Holder, their son married Marianna, the black girl from Jamaica.

Stuart threw himself into his work and quickly became recognized as one of the most brilliant microbiologists in the country. The road to Boughton was inevitable.

Together, Marianna and Stuart Holder took to Dartmoor with them the secret of Fred Bostock's death. No one ever knew how he came to die or who drove the car that killed him.

No one, that is, except Neil Jardine.

Jardine devoted the rest of the year and the first half of 1970 to his work on the Stop The Seventy Tour campaign. The South African cricket team was due to tour England in the summer of 1970 and the campaign, of which Jardine was a significant supporter, was aimed at having the tour cancelled. Jardine played his part under the leadership of Peter Hain and in due course they were successful. The tour was called off.

It is not certain precisely where or when he came to the attention of the KGB. However, a white South African, apparently committed to Marxism and vehemently anti-apartheid represented an opportunity that would fit into their plans perfectly. By the time he left Kent in 1971 he was firmly in their sights.

Jardine had achieved only moderate success in his

academic studies due to his extracurricular activities. By mid-1971, when he was due to leave Kent, he had little idea of what he wanted to do. He did not want to return to his parents in the Transvaal but the British authorities had no intention of letting him stay in the UK. A change of heart had brought a change of government. The mood of 1968 was no longer upon the country. Suddenly the priorities were inflation, the balance of payments and union strikes rather than Vietnam and the Prague Spring. It was a difficult time for Neil Jardine. He was easy meat when the approach from the KGB came.

He left England in August 1971 and flew to Embarkasi airport in Nairobi, Kenya. From there he was driven southwards into Tanzania down the interminable dirt road through Arusha, on to Dodoma and ultimately to Kongwa. One phase of his life was over – another was just beginning.

Chapter Five

London – Tuesday 13th September 1977

Harvey returned to Pritchard's office at noon as arranged. He had managed to speak to Friedland at BOSS but had made no progress in pinpointing Jardine's precise whereabouts. Apparently he had a small business in Johannesburg which he had started in late 1975. It was a recruitment agency dealing mainly with the provision and placement of secretarial 'temps'. He was thought, by the South Africans, to be something of a spent force in political terms.

When he had returned to South Africa at the beginning of 1975 he had gone back to the country club where his father still worked as manager. He found the place had deteriorated considerably. This had been hastened by some very serious floods in the Vereeniging area in early 1975. He could see no future for himself there.

He moved to Johannesburg itself to start his business. These days he was thought to be more concerned with balancing his books than bringing down the South African government. The security services still monitored his movements in and out of South Africa but until this latest incident it went no further than that. All that Friedland could tell Harvey was that Jardine was not back at his business in Johannesburg. The wheels had been set in motion with all dispatch to find him. A local BOSS agent,

Darnie de Villiers, had been allocated to the assignment.

Harvey and Pritchard spent the afternoon going over and over the information they had. Whichever way they looked at it there seemed to be only one way forward.

At 4 p.m. Pritchard looked at Harvey and said, "Well, Mark, it's dead easy and dead difficult. I will stay here and continue to chase Friedland and anybody else I can think of that might be any help. You will fly to South Africa tomorrow night and meet this man de Villiers. Your joint task will be to find Jardine and Holder; over and above that to get any virus that he may have taken, and neutralize it. We just cannot afford to let them multiply it and use it."

Harvey left the office at 4.30. He felt depressed and frustrated. He had wanted to go to South Africa there and then. Pritchard had insisted that he agree things with Friedland first.

"South Africa is BOSS's patch," he had said. "We need to go by the book. They are not natural allies; right now it's just a case of our enemy's enemy is our friend and they can be darn prickly."

"Why is that?" asked Harvey.

"If you are going to operate in South Africa you need to appreciate the delicate nature of relations between the Afrikaners and the British."

"Is that a big issue?"

"It is to some of them. I don't know how much you know about the Boer War but the Afrikaners don't remember it as Britain's finest hour. The war saw us invent concentration camps and stick tens of thousands of Afrikaner women and children in them."

"I guess I better read it up," said Harvey. "I can't say I know too much about it."

"It would be a good idea; you need to strike up a good rapport with this de Villiers guy."

Harvey needed something to take his mind off the

problem. It had been going round and round in his head. A little distance might help get things in perspective. His feet seemed to know where he was going before his mind made a conscious decision. He found himself on the escalators in Harrods on the way to the Skirts and Blouses department. Susan was there. She seemed surprisingly pleased to see him.

They arranged to meet at 5 p.m. at the staff exit.

They went together to pick up David and then go back to Susan's flat.

"Don't you ever use a babysitter?" he asked after David had had his supper and was getting ready for bed.

"Not often," she replied. "I just got used to being here. You don't get to meet too many eligible men in the Skirts and Blouses department. I never really need a babysitter."

"Well you must know someone surely."

Eventually she succumbed. A friend living above her flat agreed to look after David.

He took her to see the musical *Ipi Tombi.* Harvey did not tell her that he was going to South Africa the next day but it may have influenced his choice of entertainment. In fact they had no conversation about the matter that had brought them together. A question by Susan was stonewalled by Harvey. She realized he did not wish to pursue the subject and left it alone. They enjoyed the show finding the rhythmic singing and dancing exhilarating.

Afterwards they wandered through Piccadilly looking at the lights like a couple of tourists. Both of them lived in London – Susan in her basement flat in Cathcart Road; Harvey in a modest but nice two-bedroom apartment on the Park Hill Estate in Croydon. But they seldom did 'touristy' things. Neither of them could remember the last time they had been to the theatre.

They strolled down the Haymarket and crossed the road by New Zealand House. It was a tricky place to cross at that time of night with cars approaching too fast in order to catch the lights. Harvey took her hand as they crossed and once on the other side did not see any reason to let go.

"Have you always lived in London?" she asked.

"No, only for the past fifteen years; originally I came from Cheshire."

"Is your family from Cheshire?"

Harvey looked at the young woman beside him. These were perfectly ordinary questions; but was she trying to discover something? He decided no – this damn job was making him paranoid. He answered her truthfully.

"My mother and I were transferred away from London shortly after I was born in 1942. My father worked in the Foreign Office; we hardly ever saw him. We were sent north to get away from the bombing. It didn't work as Liverpool docks were a prime target. Many bombs dropped on the Wirral where we were."

"Do you remember that?"

"Vaguely. After the war I went to Manchester Grammar School – spent most of my time in the swimming pool."

"Were you a good swimmer?"

"I was OK," he said.

She accepted that she had got all the information she was going to get. She didn't persist further. That he had been brought up by his mother, with his father absent, explained something to her. It was obvious that he was a very strong man physically, with a definite presence; yet there was a considerate side to him. She felt that he understood women better than most men did. She smiled inwardly. Maybe she was just seeing what she wanted to see?

They went on at a leisurely pace to Trafalgar Square. They had been there about fifteen or twenty minutes when Harvey thought back to the last time he had been in

Trafalgar Square other than in a taxi passing through – New Year's Eve 1970 – with Kate. He let go of Susan's hand abruptly. He called a taxi and they went home.

Susan invited him in for coffee. The babysitter went home and they started to watch a late night film on her television. Susan sat on the floor at Harvey's feet while he relaxed on the sofa. He became very aware of how close she was. But somehow the memory of Kate that had come to him in Trafalgar Square persisted. Also, his common sense told him it would be a bad idea to become emotionally involved with Susan at this juncture. Theoretically she was still a possible suspect. At length he yawned and made to say his goodbyes.

"You can sleep on the sofa if you want," she offered. In the end he agreed.

They both lay awake in their separate rooms – wondering what the other was thinking.

Wednesday 14th September 1977

They were up early as Susan had to go to work. Harvey had left his car outside her flat and offered to take David to school and Susan to Harrods. Susan was happy and smiling. She picked up her mail from the hall table on her way out. She pulled a face at the brown envelope that clearly contained a bill and turned her attention to the other letter.

"This looks hand delivered," she said slipping into the car with a flash of thigh that took Harvey's attention away from his rear-view mirror. "It has no postmark or stamp."

They nosed out into the rush-hour traffic. Susan opened the letter. Harvey felt her sunny mood evaporate and her whole body stiffen.

"Alright?" he asked, conscious of David in the back of the car.

"Yes fine," she lied. "We mustn't be late for David."

They did not speak again until the boy had been dropped at school.

"Mark, it's from Neil Jardine." She handed the letter to him. He began to read.

Dear Susan,

It was such an unexpected pleasure to find myself on the same flight as you to South Africa. Seven years is a long time but you look as stunning as ever.

I have noticed that the British authorities have become curious about you since your return. You should know that your new friend, Mr Harvey, is one of their top men in MI7. I want you to pass this letter to him.

I am not sure whether you met Stuart Holder at university. Anyway, he has decided to join us in South Africa and is currently working to reproduce a substance he was developing at Boughton. I might add that he was doing it in direct contravention of the Biological and Toxins Weapons Convention. It is based on a newly discovered virus, Ebola. He has managed to combine it with two other viruses, myxomatosis and smallpox, to produce a highly infectious, toxic spray.

A five-hundred-millilitre aerosol container of this sprayed into a room the size of a supermarket will infect just about everyone in that room. They will begin to develop the symptoms of the new virus, Ebola, a few days later. We are now in the process of multiplying it and sealing it into containers ready to be used.

You will be familiar with South Africa's 'Apartheid' policy. One of its effects is that there are many occasions when the whites are totally separated from the blacks. This is particularly the case at night where the whites sleep in their suburban homes and the blacks go back to their townships. We will shortly have enough of this weapon to load it into tankers and tour the white suburbs of Johannesburg, Cape Town and Durban. In one night we could infect a major part of the population in each of those areas with Ebola.

Please tell Mr Harvey that we will be in touch again when we are ready to move to the next phase of our operation.

Neil Jardine

They sat in silence for several minutes while the traffic snarled around them.

Susan spoke. "Mark, what is MI7? Some sort of offshoot of MI6?"

"There is no such thing anymore," he replied. "It used to deal with propaganda and censorship of journalists working in war zones. It was disbanded years ago. He has got his wires crossed."

She looked at him closely trying to make out if he was telling the truth. "But you are not just a policeman, are you?"

"I must go to work," he said and slotted the car swiftly into the Kensington traffic.

He stopped outside Harrods.

"It's Wednesday so the store stays open until seven tonight," she said, wondering whether they would meet.

He didn't tell her he would be in the air on his way to South Africa by then.

"Sorry, I can't make it tonight; I'll call you."

He watched her disappear into the shuffling queue; just one of the five thousand funnelling into the staff entrance in Hans Crescent every morning. He wondered if he would see her again.

Pritchard read the letter from Jardine without comment other than a low whistle at one point. When he had finished reading Harvey spoke.

"What do you make of it, Chief?"

Pritchard was silent for some time and then gathered himself.

"You have to ask yourself why he has sent this letter and why he has sent it to Bennett and not you or me or someone in authority. He is not actually demanding anything so what's the purpose?"

"Just to create fear I guess," answered Harvey. As the words left his mouth he realized how lame they sounded.

"That could be part of it, but I think there's more. Read it again. What does it actually say? It's all about claiming that Holder, an Englishman, has developed an English weapon in contravention of the 1975 convention. He is aiming to place the blame squarely on the UK for this weapon. He is suggesting a British weapon could be instrumental in infecting large swathes of the white suburbs of South Africa's major towns."

Harvey nodded in agreement. Pritchard continued.

"It's very much a preliminary warning shot – possibly why he sent it to Bennett. Be that as it may he is overplaying his hand. Boughton tells me that unless someone comes into direct contact with this virus they will not develop the disease. Peters says the idea of mixing it with myxomatosis and smallpox is just that at present – an idea. We know the Soviets are trying to do it and that is why Holder was working on it. But it is very doubtful that he has succeeded in producing a viable spray in the short time he has been in South Africa. I know the Ebola virus is very toxic on its own but it would not be effective to just spray it around. I accept that, in theory, you have only to infect one person but I don't buy the idea that they can contaminate the white populations of Johannesburg, Cape Town and Durban in one night."

"Maybe not," said Harvey. "Even so it seems that in the right circumstances it could start an extremely unpleasant epidemic."

"There is one other problem Holder has to overcome. He has to put it into a flask that will be strong enough to withstand being moved around and he has to suspend it in a liquid that will prevent it from degrading too quickly. Peters reckons Holder knows enough to accomplish that – he muttered darkly about something he called DMSO, whatever that might stand for."

Harvey looked pensive.

"The fact is," he said, "Holder is probably the leading

expert in the world in this field. We have to start from the assumption that he can produce a viable biological weapon from the Ebola virus."

"Well that's for Mr Vorster to worry about," said Pritchard. "Our problem remains the same as before. We have to find Holder and neutralize anything he might be manufacturing. Preferably Jardine as well – although he is more South Africa's problem."

Pritchard read the letter again.

"I am due to see Friedland later this morning and we will progress this as we can. In the meantime nothing changes for you."

Harvey spent the rest of the morning in his office clearing some routine details.

Later that evening the British Airways Boeing 747 lumbered down the runway and roared into the night sky. He tried to sleep.

Chapter Six

Tanzania, East Africa – 1971
Cuba – 1973

Kongwa is a desolate place right in the arid heart of Tanzania. It is dry and hot; and dusty and burnt; and empty, save for an endless vista of flat-topped thorn trees and baobabs – mile after mile of parched brown earth with absolutely nothing to recommend it. Most people who have been there love it and are never free of its stark, haunting beauty ever again.

For a brief spell after the Second World War, Kongwa came to life. The Tanganyika Groundnut Scheme was centred there. Buildings and camps sprang up. But it was a debacle. It was too dry. Mighty Africa scorned the puny efforts of man and the scheme petered out with a whimper. All that remained was a large area of cleared bush, the ruins of some Nissen huts and a dumping ground for a hoard of agricultural equipment. Subsequently a boarding school for European children was housed there. That closed in 1958. Gradually the place reverted to semi-desert scrub. The process was well advanced by the time Russia's envoy, Alexander Klishenko, first set foot there.

Tanganyika achieved independence in 1961. Both China and the Soviet Union saw the opportunity to gain a foothold in East and Central Africa. China put money and expertise into a project called the 'Tanzam' railway – a link from landlocked Zambia's copper-belt to the Tanzanian coast.

If China was interested in Tanzania then so was the Soviet Union. Alexander Klishenko was dispatched to Dar es Salaam in December 1963. His visit got off to a bad start. The first part of his itinerary involved a journey up-country to the town of Iringa. The rains came early in 1963 and were exceptionally heavy. Klishenko's convoy was brought to a halt midway at Mikumi. A bridge had been washed away and there was no way round it through the mud and bush, sodden with rain. The entourage returned to Morogoro where it was decided to go via Dodoma instead. This involved a massive detour which took them past Kongwa.

It was by this quirk of the African weather that on a hot December afternoon the convoy stopped for a break at Kongwa. The Russian wandered up an overgrown track to heed the call of nature. Rounding a twist in the track he was met by a strange sight. Rows of derelict Nissen huts lay crumbling under the scorching sun in the great void of central Africa. He leaned on the iron bar gate that had once afforded an entrance to the compound. It groaned and screeched eerily in the silent vastness. He had no idea of the history of the area and, in truth, that did not matter. What did matter was the indelible impression that strange place made on him as he stood there that afternoon. Alexander Klishenko never forgot Kongwa. Later, when he was asked to suggest a suitable place to site a camp to train freedom fighters for the coming struggle in southern Africa, he did not hesitate.

By the time Neil Jardine reached Kongwa in late 1971 the derelict ruins of the Groundnut Scheme had come back to life. The huts had been rebuilt and the compound hewn once more out of the African bush. One of the most advanced guerrilla warfare training camps in the world had been born.

It was here that Jardine was transformed from a fanatical, uncontrolled anarchist into a trained and professional subversive. To start with he was subjected to a barrage of medical checks both physical and psychological. His flirtation with hard drugs was diagnosed. He underwent an arduous course of treatment to rid him of that inclination. He learned how to kill with guns. He learned how to kill without guns. He learned the secrets of the African bush; how to conceal himself and how to track an enemy. In eighteen concentrated months they turned Neil Jardine into a lethal fighting machine.

Then they started on his mind. It was during this phase in 1973 that they sent him to Cuba. The tropical palms and beaches were a blessed relief after the dust and heat of Kongwa. The purpose of the trip was to introduce him to Juanita Havanestro. She was a senior operative responsible for liaison between the Soviet organization in southern Africa and Cuba. Ultimately much of the manpower used would be Cuban. She had been entrusted with the responsibility of informing Jardine of the part he was to play in the master plan.

They allowed him a week to laze beside the turquoise Caribbean. He had worked hard. They were pleased with him. They wanted him to form a close relationship with Juanita. The treatment certainly worked and he found she inflamed him with overwhelming physical desire.

She was a strikingly beautiful young woman with skin the colour of burnt caramel, jet black, luxuriant hair, deep-set brown eyes and a wide sensual mouth. She moved with a swaying grace that enthralled him. The thin cotton of her gaily coloured skirts and blouses left him in no doubt about the promise of her supple body. She had been well chosen for her role and was a natural successor to Sara, Mary and Marianna. He made love to her hungrily in a beach chalet with the tropical moonlight reflecting on the softly moaning surf outside. If this was the revolution, Neil Jardine liked it.

But of course it was not. Jardine was there for a purpose. He had a part to play in the master plan. He had been equipped physically and now it was time for him to learn his lines.

At the beginning of his second week the atmosphere changed. Juanita summoned him to join her in a disused schoolroom. He found her with a file open upon the desk and an overhead projector loaded with a carousel of slides next to it. There was a screen behind the desk. As part of his university course Jardine had once sat in on a management training day at a large company. It looked just like that to him – except there were no other delegates.

She spoke slowly and quietly at first. He understood instantly that holidays were over. He listened to her attentively.

"We both know, Neil, that you have not been sent here just to have a nice holiday. I have a task to perform; a message to give you. You have come here to be told of the mission for which you are being prepared."

Juanita had learned her English in Canada. Her vocabulary and grammar were impeccable; only her accent betrayed the fact that it was not her native tongue.

"It is necessary for me to start by going back a few years." Jardine recognized immediately that this was a prepared and rehearsed speech. The language and phrasing were much more formal than her normal way of talking.

She pressed a button on the remote control in her hand and a slide of the Hammer and Sickle, the Stars and Stripes, and the Union Jack was projected on to the screen.

"In the period following the Second World War three powers dominated the world, the United States, Great

Britain and the Soviet Union. Gradually Great Britain began to drop out of the military race. But in fact, in one crucial way Britain has remained a major power. She is in the forefront of research into germ warfare technology. I mention this only because it is relevant to your mission."

Juanita paused to satisfy herself that Jardine was paying attention. It seemed he was. The slide changed to a picture of two nuclear missiles pointing at each other.

"The decade of the sixties saw the possession of nuclear weapons by the major powers bring about a sort of stalemate. The missile crisis here in Cuba in 1962 scared both sides and brought them up with a jolt."

A blind on one of the windows began to rattle as the wind outside got up. Juanita crossed over to it and closed the window. She did not stop speaking; merely looked over her shoulder at Jardine as she continued.

"Now America is suffering serious difficulties in Vietnam. That has dented Western morale badly. This gives us the perfect opportunity to establish Soviet leadership of the third world."

She was gradually warming to her theme. She was no longer quietly chatting to him; she was beginning to lecture, her eyes bright with excitement. She looked magnificent. Jardine had to remind himself to focus and listen.

"But the economic battle is being lost. The final blow was the total failure of the Russian grain harvest last year." A slide of a barren landscape which Jardine guessed was Russia appeared on the screen. The caption below the picture said 'Failure of 1972 Russian Grain Harvest'.

"So a decision has been taken to embark on a ten-year plan." She paused for dramatic effect. "It is codenamed 'Project Capricorn'. It involves bringing the whole of southern Africa on either side of the Tropic of Capricorn under black majority rule and Soviet influence. And you, Neil, have an important part to play in the plan."

A slide with the caption 'Project Capricorn' appeared on the screen. She looked straight at him and he realized some response was expected.

"So what's the plan?" he prompted.

"The economic sabotage of the West." She paused to allow time for her words sink in.

"Yes, Neil, this is where you and I come in; nothing less than the total economic sabotage of the Western democracies."

She sat down abruptly. The first part of her lecture was over. She had set the scene and aroused his curiosity. He was agog to know how such a gargantuan task was to be achieved and what his part in it would be.

"OK, so what have they come up with?" he asked.

She gathered herself again.

"What are the economies of the West founded on?"

"I suppose food, energy and consumer goods," he replied.

"Yes, Neil, and where are they most vulnerable?"

He thought for a moment.

"Energy perhaps," he offered.

"Exactly," she said. The slide changed to an oil derrick in what Jardine took to be some indeterminate Middle Eastern country. "Who is the largest oil producer in the world?"

"Saudi Arabia," he responded without hesitation.

"Actually, no," she rebutted him. "Saudi Arabia is the second; the Soviet Union produces more oil than anyone else. The point is that an oil crisis would hit the West far harder than us. But there is something else that Russia produces that lies at the very heart of the economies of the West."

She clearly expected an answer from him but his mind had gone blank.

"For God's sake, Neil, you are South African. What comes from your country?"

She pressed the slide remote angrily. A picture of a gold ingot flashed onto the screen.

"Gold, of course, gold," he responded.

"Yes, Neil, gold. Men have worshipped gold since the time of King Midas in Greek mythology. It was used as coinage until recent times. Even now it remains the preferred shelter in times of economic turmoil."

A graph showing a precipitously downward path became the new slide with the caption 'Western Stock Markets'. Jardine thought the lecture was becoming a little bizarre. Juanita continued unabashed.

"So our strategy is based upon oil and gold. Imagine the havoc we could cause if we seriously disrupted the supply of those commodities. What we want to achieve is a huge rise in the price of oil. This would set the Western economies back a decade or more and give time for the Soviet Union's economy to catch up."

"How do you propose going about that?" Jardine was becoming a little incredulous as Juanita's revelations seemed to be more and more fantastic.

"Israel," she said flatly.

"Israel?" he queried. "How do they fit in?"

A new slide clicked on. It was a map of the Middle East with oil derricks on all the countries supplying oil.

"Israel humiliated the Arab states in 1967. They will hit back sooner rather than later. The vast bulk of the West's oil comes from the Middle East. It has been simple to convince the Arabs that they are not charging enough for their oil. The West has been exploiting them since the beginning of the century. They can see that and are resentful. They can also see that their oil constitutes a powerful weapon to restrain the West from supporting Israel in a further war."

"Yes, granted," put in Jardine to assure her he was still with her.

"This October the Arab states will attack Israel and

will declare an oil embargo on any power that comes to her aid or supports her. They will simultaneously raise the price of crude oil to two or three times its present level. The result will be devastating. The economies of the West, particularly the weak ones like Britain, will be crippled. Inflation will take off like never before. Massive sums of money will flow from the capitalist West to the Middle East where we have much more control. In Britain they have large coal deposits but plans are being advanced to cause serious unrest in the coalfields. We aim to achieve an all-out miners' strike there next year. It will be well into the 1980s before they can mount any sort of recovery."

Jardine was stunned by the enormity of the plan's conception.

"But that's only half the story!" cried Juanita. She was back in full flow again.

"What do the West always do in times of economic trouble?" She did not wait for him to attempt an answer. "They rush into gold, Neil. So think about it; an oil crisis sparks off a stampede into gold and that is exactly where we hit them next. It's beautiful."

Jardine shook his head in disbelief. "And how are you going to arrange that?"

The slide changed and a picture of South Africa appeared.

"Do you realize how rich your country is, Neil? Do you realize that under the soil of South Africa lies sixty-five per cent of the world's known gold reserves – twenty-five per cent of the world's uranium, seventy per cent of the world's chromium, sixty per cent of its platinum, fifty per cent of its manganese and vanadium, and I haven't even mentioned diamonds."

Jardine was aware, like every South African, that his country was rich in mineral deposits. However, to hear a stock check recited in such a way stunned him. He had no idea that such a large proportion of the world's known mineral wealth lay beneath one single country.

Juanita was continuing. "The other major producer of gold is Russia. If we can cut off the supply from South Africa we would have more or less total control of world supplies of gold. It would strike at the very foundation of the Western economies. The double blow of oil and gold would create economic chaos in the West. We would then have nuclear parity, conventional weapons superiority and economic leadership."

A picture demarcating a map of the Soviet Union was emblazoned on the screen. Her triumph was complete and she looked to the South African for his accolade.

But he was not as convinced as she was.

"OK, OK," he said. "But you have not told me how South Africa is to be forced to collaborate in this plan. I hate the apartheid regime but I also know that South Africans are proud people and they will fight."

"But for God's sake, Neil, South Africa is more ripe for revolution than any other country on earth."

He looked at her with amused tolerance.

"I think you are in danger of being taken in by your own propaganda," he said disparagingly. "The blacks in South Africa are better off than anywhere else in Africa. They have their niggles, yes, but Africa is a starving continent. Ask a starving man if he wants a loaf of bread or the vote and I think you know what the reply will be. What you should remember is that the Soviets have had to build the Berlin Wall to keep their population IN. The South Africans spend millions each year mounting border patrols to keep Africans from other countries OUT. Even in Tanzania, where I have been for the last two years, there are African men packing up their belongings and making the two-thousand-mile journey to get work in Johannesburg. So if you think ideology will cause a sudden and complete collapse of South Africa you do not begin to understand the situation."

She was stunned. The vehemence of his response totally shocked her. She had no slide in her carousel to combat this objection. Nevertheless she had been well tutored for her role and she managed to find an answer for him.

"We fully accept that nothing is going to happen simply of its own accord. But, Neil, do not overestimate the impregnability of South Africa. It is strong, yes, but not invincible. You have dismissed the distress of the black population as a few niggles. You must know it is very much more than that. Think of Soweto. Could there be a place more ready to explode? Also, South Africa is vulnerable in two other ways. The first is an oil embargo. For all its mineral wealth, South Africa has no oil; it has to be imported. Secondly, the segregation of its populations makes the whites uniquely vulnerable to attack by chemical or biological weapons."

"So how is that to happen?" he asked.

Juanita returned to her rehearsed script.

A map of the southern half of Africa appeared with all the countries in different colours.

"South Africa has Rhodesia to the north, Mozambique to the north-east and Angola to the north-west. All those countries are ruled by reactionary colonial regimes friendly to her. You have seen the training at Kongwa to prepare for the escalation of a terrorist war against Rhodesia. The battle is hard but the tide will turn. History is on our side; the economy of Rhodesia will weaken, white morale will crack and Zimbabwe will be born."

The slide changed and what had been Rhodesia had become a blank, black space.

"As for Mozambique and Angola, they are Portuguese colonies and Portugal is in a parlous state after a century of fascism. While Europe is staggering from the blow of the oil crisis, the fascist regime in Portugal will be toppled and replaced by a government of the people. They will set

Mozambique and Angola free and South Africa will be exposed, its protective shield stripped away."

Mozambique and Angola were duly blacked out on the next slide.

Juanita rested and there was silence while Jardine tried to come to terms with the enormity of what he had heard. It was a strategy on a grand scale. He looked at the screen with its picture of Southern Africa – South Africa itself shaded orange, Botswana grey – Rhodesia, Angola and Mozambique remained blacked out.

"Alright, let's suppose all that comes off as you have explained. You have South Africa surrounded by Zimbabwe, Mozambique and Angola all ruled by black regimes. What then?"

And she told him.

Chapter Seven

Johannesburg, South Africa – Thursday 15th September 1977

The overnight flight from Heathrow was on time. Harvey had no difficulty in identifying Darnie de Villiers. They confined their initial conversation to the practicalities of negotiating their way out of Jan Smuts airport. Soon they were cruising down the M1 highway into the city at the legal maximum – only eighty kilometres per hour; a fuel saving measure.

It was a beautiful time of year. The full heat of summer was still a few weeks away. The delicate, lavender-coloured jacaranda trees and the vivid red of the bougainvillaea bushes made a colourful spectacle. Harvey was struck by the brightness of the light.

"Any leads on Holder's whereabouts?" he asked.

"I'm afraid not as yet, Mr Harvey." De Villiers was a hard, lean and fit looking young man in his late twenties. He had played rugby as a centre three-quarter for Transvaal. His dark hair was short by European standards; his face was tanned and serious, with earnest brown eyes that were never still.

He continued, "I think we are better off trying to find Jardine. We are more familiar with his comings and goings. We need both of them anyway and Jardine can lead us to Holder. He is known to have contacts with the

Black Liberation Party. We picked up one of their key men last night. His name is Oscar Tembi. It's a bit touchy at the moment. There's still a hell of a row going on about Steve Biko. He died in custody at the beginning of this week."

"Yes I heard. Bad business. Has Tembi told you anything yet?"

"Nope. He should be ready to tell us what he knows by this time tomorrow."

Harvey thought he was glad he was not Oscar Tembi.

"Always supposing he knows where Jardine is," said Harvey.

"He knows," replied de Villiers laconically.

His matter-of-fact tone belied the sinister implication of his words.

His attention had wandered to his rear-view mirror. Shortly he said, "There is a yellow Chev behind us. He's been there since we left the airport; could be coincidence but I'm going to try him out."

At the next exit from the motorway de Villiers held the nearside lane to the last possible moment. Then without giving a signal of any kind suddenly heaved the car off to the left. The Cortina's three-litre six-cylinder engine snarled like an angry tiger. He accelerated away down to a set of traffic signals. The yellow Chev came right after them. Any lingering doubts left in de Villiers's mind were quickly extinguished.

Soon they were cruising up a road in the residential district of Illova. Harvey noticed they were passing The Wanderers Club. He wished he had time to stop and take a look at the famous golf course; but de Villiers had other ideas.

"Hold tight, I'm going to call his bluff."

The Cortina screeched to a standstill on the left-hand side of the road. The Chev went on by them. De Villiers noticed it had an SD prefix to the number indicating it had been registered in Swaziland. It stopped a little further up the road. A thick-set middle-aged man got out.

"Quick, there's a camera under the seat."

Harvey passed it to him and de Villiers took a number of photos.

"We'll get those enlarged," he said.

Then he swung the car round in a U-turn and rejoined the motorway heading into the city.

De Villiers's boss was a tough looking Afrikaner called Van Ruyen. He had a slow laconic manner that could seem dour but behind it lay a wry sense of humour.

"Interesting job you've got yourself," he said. "Let me know if I can help."

The look on the South African's face was sardonic and Harvey found himself wondering just how much 'help' he might actually get. One hopeful thing about the present situation was de Villiers's quiet confidence. The young Afrikaner seemed a pretty cool customer and Harvey felt instinctively that they would work well together. De Villiers obviously thought it was only a matter of time before Tembi parted with the information concerning Jardine's whereabouts.

He parted with it at 11.30 p.m. To his evident surprise he was set free immediately afterwards. He presumed the police didn't want another Steve Biko incident on their hands right now.

"Where is he?" asked Harvey.

"Champagne Castle, a hotel in the Berg."

They set off for the Drakensberg mountains at 1 a.m. on Friday morning.

Chapter Eight

Champagne Castle – Friday 16th September

Neil Jardine was up early. It was a beautiful spring morning in the Drakensbergs. The crisp mountain air was alive with birdsong. He left the main building of the hotel and walked across the terrace. He continued past the swimming pool and then through a gate. This afforded access to a path leading up sharply into woodland. He walked on for a short while; then the path widened out into a clearing. Some broad timbers had been laid to permit walkers to cross the clearing. Obviously the ground flooded during the rainy season.

Jardine picked his way across. He went on a little further until he came upon a small lake. It was the most perfect mountain trout pool. He sat down on a bench underneath a large wattle tree. The water, the mountains, the conifers and the nip in the air could easily have convinced him he was in Canada or Scotland.

Jardine had much to think about. He was confused and troubled. He had retreated to Champagne Castle to be alone and sort out his thoughts. A great deal had happened since the heady days of his indoctrination in Cuba. He had been genuinely sorry to leave Juanita. He remembered her lithe and willing body with pleasure; but it seemed a long time ago.

The scenario that Juanita had outlined to him in Cuba

had run like clockwork to start with. The Yom Kippur War in the Middle East in October 1973 was duly followed by the foretold oil crisis. It struck a hammer blow at the Western economies. In Great Britain the unrest in the coal industry came to a head as she had predicted. After two general elections and a number of phased electricity blackouts in 1974, the once all-powerful Great Britain was rapidly disintegrating into a shambles. The Portuguese revolution came in on cue and Mozambique and Angola were cut free from colonial domination.

He had returned to Kongwa for a final phase of training in which they had introduced him to the murky business of intelligence, counter-intelligence, information, disinformation and the techniques of subversion. Then he had 'turned up' in Sydney, Australia in 1974. He claimed to have spent the time since leaving Kent University travelling across Europe and Asia. It was an unremarkable story for a young man of his age. His assertion that he spent some time with the hippy people in Afghanistan was never challenged.

He roamed around Australia for several months doing odd jobs. Eventually he signed on to work his passage in a cargo ship bound for San Francisco.

To his surprise he liked America. Gradually the seeds of his present confusion were sown. Suddenly he found himself wondering whether his recruitment into the Soviet ranks had come about through genuinely positive conviction; or perhaps through a chain of events that had started with student fervour and snowballed out of control. He was now twenty-five. He had left behind the hothouse atmosphere of a 1960s British university. His horizon had been raised substantially through travel.

Neil Jardine was starting to grow up.

But it was too late, much too late. His misgivings were brought to an abrupt halt by instructions to return to

South Africa in 1975. He was to get himself a respectable commercial front; the prodigal returning having sown his Marxist wild oats. He was ready to settle down and become a successful South African businessman. Jardine found the role very easy. He hoped his Russian masters didn't suspect how easy.

They gave him one other instruction. He was to return to the country club and 'mend fences' with his parents. While there he was to keep a prearranged rendezvous with Mary. They met early in the new year. In the hot African night he found he still wanted her. He took her with the urgent passion of eight years' separation. It was only afterwards that it occurred to him that she should by now have a husband and probably children. Jardine put the thought aside. The other thing he realized quickly afterwards was that they were not alone. Mary's father Johannes Zandukwe materialized from the shadows.

Jardine had not seen him since that terrible March day at Sharpeville all those years ago. The memory was a childhood nightmare. It had never left him. Zandukwe looked little different other than that he had grown a beard and was sporting a pair of rimless spectacles.

"Good evening, master."

"What are you doing here?" demanded Jardine.

"Mary went out on her own. She did not tell me where she was going. I came after her to make sure she didn't get into any danger. Now I see what she was doing and I am frightened." His voice was superficially obsequious but there was no doubting the underlying menace.

"Do you know, master, what the penalty is for a white boy raping a black girl?"

Before Jardine could reply Zandukwe turned to his daughter who stood in unashamed nakedness. She was remarkably unsurprised and unflustered by her father's sudden appearance. Too unsurprised by far, thought Jardine.

"Go home, Mary; I will deal with you later."

Unhurriedly the girl gathered her clothes and dressed herself. A few moments later Jardine and Zandukwe were alone.

"Do you prefer squash or tennis?" asked Zandukwe.

Jardine froze in disbelief. The African had used the contact question given to him at the end of his training.

"I prefer squash, it keeps me in better shape," he replied.

It turned out that part of Jardine's duties would be to provide support to Zandukwe. An operation was being mounted in Soweto. For the next six months Jardine built up his staff agency in Johannesburg by day. On two or three nights each week he obtained information to be passed on to Zandukwe. They met at weekends. Mary was no longer in evidence.

Zandukwe finally engineered an uprising in Soweto in June of 1976. Jardine had his reservations. But he was in too deep and there was no way out. It only needed Zandukwe to blow the lid off his communist affiliations, let alone accuse him of raping Mary, and he would be in a whole lot of very nasty trouble with the South African authorities.

For some months after Soweto they left him alone. He immersed himself in his business which was growing nicely. Then one day in June 1977 one of the girls he was interviewing for a part-time secretarial job asked him, "Do you prefer squash or tennis?"

He learned that Juanita was in Johannesburg. She had information that a blood sample, originally from Zaire, was being couriered to the South African police forensics unit. Jardine was instructed to intercept it and take it to a facility that had been set up on an old South African brewery's site.

Then he was sent to England. His mission went more

easily than he had anticipated. Stuart Holder had been threatened with the exposure of Marianna's guilt over Fred Bostock's death. He was in a torment but ultimately his concern for his wife prevailed over everything else. He agreed to fly to South Africa and work on analysing the blood sample sent from Zaire. Juanita had told Jardine that they suspected it contained this new virus that had now been named Ebola.

Holder's task had been to seal the virus within suitable aerosol type canisters so that it would not rapidly degrade. For a man of his knowledge and experience this was not an impossible task given the facilities on site. Jardine's instructions were that Holder should produce three separate canisters. They were to be hidden in three different locations far apart from each other. It was left to Jardine to choose the locations. Once he had hidden the canisters he was to advise Oscar Tembi of their precise positions.

Accordingly Jardine had obtained three five-hundred-millilitre canisters from Holder. The Englishman had by now confirmed that the virus in the blood sample was indeed Ebola. The canisters were much heavier than Jardine had expected. The toxic liquid had to be housed within a three stage packing – the actual toxin in something similar to a vacuum flask, a secondary watertight and leak-proof receptacle and a robust outer packaging.

He had buried one of the canisters in the glade by the river where he and Mary used to meet. He had taken another one to Cape Town and buried it in a remote spot on the slopes of Table Mountain. He took the third one to Durban. Unbeknown to anybody he had bought a small chalet at a place on the coast north of Durban. He had buried the third canister in the grounds of this chalet. He was confident that nobody other than himself had any idea of the locations of the three canisters.

So now he sat at that mountain trout lake, on that Friday morning, trying to bring some order to his thoughts.

Harvey and de Villiers had approached the Drakensbergs at dawn. The mountains were a breathtaking sight. The flat, monotonous landscape of the Orange Free State had given way to rolling country at the foothills of the mighty range. Suddenly the view soared up to the clouds in the majesty of Cathedral Peak.

They had left the tarmac road when they turned off the main highway. Twin jets of dust spurted from the rear wheels of de Villiers's Cortina as he thrashed it over the corrugated dirt road. The dust rose to hang in a pall in the dawn air, testimony to their passage. It remained long after the growl of the three-litre engine and the clumping of the suspension had faded into the vast African silence.

Gradually the road became more winding and steep. On arrival they parked the car and went into reception. Despite the early hour there was a smiling receptionist to welcome them. Her smile froze when de Villiers identified himself. It took only a few moments for her to recognize Jardine from their description. She told them that he had gone for a walk up towards the trout lake.

Harvey went up after him swiftly and silently. De Villiers stayed some distance behind to provide cover in case Jardine became violent or tried to make a run for it. Harvey recognized Jardine immediately from the footage of the Grosvenor Square riot and the photographs which he had studied before leaving on this assignment. He crept up behind him like a cat.

"Good morning, Mr Jardine."

Jardine remained silent. He had heard the two men approaching but reasoned that if they were friendly he had no need to move and if they weren't it was too late to take evasive action.

Harvey came forward and stood behind the bench upon which Jardine sat.

"My name is Mark Harvey; I am from British Intelligence and have come to act as the go-between. We require to know the whereabouts of our man Stuart Holder."

"I think you will find Mr Holder is *our* man not yours," answered Jardine. "There is really nothing to discuss. When we are ready to move we will advise you as to what we require in exchange for the supplies of your illegal virus that we have. Either the conditions of our ultimatum will be met or a threat to release the virus will be activated. End of story."

"First of all, we categorically deny that you have any substance appropriated from the United Kingdom," answered Harvey. "Our work in the field of biological weapons is entirely defensive and therefore legal. It is devoted to developing a vaccine to protect our country in the event of a biological attack."

"Dream on, Harvey. We have Holder and he knows everything there is to know. He has made it quite plain to us that if we release this substance into a residential area it will infect thousands. I assumed you knew that. We certainly do."

"What you must also know," retorted Harvey, "is that it is only a matter of time, a short time, before we locate Stuart Holder and arrest him and your kingpin will be removed."

"Too late. He has already distilled enough to cause widespread infection in the white residential areas of Johannesburg, Cape Town and Durban. No one will be alarmed at the sight of a street-cleaning lorry slowly moving up and down the suburban streets. It will be too late by the time they realize that it is releasing a deadly spray."

Harvey was silent for a few moments.

"You must know that all you will achieve is to unite the whites and cause them to fight back in the most deadly way. South Africa is a very strong country."

"It is at the moment but how do you think they will feel after a night on Boughton's biological weapon – thousands developing the most horrible disease imaginable."

Harvey answered immediately. "Whatever you have it is not Boughton's biological weapon. Boughton does not have one."

"Get real, Harvey." Jardine sounded contemptuous. "Britain is up to its neck in biological warfare. What we have is exactly what Holder was working on in the UK. It is called EV77. If it is released into the atmosphere it will infect thousands. There would be widespread chaos; a chaos that would necessitate the Soviet forces in Angola and Mozambique to move in to ensure the safety of the black population from any reprisals planned by the South African military."

So there it was; the blatant threat of Soviet military intervention. Harvey was confident now that Jardine was over-playing his hand. The idea of a street cleaning lorry touring white suburbs spraying Ebola virus into the atmosphere was fantasy. There was no way Holder had had time to combine the Ebola virus with myxomatosis. The substance as it presently existed was no doubt highly toxic but only in the case of direct contact. It was possible that a few people could become infected and then it might spread. Nevertheless the blanket coverage that Jardine was threatening was unrealistic. In addition to that the Soviets would be well aware that any overt and direct military intervention in South Africa would be bound to bring a Western response.

However, South Africa had few friends in the West and covert terrorist activity was far more likely. Furthermore the Ebola substance that Holder had produced might be crude and difficult to use effectively in its present form but it still represented a potent threat. Harvey was mindful of Pritchard's instructions to find and neutralize it as a priority.

Some action was required to break the deadlock. They were just bandying words.

Jardine sounded smug but Harvey definitely got the feeling that he was not nearly as confident as he sounded. He must know that the sort of atrocity that he threatened would bring the wrath of the Western world down on him. If he knew anything about the Soviets he would know also they would leave him to his fate without compunction.

"Enough, Jardine." Harvey dropped the civilities to indicate that the circling around each other was over. He was now taking charge. "We are taking you back to Johannesburg for formal questioning. On your feet."

Jardine briefly considered making a run for it but assessed that it would be futile. Harvey was clearly young, fit and strong. Any accomplice – there was bound to be one – would be equally so. He decided to go quietly.

The journey back to Johannesburg was a nightmare. Both Harvey and de Villiers were very short of sleep. The heat of the day was stifling. The road seemed endless. They had to watch the handcuffed Jardine like a hawk. He may have come quietly but he was a formidable foe and nothing could be assumed.

They arrived back in Johannesburg in mid-afternoon and went straight to de Villiers's headquarters. Jardine was turned over to Van Ruyen who gave instructions that he was to be left entirely alone. Harvey and de Villiers then sank into blissful sleep with instructions to be awoken at 6 p.m.

They felt terrible when they were awoken. But they were young and fit. After a shower and a change they were refreshed; ready to go to work again.

"What's your thinking?" de Villiers enquired of Harvey

"We have to get under Jardine's skin. He seems very smug on the outside but I get a definite feeling that he doesn't believe in this plan nearly as strongly as he makes out. He is largely mouthing off stuff that has been drummed into him by someone else. If we can turn him maybe we can get to Holder and impound the virus before it gets sent to all corners of the country."

"How do you propose to set about turning him?"

"Good question. Any ideas?"

De Villiers was silent for a few moments and then spoke.

"I don't think it's any good merely talking to him. We will just go round in circles. We want to change his behaviour. You can do that two ways. One, by having a powerful enough sanction to force him to change. Short of torture – not desirable with the Biko business so fresh in memories – we do not have that. The only other way is to work on his attitude and, by changing that, change his behaviour."

"Quite the psychologist, aren't you, Darnie," said Harvey. "But you are right; we need to show him some action that will bring home to him that he is going down a dead-end."

De Villiers was thoughtful for a few more moments.

"I have an idea but I need to get official approval at the highest level."

"What's your plan?" asked Harvey.

"Let's see if I can get it approved first," he said.

Chapter Nine

Friday Evening 16th September 1977

They left Johannesburg by car at 8 p.m. Jardine was bound and blindfolded. The necessary approval had been sought and obtained to take him on the journeys proposed; also to gain access to the sites de Villiers wished to enter.

Jardine could not be sure in which direction they were travelling. However, he was aware that the journey was around twenty to thirty minutes. He guessed, correctly as it turned out, that they were still in the area between Johannesburg and Pretoria. It was clear from the noise and windswept feeling he got on alighting from the car that they had arrived at some sort of airbase. They had passed through three separate checkpoints. It was obviously a very well-guarded facility.

After guiding him into a building and descending in a lift they took the blindfold from his eyes. They allowed him a few moments to acclimatize to the fluorescent lighting.

He was in something that resembled an underground car park. They were escorted by a man in South African Air Force uniform along a corridor towards some double doors. At these the officer punched in a number to the lock on the door. As it swung open they were met by further air force personnel. An exchange took place. A further walk brought them into a huge underground warehouse and Jardine stood dumbfounded at what he saw: as far as the eye could see stretched row upon row of crated aircraft and aircraft parts. They boarded a golf buggy and started to travel along the rows.

Jardine was aware of the stated strength of the South African Air Force but this clearly exceeded anything he had been led to expect.

"You see, my friend," de Villiers started, "this is an air force like no other in Africa. You may have been led to believe that sanctions have robbed us of modern aircraft and the parts necessary to keep them in the air. Believe it no longer. Believe instead that it is a national characteristic of the French to have a particular respect and desire for gold. It is also true that they manufacture some of the best military aircraft in the world. Believe also that South Africa is the one country in the world that can meet their greed for gold. All the sanctions so loudly trumpeted by the Western powers will never overcome those basic facts. We have all the men necessary to fly these planes, and all the spares necessary to keep them in the air. In effect, Mr Jardine, you are looking at one of the largest, best equipped and best trained air forces in the world, let alone Africa. If you think a few Cuban cowboys are going to put much of a dent in this lot… forget it."

Harvey felt the need to intervene. De Villiers was allowing his patriotism to colour his tone. If allowed to continue further he ran the risk of antagonizing Jardine to the point where he would simply close down.

"Impressive, I think you will agree," he interjected. "But we haven't brought you here just to show off all this military hardware – awesome as it is. Our purpose is to try to bring home to you that you have seriously miscalculated. South Africa is nowhere near ready to capitulate. If you unleash the so-called EV77 all you will achieve is an atrocity. In the long run the ordinary black man, woman and child in South Africa, will be the main victim.

He looked closely at Jardine trying to tell whether he was getting through. One thing he did know; Jardine was shocked. Nobody could look at that vast display of naked air power and remain unmoved.

He pressed home his point. "You know yourself that they played their hand too soon in Soweto last year. It has just fizzled out. Bit by bit the kids have gone back to school and things have got back to normal. South Africa is a lot further from revolution than the outside world believes. You know that yourself from living here."

He stopped to let his words sink in. Silence fell in that vast underground warehouse. Somewhere water dripped unnaturally loudly in the tension laden atmosphere.

"All these are still crated up," said Jardine as he gazed at the seemingly endless rows. He turned to Harvey and in his eyes was defiance not defeat.

"Now let me tell you something, Mr smart-arse Harvey. Soldiers, sailors and airmen run on food. Aircraft run on fuel. Without the fuel to fly them all this is just bravado. Your whole effort will grind to a standstill because South Africa has no oil. An embargo which will surely come will cripple you in weeks if not days."

De Villiers rejoined the conversation.

"I think we have seen enough here for the time being. We have some other visits to make." He turned to the air force officer. "Is our plane ready?"

"Your aircraft awaits you," responded the officer with an almost imperceptible emphasis on the word 'aircraft'. He did not like his pride and joy being called a plane.

"Good, let's go."

Fifteen minutes later they were in the air heading south-west. Jardine could not see any instruments and could not be sure how far or fast they were travelling. He could see the night lights of Johannesburg away down to his left. He knew that they were somewhere south-west of the city when the aircraft began to circle and lose height. Ten minutes later they were on the ground once more.

It took him a little time to realize what the new site was. It seemed like just another military base. Soon enough he understood. Having gone through two further checkpoints he was ushered into a large lift. The doors clanged shut and the lift started to descend thousands of feet into the ground. He was being taken down a mine.

"You are wasting your time," he said with more nonchalance than he felt. Inwardly he was reeling from the sight of that vast underground arsenal of aircraft. "I've been down a mine before and everyone knows you've got gold. All the gold in the world will not buy you oil if no one will supply it. I'm not going to be impressed by a gold mine."

"I think you might change your mind about this one," retorted de Villiers.

"Oh, what's so special about it?

"Well for a start no gold has been mined here for over twelve years…"

Further conversation was brought to a halt by the lift finally coming to a standstill. The gates hissed open. De Villiers motioned them out and they boarded another golf-buggy-like vehicle. This one was on rails. They travelled for a few minutes and de Villiers brought it to a halt. He got off and waited for the others to do the same.

Then he led them slowly in a gigantic circle round a huge cylindrical edifice. It was like walking round the catwalk of a huge gasometer.

"What was it you were saying about aircraft, tanks and ships? What was it you said they needed?"

"Oil," replied Jardine flatly, beginning to understand.

"Oh yes, oil," repeated de Villiers. "You see, one of the problems of stockpiling oil is knowing where to put it. Storage tanks above ground are obvious and easily targeted. Even buried to a reasonable depth they are vulnerable. But, Mr Jardine, just suppose you could bury it a mile below the surface; just suppose someone else had conveniently dug the hole for you? Are you getting my drift?"

"Are you telling me that you are using a disused gold mine as a giant storage tank?"

Jardine was inwardly amazed but covering it well. He could see immediately that a disused gold mine provided the perfect place to store oil. Its depth made it invulnerable to anything short of a nuclear bomb.

"You are nearly there," said de Villiers unable to keep a note of triumph out of his voice. Not one gold mine – this is just one of many. How many defunct gold mines do you think there are on the Rand? Don't try to answer; just take it from me that South Africa has enough oil stored to withstand anything anyone might throw at them – weeks; no, months; forget it; years, my friend, years."

Jardine was shaken but still thinking.

"That's all very well but to store oil you have to have it in the first place. South Africa has none of its own and the world is universally hostile to you. So where do you plan to get it?"

Harvey had remained silent deliberately. This was a gigantic poker game being played out between the two South Africans. De Villiers seemed to be handling the situation better now. He had got his antipathy to Jardine under control. He was reasoning with him rather than threatening him. The outcome was crucial to their plan to turn Jardine; but the latter was proving depressingly hard to convince. Even Harvey was wondering how de Villiers would rebut this latest objection from Jardine.

The answer when it came astounded even him with his simplicity. He wondered why he had never thought of it himself.

"Let me ask you something." De Villiers looked

straight at Jardine. "What has South Africa got other than gold that makes it so interesting to the Soviets? You already know, but in case it is escaping you for a moment, I will tell you. It has an absolutely crucial position on the map. It overlooks the sea lanes round the Cape. Unless you go through the Suez Canal, which is severely restricted and easily blockaded, the only way to get a ship from east to west is round the Cape of Good Hope. So what would Soviet control of those sea lanes mean, Mr Jardine?"

"It would pose an enormous threat to the West's oil lifeline," countered Jardine.

"Quite so. But think about it. Trade is a two-way affair. Something that threatens a customer can also threaten a supplier. And if the commodity in question is the only significant source of income to that supplier, he could get very jumpy, hey, Mr Jardine?"

De Villiers paused for effect and then continued, "When people get jumpy they take precautions. Spare a thought for the Shah of Iran. His country is bordered to the north by the Soviet Union. He could easily get a feeling of insecurity when he stands on that border and gazes north. He knows he has nothing to fear from the West so why do you imagine he is building his armed forces as fast as he can? Soviet dominance of the Cape sea routes would be a disaster for him; they are his way to the outside world and the nations who buy his oil. Self-preservation tells him he is better off with South Africa in the Western camp. After Russia and Saudi Arabia, Iran is the largest oil producing country in the world. Now, Mr Jardine, ask yourself where our oil comes from. Paying in gold is always an added attraction too. Do you think he keeps us short? The world at large gives South Africa weeks if it faces an oil embargo. Look around you and know that there are several facilities like this one; how long would you give us – years, my friend, several years –

as things stand today we could survive for four years and it is getting longer all the time."

There was silence in the cavernous gold mine; both Harvey and Jardine knew that what de Villiers had said made utter sense. The thought that South Africa might have a powerful ally in the Middle East was very sobering.

De Villiers studied Jardine's demeanour intently, searching for any sign that he was about to crack. As their eyes met he thought for a moment that he had prevailed. But the reality followed quickly.

"Well, if South Africa is getting stronger every day, the sooner we strike the better," came the response from Jardine.

But the wording betrayed his ambivalence. It was long on bravado but short on conviction.

Jardine was continuing, "All the tanks, ships, aircraft and guns in the world are helpless against EV77. It is the ultimate weapon; and we have enough now to wipe out all life in swathes of your white suburbs."

De Villiers looked hard at Jardine. "No, my friend, it won't work. You may wreak dreadful destruction but you will not wipe out all life as you put it. Rest assured you will not defeat South Africa with it. It would take a full-scale land, sea and air invasion to take South Africa. I can tell you that will not happen for the reason to beat all reasons."

De Villiers turned on his heel and climbed back on the rail buggy. They rode in silence back to the lift shaft. Soon they were airborne once more. As far as Jardine could tell, they were heading in a westerly direction.

Saturday 17th September 1977

Night was beginning to give way to dawn when, at last, the engine note changed and they started to descend. As the sun came up Jardine could see at once that they were flying over the Kalahari Desert, one of the largest deserts in the world.

"We are not going to land here; there will be no need," said de Villiers. "Shortly you will understand why no country on earth will ever attack South Africa."

Mark Harvey saw it first, with a sinking feeling that had nothing to do with the descent of the aircraft. He had seen its like just once before. On that occasion he had been deployed on a mission during the Yom Kippur War. He had seen, in Israel's Negev Desert, something very like the site which he now saw below him.

But Neil Jardine had not seen anything similar before and at first looked somewhat perplexed.

"What are you trying to tell me?" he asked.

"Have you any idea what you are looking at?" de Villiers questioned him.

Jardine was silent for some time; then realization began to dawn upon him.

"If you are trying to tell me that this has something to do with the so-called South African nuclear programme, then pull the other one. South Africa likes to hint that it has nuclear weapons but no way is that true."

De Villiers, looking directly at Jardine, produced two pieces of paper and said, "When you see this you will understand. I had one hell of a job to get security clearance to show it to you. It will be obvious why. Believe me, Mr Jardine, we are not playing games here."

With that he handed the two sheets of paper to Jardine.

SECRET

August 19, 1977

The Honorable
R. F. Botha
Minister of Foreign Affairs
Pretoria

Dear Mr. Minister:

President Carter and I have been closely following the dialogue between our governments concerning allegations of a nuclear weapons program in South Africa. Ambassador Bowdler has already conveyed to you the nature of our concerns.

In your conversation with him, you asked to be provided with the evidence that had led us to express doubts about the purposes of the Kalahari facility. Our experts have concluded, on the basis of experience with analogous installations, that the most likely purpose of a facility--like the one in the Kalahari--is to conduct underground tests of nuclear explosive devices.

The facility that concerns us is located in the southern part of the Kalahari Desert, about 100 km. south of Botswana and 145 km. east of Namibia at approximately 27-45 S, 21-27 E. It consists of:

(a) A drill rig and associated facilities;

(b) A square lattice tower in a cleared area enclosed by a wall, about 1 km. from the drill rig;

(c) An area, about 3 km. from the square tower, containing a pad; this area is connected to the tower area by power or communications lines;

SECRET

(d) A secured housing area 15 km. from the tower area, containing approximately ten buildings;

(e) A hard-surface airstrip approximately 1,600 meters long and 3 km. from the housing area. In addition, the entire area is surrounded by an outer patrol road.

We are prepared to show you photographs from which this data is derived.

I believe the only way to resolve existing doubts is to permit a prompt visit by a small U. S. technical team to inspect the location in the Kalahari Desert, which we have identified as a possible nuclear test site. I believe that it is in both of our governments' interest that this visit take place no later than Sunday, August 21, before the start of the Lagos conference, where some will seek to exploit politically, to our mutual disadvantage, the uncertainties raised publicly by South Africa's nuclear activities. Our experts are prepared to leave for South Africa at a very short notice.

I hope that with your government's cooperation we can quickly put this matter to rest.

Sincerely,

Cyrus Vance

When he had finished reading it Jardine looked up, defiance still in his eyes.

"OK, so we are looking at a facility to carry out underground tests on nuclear weapons. But where are these weapons made? How do I know they are ours and this is not just a site provided by South Africa for the use of the United States or Great Britain?"

De Villiers spoke slowly and with emphasis.

"You are right; the research and development does not go on here. That happens at Pelindaba, west of Pretoria. I regret that I was refused permission to take you there but I can assure you that the programme is ours. The point is that no power on earth is going to attack South Africa knowing that the retaliation will be nuclear. Believe it, Mr Jardine."

De Villiers and Harvey looked hard at Jardine who was staring straight ahead.

"You bastards," he said softly.

De Villiers knew at that moment that he had won. As the pilot swung the aircraft round to head back the way they had come, he reflected upon the fear that the ultimate weapon induced in all who confronted it. It took a little longer but the end result was inevitable now. Jardine's spirit had been broken by what he had seen and learned in the dawn sun of the Kalahari Desert. By the time they landed back in Johannesburg Jardine had agreed that he would tell them where Stuart Holder and his unit was. However, he was refusing to part with the information until he was paid one million rand.

Harvey and de Villiers were triumphant but deathly tired from lack of sleep. The tension and the drama that had been played out that night had drained their last reserves. They were hard-trained and two very skilled operatives but they were human. Their concentration slipped for just a moment. But it was a moment long enough for them not to notice the yellow Chev in their rear-view mirror. When de Villiers did see it, it was too late. He was trapped between the sloping bank on his left and the yellow Chev on his right. Neat as a circus stunt the Chev flipped the Cortina sideways and then over into a roll. As accidents went it was not remarkable and not particularly dangerous but it was very effective. The Cortina slid to a halt upside down on its roof.

Two men appeared running from the archway of the motorway bridge they had just passed under. As Harvey fought to free himself from the stationary car he felt the sharp prick of a hypodermic needle in his arm. An ambulance had pulled down on to the carriageway from the bridge. Within minutes Harvey, de Villiers and Jardine were riding unconscious in the back of the ambulance.

Chapter Ten

London 6.30 p.m. – Saturday 17th September 1977

Geoffrey Pritchard drove his Volvo homewards. The Saturday evening traffic south of the Thames was not heavy. He was a troubled man. The news had been uniformly bad all day. The Soviet build-up of arms and supplies to Mozambique had continued unabated. Cuban troops were being ferried across from Angola to join the forces massing on the Rhodesian and South African borders.

He was frustrated by the American reaction. He knew there were plenty in high office there who could not even point out Rhodesia on a map. Since the departure of Henry Kissinger – a rare exception – he felt they had no real strategy on Rhodesia and South Africa other than to fire-fight.

The South African authorities seemed to have gone into shock. They had more or less stopped communicating altogether. The Steve Biko affair was consuming all of their attention. They seemed not to comprehend the seriousness of the EV77 threat.

News of the disappearance of Harvey, de Villiers and Jardine had reached Pritchard from Van Ruyen in mid-afternoon. To cap it all, just as he was leaving the office, he had learned from Edward Jefferson, the Chief of Security at Harrods, that Susan Bennett had not returned to her department after her lunch break. Nor had she arrived to collect her young son. He was now being cared for by the parents of one of his school friends.

In short, things were not going at all well. The Soviet plan was seemingly to create a sense of panic among the South African whites as a prelude to a 'spontaneous' uprising of the black majority. This would, in turn, lead to intervention by the Cuban troops 'to restore peace'. The way things were going it might even work, thought Pritchard. He gave an inoffensive cyclist a savage blast on the Volvo's horn.

There was nothing he could do now but sit and wait for some news from South Africa. His enforced inactivity frustrated him beyond words. He wished to hell he hadn't given up smoking as a New Year's resolution. He would have given a month's salary for a Rothman's king size at that moment.

KENYA
TANZANIA
DODOMA
KONGWA
DAR-ES-
SALAAM
MOROGORO
IRINGA
MBEYA
MUFINDI
ZAMBIA
MALAWI
MOZAMBIQUE

Chapter Eleven

Kongwa, Tanzania – Sunday 18th September 1977

Harvey awoke slowly. Every time he drifted towards consciousness he evaded reality by kidding himself he was still asleep and dozed off again. At length he accepted the inevitable and sat up.

He had no idea where he was. All he did know was that he was alone in a small room and his head hurt. Judging by the heat he was still in Africa but where exactly in that enormous continent was a mystery. He had been separated from de Villiers and Jardine. He allowed the fuzziness caused by the drugging and the journey to clear. He took stock of the situation.

Neither he nor de Villiers knew where Stuart Holder was or where the supply of what was now called EV77 was being held. Although Jardine had crumbled and agreed to tell them where both were, he had refused to actually spell it out there and then. He had resolved to salvage something out of the situation for himself. He was demanding one million rand as a payment for the information sought by Harvey and de Villiers. He had refused point-blank to give up that information until he saw the money.

Now that they appeared to be in enemy hands, Harvey was not sure that Jardine would keep his word. He could recover his nerve enough to play the part originally mapped out for him. He would not want his masters to realize the extent of his intended treachery. He might well be more scared of the Soviets than of Harvey himself and de Villiers.

Harvey reflected that the whole situation was bizarre. BOSS was not a natural ally of the UK. As Pritchard had said it was really a case of my enemy's enemy being my friend. Then again, which side was Jardine now on? Probably best to assume he was still the enemy. There was nothing Harvey could do about any of this in his present circumstances. His priorities were clear – to find out where he was, how he was being held, and to escape.

He got to his feet and found that he did not feel too bad. He was very fit and was quickly shaking off the aftermath of his abduction. The room was about ten feet long by six feet wide. There was a bed along one wall. There was no window. A bucket in one corner served as a toilet. The one surprise was a wash basin and hand towel in the other corner; a touch of luxury which was never explained. Gratefully he made use of it to clean himself up as best he could. The car crash, although not seriously injuring him, had left some scratches and bruises. He paced up and down for some time, then decided to sit and wait for something to happen.

That something took a further hour and turned out to be footsteps outside his cell. They were followed by the sound of keys clanking in the lock and the door was swung open. To his surprise he found himself confronted by a strikingly beautiful girl. He judged her to be of Caribbean origin; beautiful in all aspects except her eyes, which at that moment were hard and merciless.

"Good morning, Mr Harvey," she said briskly. "I trust you slept well."

Harvey knew that she could not have given a damn whether he had slept at all but she was continuing. "You are no doubt wondering where you are, who we are and what we want with you. I have come to tell you these things."

Over her shoulder, Harvey could see two heavily armed Africans. Making a run for it was not an option.

"My name is Juanita Havanestro and I am working in alliance with the Black Liberation Party of South Africa. You are being held in central Tanzania and will continue to be held here until we have completed our operations in South Africa. We decided to act against you as we had become concerned about the reliability of our man Jardine. We suspected that you would break him and that he would give away details of our plans. What happens now is that you will be given some food and then attend a meeting. I will then explain what we require you to do."

With that she turned on her heel and swept out of the cell.

Thirty minutes later some food arrived. It was a maize-meal mixture which the local Africans call *posho* and it was pretty solid but Harvey was hungry enough to force some of it down.

Gradually the morning wore on and the heat began to build. Harvey started to wonder when the promised meeting would take place. He heard footsteps approaching. Once more the door was thrown open. He was handcuffed and taken to a larger hut facing what he judged to be the main compound. He still had no idea where he was other than that he was in central Tanzania. It wasn't a country that figured very highly in his training or experience and the only town he really knew of in Tanzania was Dar es Salaam. However, he knew that was on the coast and not in the centre.

On entering the new hut he found Juanita sitting on the edge of a desk on one side of the room. She was clearly in charge and she motioned the guards to seat Harvey in front of her – slightly to one side. Two more guards arrived bringing with them the handcuffed de

Villiers. He was placed beside Harvey, slightly to the other side of Juanita. The guards backed off with all four of them standing behind the two prisoners. They were clearly ready to put a premature end to any idea either of them might entertain of escape.

"Let me come straight to the point," said Juanita without preamble. "Jardine is causing us quite a lot of difficulty. It was his responsibility to get the weapon, which is called EV77, put it into three canisters and hide them. He now declines to tell us where the canisters are unless we make an exorbitant payment. We consider it is very likely he has, under duress, entered into some deal with you. Clearly he is not reliable any more. Accordingly he is to be relieved of any further responsibility. His role in the operation is to be taken over by me. I will deal with him in due course. Meanwhile, I require you to tell me everything you know regarding the whereabouts of the canisters."

Harvey decided it was time to put a word in.

"Well, I can save you some time. We do not have any useful information. Whilst Jardine had agreed to lead us to the hideout where the EV77 is manufactured, he was not prepared to tell us the location until a payment was made. Before that was considered your people intervened and brought us here – wherever 'here' is."

"Here is a place called Kongwa. I do not need to be told where Holder worked on the toxin. I know that. What I need to know is where the canisters are now and where Holder has gone. Please don't waste my time telling me you don't have the information. Jardine has told us you do."

"He would say that, wouldn't he?" replied Harvey thinking he sounded like Mandy Rice-Davies.

"Come, Mr Harvey, you and de Villiers were with him all night. That is usually long enough for BOSS to get any information it wants out of someone." She looked pointedly at de Villiers.

De Villiers spoke for the first time.

"Does he look as though he has been harmed?"

"No, I admit that he does not. That might just mean the threat was enough to make him talk."

Harvey cut in again.

"Well the reality is that we don't know. All you are doing at present is wasting your own time."

The young woman flushed with anger; she did not like being spoken to in such a dismissive way. She looked at one of the guards.

"Get the girl," she barked.

To Harvey's horror a very frightened-looking Susan Bennett, similarly handcuffed, was brought in to the hut. She was seated on a chair at the side of the desk on which Juanita still perched. She was made to sit, like Harvey and de Villiers, with her hands behind her back, tied to the chair and handcuffed. It was a position that forced her torso to be thrust forward. She looked pale. Her blonde hair was dishevelled and her face was streaked with dust. Her skirt was split down one side and her blouse was torn in two places; the legacy of some struggle when she was kidnapped, Harvey supposed.

"We decided to bring Miss Bennett to Kongwa as we know both de Villiers and yourself have been trained in resisting questioning. In the end anybody will talk but 'in the end' is not soon enough for us. We want information and we want it now. Knowing the quaint concern you English have for what you patronisingly call the 'fair sex', I reasoned that you would be persuaded to talk more easily if the girl was threatened. Let me explain."

Juanita motioned towards the doorway for someone to enter. A further guard appeared carrying a large oblong package which was covered with a blanket.

"Go ahead, Victor," commanded Juanita. Victor paused and then, with a flourish, whipped off the blanket covering the large oblong package he was carrying.

Susan gasped.

Harvey had been shocked when she had been brought into the room. She was the last person he had expected to see in the prison in which he appeared to be confined. In frustration he rocked the chair to which he was bound.

The package was a glass tank. Inside the tank were two of the most fearsome snakes any of them had ever seen.

"Nice, hey?" taunted Juanita. "Do you know what they are?"

Nobody spoke.

"They are black mambas; the most aggressive snake in Africa. They are not uncommon here in Kongwa. A bite from one of those is fatal. It will kill you in anything between twenty minutes and eight hours of agony. Because it is so aggressive, it will attack unprovoked. Show them, Victor."

Victor's gaze turned towards the terrified Susan. He advanced slowly to stand in front of her. Clearly relishing what was coming next, he reached down and started to unbutton her torn blouse.

Harvey watched, desperate to stop what he could see was going to happen. He had to do something – anything.

"Alright, you have made your point," he said.

But Victor was not to be denied. Having unbuttoned the blouse he pulled it down over her shoulders, tearing it further in order to get it far enough down. Taking a wicked-looking sheath knife from his hip he ran the point of the cold steel slowly down the line of the girl's cleavage. Then with a swift jab, cut the V at the front of her bra causing it to fall away and leave her breasts exposed in an appalling humiliation. More quickly then, he cut the straps and removed the mutilated garment. He threw it on to the floor. She sat there, her eyes wide in terror. Harvey had never felt so helpless in his life. He had nothing to bargain with. Juanita clearly did not believe it, but the truth was he did not have the information she wanted.

The two African guards behind Harvey closed up. One jabbed the barrel of his gun into Harvey's temple; the other took a fierce arm lock around his neck. De Villiers was treated similarly. There was no way either of them could move. They watched in horror as Victor produced a heavy gauntlet which he pulled on to his right hand and arm. Then turning to the glass tank he carefully reached down into it and grabbed one of the snakes behind its head. Its tail swung sickeningly as he moved towards Susan. Harvey could hardly bear to look. It was obvious what was going to happen. Victor stepped towards Susan. She screamed in terror as he dropped the writhing snake around her bare shoulders.

There was complete silence in the room. Her scream died away. They watched unable to do anything to stop the horror unfolding before their eyes.

Nothing happened. For a few moments the silence continued. And then Victor began to laugh and laugh. The snake was a rubber replica and just hung around her neck where he had placed it.

"Alright, Victor, that will do for the moment. I think Mr Harvey understands now the consequences if he refuses to cooperate. Believe me, my friends, the other snake in the tank is not a replica. It is very real indeed."

She looked ominously at the cornered Englishman.

"Right, let's start at the beginning, shall we? I want you to tell me everything you know about our operation; everything that your superiors in London know; I want to know what they, and the South African authorities, are planning to do about it. I advise you to tell the truth because Victor and his friend are going nowhere. I will be forced to let him go to the next stage if I think you are stalling. I don't think I have to tell you what that next stage will be." She looked at the snake that was slowly writhing in the tank. Then she swung her gaze deliberately onto Susan.

From the moment he saw the snakes, Harvey had been desperately trying to think of what he could say to stave off an attack on Susan. In truth he knew very little that would be valuable to Havanestro. He decided he would just start at the beginning and relate the entire sequence of events. He hoped against hope that either he or de Villiers would be able to think of something to cause a disturbance and somehow get away from the guards. That did not look a very promising prospect. As his story developed, no inkling of a way out manifested itself either to him or to de Villiers. He just droned on wondering what would happen when he reached the end.

He never did reach the end. He had got as far as the interrogation of Oscar Tembi when there was a sudden commotion outside. There was some shouting followed by a few shots and the sound of people running. Then the sound of a vehicle being started up and driven away at high speed. An African burst into the hut.

"*Memsahib!* Bwana Jardine has escaped!" he shouted.

Juanita swore in a language none of them understood and jumped down from the desk.

"Keep them here until I return," she shouted and hurried out. A few moments later there was the sound of another vehicle being driven away. Harvey placed them as Land Rovers from the noise.

Silence fell in that small room. The guards, other than Victor, had gone with Juanita although it was doubtful that was what she had meant to happen. Harvey and de Villiers realized that if they were ever going to get away it had to be now. There was no way of knowing how long she would be gone, how quickly she would realize that only Victor remained with the prisoners or what other guards there might be on site. But Victor was large, powerful, watchful, and above all, armed. The keys to their handcuffs were lying tantalizingly on the desk where one of the departing guards had thrown them. Presumably they had thought Victor might need them.

Gradually it dawned on Susan that she was the only one of the three with the ability to distract Victor's attention. That might give the other two a chance to start something. She was very aware that his eyes kept returning to her naked torso. She looked up at him and in a conciliatory tone said, "Please would you give me my bra back."

Victor said nothing. He gathered together the pieces of her bra that were strewn on the floor. With obvious relish he dropped them into the waste-paper basket behind the desk. Then he walked round to the front of the desk again and stood over the horrified girl. With a sneer he raised his right hand and made to place it full on her left breast.

He never made it. Harvey and de Villiers were handcuffed and tied by their arms to their chairs but their legs were free. The African had no idea of what was about to happen. Taking the chair with him Harvey sprang up behind Victor. He kicked him with all the considerable strength in his right leg, squarely in the groin.

Such was the force of the kick that Victor's fifteen-stone frame left the floor and toppled sideways to the ground. He let out an agonized roar as he fell clutching his groin. At that moment two further kicks, one from Harvey and one from de Villiers, caught him on the back of the neck with two sickening cracks of such ferocious power that Susan thought they would have felled a tree. They certainly felled Victor.

If the circumstances had been different the next few minutes could just possibly have been the funniest of their young lives; three people, all with chairs attached to their backs, attempting to manoeuvre themselves into a position from which they could retrieve the keys to their handcuffs. But the circumstances were not different. They were desperate to free themselves before anyone else appeared. Susan's semi-nudity made her angry and embarrassed in equal measure as well as scared. Harvey learned that she was capable of a stream of expletives.

"I don't suppose that is common parlance in the Skirts and Blouses department at Harrods," he said.

"You might be surprised," she retorted

It was five minutes of the most desperate urgency, however, and not in the very least amusing to any of them. They were terrified that, at any moment, Victor would come back to life or a guard would appear or Juanita would return. Their fear gave them superhuman strength to contort themselves into every possible and seemingly impossible position. Finally de Villiers managed to grasp the keys. With difficulty he released Susan's handcuffs. In turn she released the two men. Quickly she rearranged her blouse. It was in a poor state but still just enough in one piece to cover her. It would have to do.

Harvey peered gingerly out of the window. There were a number of vehicles in the compound, mostly Land Rovers, but no hope of reaching any of them without being seen. They did not know who was still around, where they were or what arms they had. The only sensible course of action seemed to be to try and slip away from the camp as unobtrusively as possible. This meant going into the bush away from the road. Harvey assumed there would be a way of doubling back when they were far enough away. This would allow them to reach the road he presumed was at the end of the track leading out of the camp.

"We'll go out of the window," he said, and they did, slipping away behind the compound and into the bush. It was slow and painful progress. They discovered quickly that there are many thorns in the bush around Kongwa. They inched their way cautiously in a circle to take them back out of the camp. The place was ominously quiet.

Obviously the routine of everyday life had been seriously disrupted for there was a noticeable lack of activity about the place.

The arid scrub did not offer much cover. It had originally been much thicker but a great swathe had been cleared in preparation for the Groundnut Scheme. They set off as stealthily as they could. De Villiers turned out to know exactly how to make the maximum use of what little cover there was. They started to work in a circle so as to return to the road.

Perhaps they turned back a little too sharply or perhaps Victor was more resilient than they thought. Whatever the reason, suddenly he appeared from behind a baobab tree. Harvey could hardly believe that the African had recovered so quickly – but there he was. The black mamba had gone but in its place a pistol in his right hand was pointing very threateningly straight at Susan.

"Stop!" he cried. "I will shoot."

A Land Rover engine came to life somewhere close by in the camp. Someone was coming to assist Victor. Harvey felt sick. They had just managed to get away from a seemingly hopeless position only to be recaptured in minutes.

Suddenly they were fighting to stay on their feet. Their faces, hands and all exposed flesh was being lacerated by sand. It was as if a thousand men were at work with sandpaper on them. They were engulfed in a red dust-devil some hundred feet high – a not uncommon occurrence in Kongwa.

The swirling monster passed over them relatively quickly. Its path was taking it straight towards the incoming Land Rover. The driver saw it rather late and took desperate avoiding action. The Land Rover slammed into the baobab.

The tree was home to a beehive and the impact of the Land Rover dislodged it. A swarm of bees dropped out and onto Victor and the driver of the vehicle.

"*Wembembe! Wembembe! Angalia! Hatari! Wembembe!*" shouted Victor.

"What's he shouting?" called out Susan.

De Villiers was the first to realize what was happening. "Bees!" he screamed. "Leg it as fast as you can go. Just hope they stick with the two Africans."

"Are they dangerous?" asked the English girl.

"Dangerous!" responded de Villiers. "They are more than dangerous; they are bloody lethal."

The bees descended on the two hapless Africans. They fought desperately, tearing at their clothes. They ran screaming and waving their arms. They rolled in the sand. They tried in vain to cover their faces. Victor slumped to the ground. The Land Rover started reversing, veering wildly from side to side. The driver was still tearing at his clothes and exposed skin.

The diversion enabled the three escapees to put distance between themselves and the camp. They did not know precisely where they were but de Villiers had a natural feel for the bush and was confident that they would soon come upon a road. In a relatively short time he was proved correct. They discovered that it was a loop off the main road. They continued on and eventually took refuge in a culvert under the main highway from Morogoro to Dodoma.

They heard a car approaching. Peering from the ditch they could see a station wagon bearing down on them. They left it as late as they dared; then Susan leapt from the culvert into the road, the damsel in distress. The vehicle was a Peugeot 404 estate car and it pulled up in a cloud of dust. She was relieved to see that it contained only one occupant, a European man. She ran forward and opened the passenger door.

"Please, we need your help," and with that Harvey and de Villiers came scrambling out of the culvert.

"Have you passed two Land Rovers going in the opposite direction?" asked Harvey.

"No," replied the young man looking from one to the other of them with a puzzled expression on his face. "I haven't passed a thing all the way from Morogoro except one bus."

"Please will you take us the way you are going then?" asked Harvey. "I'll explain as we go."

The young man hesitated for a few moments; but it is inbred in Europeans in Africa to help each other. The presence of a woman made him feel doubly obliged. Soon they were leaving Kongwa behind.

It took a little time to explain to the man, Robin Crawford, what three people, all in a dishevelled state, were doing in the middle of Africa with no real idea of where they were. Harvey saw no point in beating about the bush; they were going to need this young man. He told him as much of the truth as he could without mentioning the EV77.

They learned that Crawford was going to Dodoma; a town more or less in the middle of Tanzania. He told them it was about fifty miles west of Kongwa; an hour's drive.

They stopped a couple of times to enquire of Africans on the road whether they had seen two Land Rovers pass. They soon discovered that they had. It was clear that Juanita also was going the same way. When they reached the outskirts of the town they made further enquiries. It became apparent that they had gone straight through Dodoma and south towards Iringa. By this time Crawford knew enough to know that he could either drive on or hand over his car. He elected to drive.

Harvey guessed that they must be about forty-five minutes behind the Land Rovers. He knew that the Peugeot would cover the ground more quickly.

Crawford volunteered the information that Iringa was

about 160 miles south.

"There's a long winding escarpment just short of Iringa," he said. "That should slow the Land Rovers more than us. We may be able to catch them there."

Apparently he travelled the road frequently so knew it well. It was clear that fuel was going to be a critical factor in this pursuit. Here again the Peugeot would outperform the Land Rovers unless they had diesel engines.

"No, they've got petrol engines; I heard them when they drove out of the camp." De Villiers was adamant.

Crawford made Iringa in just under three hours. They pulled into the Caltex station in the main street of the town. It was here that they learned that Jardine was armed. He had shot down all four of Juanita's guards. They learned from a very shocked attendant that he had pulled in for fuel and had only taken on a little when the second vehicle appeared. After the skirmish both Land Rovers had then gone screaming out of Iringa southwards; they were less than five minutes ahead. Crawford looked askance at the four dead Africans sprawled on the forecourt of the filling station. But he was not about to hand over his car. A police Land Rover, siren wailing, made up his mind for him. They were on their way again almost immediately.

It was on another shorter escarpment directly out of Iringa that they first saw the two Land Rovers. They had turned to the right and were heading south down the road to Mbeya. As the Peugeot slewed down the winding road Harvey could see down below, to the right, that the two Land Rovers were about half a mile apart.

"This could go on forever!" shouted Crawford. "Mbeya is more than two hundred miles down that road."

"Just catch them up and then hold station about two hundred yards behind them. They will both run out of petrol before you do."

"You hope!" replied Crawford with feeling.

Neil Jardine was a desperate man. He knew he had shot and at least wounded Juanita's guards. He did not know whether he had got them all. He was not increasing his lead over her at all; he had only taken on a minimal amount of fuel at Iringa before she caught up with him. The country was now so open that he could see no way of losing her.

He had travelled about fifty miles out of Iringa when he began to feel panic rising. His petrol gauge was dipping perilously close to empty. He knew he would run out of fuel within the next twenty or thirty miles. He presumed that Juanita must be in a similar position. She would not have had time to put very much in after he had roared out of the Caltex station. He did not feel like gambling his life on who would run dry first. He needed a more winding road and more cover to make some sort of a stand.

All these thoughts were racing round his mind when he reached a turn-off at a place marked 'John's Corner'. He chose to go left off the main road onto one which looked less made-up. He hoped it might offer the sort of terrain that would be more helpful to him. He saw from a sign that he was heading into the Southern Highlands of Tanzania. Perhaps he would find what he sought up there.

The vehicles slowed gradually as the altitude began to reduce the power of the engines. The road began to climb towards rainforest. A sign indicated that he had reached a district called Mufindi.

Desperate that he would run out of fuel, he decided to take a chance. He took a left turn onto a dirt road. He noticed a large board identifying the place as 'Section 9 of The Highlands Tea Co Ltd'. The main reason he had chosen that precise moment to turn was that he had been, for a minute or two, out of sight of Juanita. But it was the dry season in Mufindi. There had been no rain since May.

His progress was obvious for all to see by the cloud of dust that hung in the air.
Juanita did not hesitate. She went in after him.

She had her own worries. She was also desperately short of fuel and she had no idea who would run out first. She had a hand-gun but she was alone now and Jardine was armed. Thanks to the training he had been given, he was a formidable enemy in this type of terrain. She could not see any alternative but to follow him and wait for the crunch to come. She was not prepared to give up. So she drove on, her mouth dry with suspense and choked with dust.

The Peugeot followed behind them. They had no immediate fuel worries but they did not have a gun between them; moreover, Harvey did not like the way the country was becoming much thicker in vegetation and more densely wooded. There were too many places where Jardine could disappear. He was still their quarry and their only hope of locating Holder and the canisters of EV77.

Jardine hurtled on through a camp and past some single-storey buildings. All the while he was looking for a place to make his stand. He forked right after the buildings and then took a left turn. He went roaring up an incline between two fields of what looked like low laurel bushes. He had passed a few African huts when he saw a bungalow off to the left. He slewed the vehicle into the driveway and came to a shuddering halt.

He had noticed a board marked 'Kilimatembo' and presumed that must be the name of the place. He leapt from the Land Rover and ran onto the veranda of the house. He pushed open the French windows. He found himself in a large room with an open fireplace and four doors leading to other rooms. He chose the one on his immediate right, guessing correctly that it was a bedroom.

It afforded a good field of vision of the driveway. In a few short moments he had barricaded himself in and was crouched at the window. He had an automatic pistol and enough ammunition to put up a stout defence.

Neil Jardine was ready for the showdown.

Juanita saw, by the dust from Jardine's Land Rover, that he had come to a halt. It was obvious that he had holed up in the building. It was an old colonial, settler-type bungalow with white walls and a green corrugated iron roof. She was about three hundred yards short of it when she saw the sign 'Kilimatembo'. She went a further hundred yards and then decided to stop. She knew that Jardine had a gun and would not hesitate to use it. She did not fancy driving up to the front door and allowing him to take a free shot at her. She despised him for his treachery but she knew he was as dangerous as a cornered wild animal.

The Peugeot, in turn, pulled up a further hundred and fifty yards behind Juanita. Harvey had no idea whether Juanita was aware of the station wagon following her. It made little difference anyway. All he could sensibly do was to sit tight and preserve any element of surprise that he had. He must pick his moment to strike.

Shortly he became aware of the sound of an engine labouring up the hill behind him.

A few moments later a battered old Ford Anglia van appeared. A young man dressed in shorts and a shirt climbed out of the van.

"What's going on here?" he asked

"Is that your house?" replied Harvey.

"Yes it is. I was on my way back to lunch when I saw the dust from your cars. I don't get too many visitors up here and was curious."

"I would leave lunch for a bit if I was you, Mr Errr..."

"Evans," supplied the young man. "Dennis Evans."

"Well, Dennis, it's like this," explained Harvey. "There is a dangerous criminal holed up in your house. In the Land Rover just up the road ahead of us is one of his accomplices with whom he has fallen out. My colleague and I–" he said, indicating de Villiers, "–are from the police authorities and are trying to apprehend the man in the house before the woman in the Land Rover either kills him or gets killed by him."

"Woman?" echoed Evans in surprise.

"Yes, woman," confirmed Harvey. "But don't let that fool you; she is as dangerous as half a dozen men." He paused and turned his attention to the road ahead of them.

"Robin here says this stuff on either side of the road is tea. Presumably the sign saying 'Kilimatembo' is the name of this tea estate. Is that right?"

Evans looked somewhat taken aback that someone in the middle of the tea growing area of Tanzania apparently didn't know what tea looked like. But he was having a surprising morning so he just answered the question anyway.

"Yes, that's tea alright and the name of the estate is Kilimatembo. In Swahili *kilima* means hill and *tembo* means elephant so basically you are in a place called Elephant Hill; but don't worry, there haven't been any elephants here for years. The occasional leopard maybe, but no elephants."

Harvey ignored the slightly amused tone and asked, "Is there any way we can creep up on the Land Rover without being seen or heard?"

"Yes," replied Evans. "The tea on the left is too low but on the right it is in its final year before pruning. As you can see, it is chest high so we could crawl along beneath it and I could bring you out exactly opposite the Land Rover."

Like Crawford before him it never occurred to Evans to do anything but help a fellow European.

"I suppose you haven't got a weapon of any sort have you?" enquired Harvey.

"Not with me; there's a shotgun in the house but in the van I do have a pruning knife. You can make a hell of a mess of someone with one of those."

He went to the Ford van and returned with a knife. The handle was about a foot long with a short hooked blade on the end, giving the implement the appearance of the letter J.

"Right, Darnie, you stay here with Susan and Robin while Dennis and I will attempt to take Havanestro by surprise."

They set off through the tea. Harvey had learned from Evans that the uniform height to which the tea grew was called the 'table'. It was plenty tall enough to cover their approach as long as they crawled. Indeed the greater danger was that they would be heard rather than seen. They kept well away from the road until they reached a point where they were level with the stationary Land Rover. Harvey risked a peep over the tea table. Juanita was sitting at the wheel of the Land Rover staring intently at the house. She was obviously trying to make up her mind whether to go in after Jardine or be patient and wait for him to make a move.

It was clear to Harvey that there was no way they could creep up on her without her hearing. He ducked down again quickly and whispered as much to Evans.

"It's 2.30 p.m. now," whispered Evans in reply. "Work stops at three for the day on the estate. Some of the labour force will walk back along this road to their huts. They will be chattering and laughing and will make enough noise to drown out our approach. I suggest we just wait."

Harvey saw no alternative. He was worried that Juanita

would make a move but in the event his concern proved groundless. She remained sitting in the Land Rover clearly thinking that patience would pay dividends in the end.

At 3.15 they heard the first of the Africans returning from the tea fields. They were walking along the road chattering and laughing exactly as Evans had predicted. Some of them were singing and altogether they were making enough noise to enable Harvey and Evans to move. They crawled right up to the side of the road being careful to avoid being seen by any of the Africans who would have given away their position immediately.

Then Harvey got the break he needed. Two African stragglers were approaching along the road and he could see that they were both in an advanced state of inebriation. He could hardly believe his luck. Evans could have told him that it was a regular occurrence at this time of day. They approached and stopped a few yards away from Juanita's open window.

"*Jambo, Memsahib*," said one of them as a greeting.

"*Camwene*," replied the other, using the tribal language of the local Wahehe tribe rather than Swahili.

They stood and giggled as Juanita made no reply. She simply ignored them. Then one of them lurched towards the Land Rover. He came from the front. As the Cuban girl watched him Harvey struck from behind. Before she knew what was happening she found an arm thrust through the side window and a wicked looking knife hooked hard against her throat.

"Just don't move, not even an inch," he snarled at her. "Evans, come and give me a hand."

Evans rose from the tea and came towards them.

"*Toka! Toka!*" he shouted at the two startled Africans who took off as fast as their impaired sense of balance would permit.

"Get into the Land Rover through the back and pick up the gun that is on the seat beside her."

Juanita considered taking a chance and going for the gun; then she thought about the steel pressing on her throat and the steadiness of the hand that held it. She decided that she wasn't ready to die just yet.

Evans climbed into the vehicle from the back. Only a short time ago he had been going home for lunch. Now here he was apprehending a dangerous criminal. Things were getting a little out of control, he thought. He reached gingerly over the back of the seat for the gun but the girl did not move and he retreated out of the back door the way he had come.

"Do you know anything about guns?" asked Harvey.

"Yes I do and this one is loaded and ready to fire."

"OK, let me have it." He held out his left hand and Evans passed it over to him. In a moment he had the girl covered by it.

"Alright, baby, let's go very slowly." He motioned her out of the back of the Land Rover to minimise the chance of Jardine shooting at them. They crawled back to the Peugeot using the tea as cover.

"Have you any rope?" Harvey asked Evans.

"Yes, in the van – I'll get it."

De Villiers trussed the girl up with her wrists lashed to her ankles and shoved her unceremoniously into the back of the station wagon.

"One down and one to go," said Harvey. "Darnie, I suggest you, Susan and Robin stay here and make sure madam does not move. If she even as much as yawns, hit her with this as hard as you can."

He handed him a tyre lever that he had found in the well under the passenger seat of the Land Rover.

"Dennis, you come with me and see if we can flush Mr Jardine out."

"I hope he hasn't flown already," responded de Villiers.

"I doubt it. If I was him I would wait for darkness before trying to make a run for it."

The two of them went back into the tea and crawled along towards the house. They did not want to give Jardine a target. He had probably seen what had happened to Juanita. They did not know which room Jardine would have holed up in.

Evans said that the front bedroom was the obvious choice; it afforded a view down the drive.

"What he probably doesn't know," said Evans, "is that the drive has two entrances. An 'in' at the front and an 'out' at the back. I suggest we circle round and approach the house from the rear."

"OK," agreed Harvey. "But quietly; this guy is seriously dangerous."

They made their approach as Evans had suggested. They found the servants' quarters at the rear of the house. Evans's cook was looking decidedly apprehensive but able to confirm that the stranger, the *mgeni*, was indeed in the front bedroom.

They entered the house through the kitchen and went via the dining room into the living room. Harvey motioned Evans to stand well clear of the bedroom door.

"Jardine!" he called out. "It's me, Harvey! We have got the girl. You can come out now."

There was a fairly lengthy silence as Jardine digested this new and somewhat unexpected turn of events. It was a difficult decision for him to make. He wanted to pursue his million rand but he did not want to walk straight into the arms of the enemy. He preferred to remain free to continue negotiations. At length he made his decision.

"Thanks for the offer, but no thanks. I'll stay here for now. If you want me you'll have to come and get me. I warn you that will not be easy."

"No problem," responded Harvey. "I have nothing else on today. You'll get hungry and thirsty sooner or later."

And so they sat. Harvey saw no point in risking bloodshed trying to force the pace.

He asked Evans to get his shotgun. Then he sent him back to the others. They were to bring the Peugeot up to the house. Some twenty minutes later it nosed cautiously into the rear entrance of the drive.

Time wore on. There were a few desultory exchanges of conversation with Jardine but nothing that led anywhere. Evans noticed bloodstains on the living room floor. They deduced that Jardine must be wounded; how seriously was not known. Perhaps that was why he had not made a run for it when Juanita was being captured. Or possibly he had not been able to see exactly what was going on and preferred to wait for darkness to make a move.

Dusk quickly gave way to night. At an altitude of six thousand feet above sea level they found the heat of the Mufindi day dissipating quickly. Evans lit a log fire. He also lit two paraffin lamps. The bungalow had no electricity supply.

It was after nine when Jardine made his move. He guessed there was only one gun against him and that Harvey probably had it outside the bedroom door. Obviously they would have posted de Villiers in the garden somewhere but he would have to take that chance. He went out through the front window of the bedroom like a cat and was round the corner of the bungalow before anyone had time to move. His aim was to lose them in the surrounding forest.

But de Villiers was quick. Although Jardine was running, as soon as his feet struck the ground he had to sprint down the back drive to keep de Villiers at a distance.

Meanwhile Harvey came bounding out of the kitchen

door and joined the chase.

Jardine raced down the road behind the house. It led down quite sharply into the dwellings provided for the estate labour force. It consisted of an encampment of several rondavels and some rectangular huts laid out neatly in symmetrical rows.

Jardine dived behind one of the rondavels for cover. Harvey immediately gestured for de Villiers to hold position. He started to inch his way towards the rondavel. Jardine had just decided to make a dash into the nearest hut and take a hostage, preferably a child, when it appeared.

'It' was a mongrel dog, a *shenzi* as the Africans call them. It came sloping out of the darkness across the camp. Harvey froze in his tracks. The dog was running in a completely erratic and random manner, leaping into the air from time to time and emitting the most blood curdling noise somewhere between a howl and a scream. Its jaws were covered in frothing saliva. In the moonlight it was one of the most terrifying sights that Harvey had ever seen – and he had seen a few. But he had never seen rabies.

He raised the shotgun to shoot it but, before he could get a shot in, it disappeared behind the rondavel where Jardine had taken cover. In a silent frenzy it attacked the terrified man. Jardine erupted with a scream of terror. He leapt out into the open with the crazed animal clinging to his arm by its teeth. Harvey recalled the blood on the living room floor in the bungalow. He realized Jardine probably had an open wound. In the end Harvey managed to shoot the wretched animal without killing Jardine.

"Just hold it there, Jardine," shouted Harvey. "Pull yourself together and don't move one step further." His voice cut across the night.

"For Christ's sake I've been bitten by the bloody thing. I've got to get to a hospital and have the jabs," screamed

Jardine.

"Just shut up and listen." Something in the tone of Harvey's voice stilled Jardine.

"I will drive you to the nearest hospital and you will get the jabs you need but first you will tell me where Holder is and where you have hidden the canisters of EV77."

Jardine was hardly listening. He was focused totally on the dreadful event that had just befallen him.

"Come on, man, there's no time to waste," he shouted. "I need those injections like now."

A cold fury gripped Harvey.

"So," he spat out, "it's alright for thousands of your innocent countrymen to die of Ebola but not alright for Neil Jardine to die of rabies. Wake up, you little shit. I don't give a damn if you never get the injections. If you die in crazed agony it will be nothing to me, so don't hold out on me one minute longer. Give!"

Jardine was still enough in control to recognize that Harvey was deadly serious. His fear at being bitten by the rabid dog was overriding all else. Suddenly his political beliefs and his desire for money seemed totally irrelevant. He just stood in the African night gripped by a primeval terror he had never before known.

"OK, OK, OK," he screamed. He told Harvey where Holder was working.

They made space for him behind the back seat of the Peugeot. With Harvey and de Villiers flanking Juanita in the back seat and Susan and Evans squashed into the front, Crawford set off towards the main road. They learned from Evans that the tea company had a hospital near its head office about half an hour's drive away.

Harvey used the journey to take stock of the situation. He had no way of knowing if Jardine had told him the truth. Assuming that he had, Holder and the EV77 manufacturing unit were in Johannesburg in a disused building belonging originally to South African Breweries.

Pritchard had said that it would be easy to hide a laboratory in a pharmaceutical company. A brewery seemed to fit the bill just as well. Quite how much of the stuff had been got outside the unit he did not know. That was not his immediate concern. His immediate concern was quite simply stated but not at all easily accomplished. He had to get back to South Africa. How he was going to do that he had no idea. He would have to think of something – and fast.

His thoughts were ended by their arrival at the hospital. The doctor was called. He was naturally taken aback to find a man and a woman both bound so they could barely move. Harvey took him aside and told him that they were accomplices in a criminal gold-smuggling gang; that de Villiers and himself were to escort them back to South Africa to be charged. The doctor looked less than convinced but seemed to accept that it was not really his business. On the other hand a man who had been bitten by what sounded like a rabid dog was. He agreed to give Jardine the first of the vital injections. He assumed that the man would stay under his supervision until out of danger. Harvey had no intention of letting him stay or staying with him but saw no point in complicating matters by telling the doctor that at this point. In any case it was now approaching 11 p.m. and they were all exhausted. They had not eaten. The doctor roused his African cook and offered them bacon and eggs at his house.

Afterwards they returned to the hospital. The doctor explained that what had originally been the isolation ward had now been turned into guest quarters. There was sufficient room to accommodate them all. All that is except for Robin Crawford. He asked to be allowed to return to Dodoma where he had a job to go to. Harvey took him to one side.

"You do realize that nothing that you have seen or

heard must ever pass your lips."

"Yes, of course," replied Crawford. "The fewer people who know I was ever here the better, as far as I am concerned. I have to live and work in this country."

Harvey looked directly into the eyes of the young man.

"Well, I must impress upon you that discretion is paramount in this case; and as a matter of fact I wouldn't go anywhere near Kongwa for as long as possible."

"You're telling me. Don't worry, Mr Harvey, I'm out of here and will never speak of it again."

Harvey's experience told him that Crawford probably would speak of it again but he couldn't keep him as a prisoner forever. There was really nothing to be done but to let him go. Harvey was not a man to spend time worrying about things he could do nothing about. Once he had made a decision that was the end of it. Crawford left and Harvey put him out of his mind.

He arranged for Jardine and Juanita to be firmly roped to their beds and de Villiers volunteered to sleep in one room with them. Harvey, Susan Bennett and Dennis Evans took the second room. There was much to be thought about and done. But now they slept.

Chapter Twelve

Chimoio, Mozambique – September 1977

Richard Masingi was not a happy man. He was second-in-command at Chimoio Guerrilla Training Camp. Chimoio lay in the north-west quarter of Mozambique some fifty miles from the eastern Rhodesian border. There were upwards of nine thousand personnel at the camp which had been set up as a base from which to conduct a bush war against Ian Smith's Rhodesia. The leader of the Zimbabwe African National Union (ZANU), Robert Mugabe, had established his headquarters there after his release from prison in 1974.

The command unit of the camp was situated approximately twelve miles north-east of the actual town of Chimoio. This was the military headquarters for the Zimbabwe African National Liberation Army (ZANLA).

Masingi's personal base was at a place named Chaminuka Camp. He commuted daily to a further camp called Takawira Base Two Camp. This was a few miles to the north-east. Most of the military training was undertaken there.

Although standing at an altitude of two thousand feet, the climate was hot and humid. The most prominent feature at Chimoio was Mount Bengo, an edifice of rock that resembled the head of an old man. The native Mozambiqueans attributed spiritual status to this rock.

When the rains came, it seemed as if the old man was shedding tears as the water rolled down the side of his face.

Richard Masingi had rather too many problems on his mind to be able to appreciate this superstition. He was beset by plotting and scheming within his own ranks. There were those among his men who wanted to mend fences with the Zimbabwe People's Revolutionary Army (ZIPRA) their brothers based in Zambia. They wished to launch a united offensive against Rhodesia. Masingi regarded such an idea as totally naïve. Getting the whites out was just the start. What really mattered was *who* got them out. It had to be ZANU, and then ZANU would rule Zimbabwe.

Even if he decided to listen to his dissidents and try to unite with ZIPRA, his opposite number there, Joseph Ngaya, would have none of it. It seemed to Masingi that he and Ngaya spent far more time and expense decimating the ranks of each other than ever they did on their combined efforts against Ian Smith.

Masingi hated the white regime in power in Rhodesia. However, he knew the Rhodesian forces were to be respected. He also realized that the divisions in his own ranks allowed the wily Smith to play one off against the other.

There was only one compensation. There was a torrent of arms and military equipment being air-lifted into the base. He could get his hands on some of that one day.

ZAMBIA
ZIMBUE
FINGOE
ZUMBO
ZAMBEZI RIVER
CAHORA
BASSA
LAKE KARIBA
MOZAMBIQUE
RHODESIA
CHIMOIO

Chapter Thirteen

Mufindi, Tanzania – Monday 19th September 1977

Harvey awoke early the next day. It dawned clear and bright. The highland air gave a crispness to the morning that he associated more with Scotland than Africa. He did not seem to be suffering any ill effects from the altitude of six thousand feet. Altogether he thought he could get to like this place.

Despite the freshness of the early morning, the latent power of the sun presaged a warm day. It was spring in Mufindi and the temperature would reach well into the seventies by noon. Harvey needed time to clear his mind and order his thoughts. The events of the previous day had unwound so swiftly that he had been forced to react to them rather than control them.

He slipped out of the hospital wing and down a track at the end of the drive. As he strolled through a belt of wattle trees he found himself on what was, unmistakably, a golf course. The dew was still visible on the fairways. The whole morning had a magical 'Garden of Eden' quality about it. He wished he had no more to do than to play some golf.

But he did have more to do; much more. He had to get all of them back to South Africa – and he had to do it fast. He thought about getting hold of a car or Land Rover and driving down to Malawi or up to Kenya. He was very unenthusiastic about either option. The time element was against him and anyway there were too many problems about travelling across hostile borders to make it viable. The expanse of grass in front of him reminded him of a small airstrip in Hampshire where he was accustomed to landing, after flying from Biggin Hill. It made him think that, if somehow he could get hold of a light aircraft, the best plan would be to fly out of Tanzania. But where was he going to get an aircraft from in the middle of Africa?

He turned to look back up the fairway and was surprised to see Susan walking towards him. He found himself wondering about his feelings for her. He recalled his first girlfriend, Jenny. She was a sweet girl and worshipped him. She was a fine swimmer. They had met when he was in his last year at Manchester Grammar School. He was their freestyle star and subjected to intense training there. The relationship had died when he left school and joined the Metropolitan Police. He was sent to Hendon for his training. Jenny's successor had been Christine. He remembered her with a mixture of fondness and pain. He had really liked that girl but he was able to admit to himself, now several years had passed, that she was a flirt. She would never commit solely to him.

Then came the love of his life, Kate. She was an agent in MI6. By the time they were both thirty they were ready to settle down and marry. Then Kate had been sent to East Pakistan in 1971. The country was in the process of a struggle for independence from Pakistan. Eventually it became Bangladesh. There had been far more involvement by the major powers than was realized at the time. The United States supported Pakistan. Britain, as the ex-colonial power, had been in a difficult position. Harvey would never forget the day he received the news that Kate was missing. She was never found. The agony of not knowing had been the worst thing. In the end he just had to accept that she was gone, probably dead, and get on with his life. It had not been easy. He had taken it badly. More than once Geoffrey Pritchard had been forced to reprimand him for taking too many risks with his life during their time together in Northern Ireland.

For the past six years he had not had a serious relationship. He had taken Pritchard's PA, Lesley Joyce, out a few times. It was enjoyable but was never going to lead anywhere. Now, suddenly, here was a young woman barging into his life. At twenty-eight she was seven or eight years younger than him but she seemed mature. His mode of life – frequent unpredictable trips away from home – had made him something of a loner.

He had been enjoying the solitude of the early morning. Normally he would have been irritated to have someone else intrude. But, somewhat to his surprise, he had to admit to himself that he was not displeased to see her.

Susan had managed to borrow some clothes from the doctor's wife. She was wearing a plain turquoise skirt and a floral print cotton blouse. She clearly had not been able to borrow a replacement bra. Harvey was very aware of the movement of her body beneath the light fabric.

She stopped a few yards short of him to take off the rubber flip-flops she had borrowed. They were becoming slippery on the damp grass. She came towards him holding them in her left hand. As she reached him she held out her right hand for him to take.

"Isn't it a glorious morning?" she said.

"Perfect," he answered.

A look of tension crossed her face; she withdrew her hand and turned away from him.

"Not quite perfect," she said. "I haven't said anything about it yet but I am worried sick about David."

"When did you last see him?" he asked.

"When I left home for work on that last morning; Friday."

"Who do you think will be looking after him?"

"After school he was due to go to the Hiltons, in the flat above mine. They know him well and have always been very helpful. I am assuming that he went there as planned. They know the telephone number of my parents in Kent. I'm hoping they will have come to take over and look after him. I've no reason to suppose anything else might have happened but we seem to be mixed up with some very ruthless people."

"How were you taken?"

"I decided to eat my sandwiches for lunch in the park; near to where we sat on that first evening. On the way back I must have been abducted. I don't remember much about it, except for someone approaching me to ask the time. The next thing I knew I was in that little room at Kongwa. Naturally my first thought was for David but there is just nothing I can do for him. Is there any way you can find out if he is alright?"

"I can try to get a message to Pritchard, my boss, but it will be difficult while we are in Tanzania. The moment I make contact I am laying us open to being located. I will do my best though. Do you remember anything about your journey from London to Kongwa?" He was a little curious as to how she had just materialized in Tanzania.

"Well it must have been by air to have been so quick; I can only suppose it was in a private plane."

"I guess so," mused Harvey. He was wondering if now would be a good time to pursue the reservation he still had about Susan Bennett's story. She had been vague about her parting from Jardine in 1970. Harvey felt uneasy about it. It must have been clear in her mind if it was a difficult scene. She had implied that it had been tense as she had given Jardine his marching orders at the time.

"Sorry to come the policeman on you but I need to clear something up." He decided a direct approach was best now he knew her fairly well.

"Oh? What?"

"Your parting from Jardine in 1970. I just feel you held something back when you told me about it."

She was silent for a moment. Then she looked directly at him.

"Bloody hell, Mark, you don't miss much do you?"

"It's my job, Susan."

"Yeah, OK. To be honest it is something I am not very proud of and did not see that it was relevant. That's why I didn't go into it."

"Now would be a good time."

Susan thought back to that heady day in May 1970 when the South African cricket tour had been called off. She decided to tell Harvey the whole story – well almost.

"One of the guys taking part in the campaign was called James Fingleton. He was from North Wales and lived just on the mainland side of the bridge spanning the Menai Straits. He was really very keen on me. He was desperate for me to go to his home and meet his parents. I had nothing else planned and a trip to North Wales sounded interesting enough. I agreed to go with him. Neil Jardine managed to get himself onto the trip as well. He was no particular friend of James; to be honest they were in competition over me. Although he had no wish to go to Anglesey, Neil was damned if he was going to let Fingleton have the field to himself."

Susan seemed a little embarrassed to admit that two young men were fighting over her. Harvey smiled as she continued.

"The atmosphere was exhilarating. We hadn't really expected to get the tour completely called off but that's what happened. The invitation for the South Africans to tour was officially withdrawn on Friday 22nd May. On that evening the three of us travelled north by train. There was plenty of drink flowing and the celebrations continued the next day. On the Saturday evening James had been invited to a party near his home. He asked Neil and me to go along with him. In truth it was a pretty uncomfortable threesome. In the event the party never happened. The parents of the girl organizing it got wind of what was going to happen. They locked up the house and removed themselves and their daughter from the scene."

Susan paused and looked at Harvey to see if he was still listening.

"Go on," he said.

"By this time we had been joined by a group of teenagers who had also been invited. They all decided to go down to what they called 'the tube' – and we went along. The tube was a nickname the kids had for the railway across the Britannia Bridge. It stemmed from the structure of the bridge which spanned the Menai Straits from North Wales to Anglesey. It consisted of rectangular iron tubes supported by masonry piers. The trains ran inside the tubes. To go there was just the sort of crazy idea young people get on a Saturday night when they have drunk too much."

Susan gave Harvey a rather embarrassed look and then continued.

"It was very dark inside the tube and one of the teenagers found a discarded book lying on the ground. He picked it up, tore out a page and James produced a lighter. The paper caught fire more violently than the boy had expected. He dropped it to prevent his fingers getting burnt. It landed on some wooden sleepers on the track and the tar covering them caught alight. The fire spread with terrifying speed – I just couldn't believe how quickly it happened. The roof of the structure was wood. It burned easily. The length of the tunnel acted like a gigantic draw. The flames spread, literally like wild-fire, from the mainland side towards Anglesey. We just ran for our lives."

Susan seemed to hesitate and Harvey had to encourage her to continue again.

"James and I dived behind a bush while Neil ran on some distance further. We watched in horror… the bridge was a famous landmark. I didn't know it then but found out afterwards it was built by Robert Stephenson and had stood since 1850… anyway it just burned from end to end in front of our eyes."

Once again Susan paused; she was finding it difficult to tell the whole story to Harvey – especially the next part.

"OK, so…?" he encouraged her.

She had no intention of telling him exactly what happened next. The tension and excitement seemed to do something to her mood. It just rose up inside her. As she and Fingleton lay behind the bush she suddenly moved towards him and pulled him onto her. Nothing seemed to matter but the urgency of her desire and in a moment he was inside her and she was crying out in passion.

How was she going to get over this bit – best just miss it out, she told herself.

She took up the story again…

"The teenagers had disappeared into the night with Neil. The bridge itself was irreparably damaged. It took the fire service nine hours to bring the flames under control."

Anger darkened her eyes.

"The rat Jardine saw his chance to destroy James and sent an anonymous tip-off to the police implicating him. In due course James was apprehended. However, his explanation that it was just an accident was ultimately accepted… So you see, Mark, it has nothing to do with this matter." Susan was anxious for Harvey to believe her.

"Ultimately there was no prosecution; the fire was deemed an accident. But Neil and I had a violent row. I was appalled at his attempt to incriminate James. I have always felt very bad about the incident. The shame haunts me. Whilst most of the group were kids of fifteen and sixteen, we were in our early twenties. We should never have let it happen."

The sun was beginning to get into its stride and Mufindi golf course was noticeably warming up. Harvey was silent for what seemed an age to Susan and then he burst into laughter.

"You bloody little vandal – you burned down the Britannia Bridge and that's what you have been keeping from me!" Susan started to laugh as well.

Susan's expression changed.

"Mark, please try to check about David for me. Juanita told me he had not been taken or harmed but I won't be entirely convinced until I know it from someone I trust."

Harvey paused and then decided to ask her.

"Susan."

"Yes."

"Would you be prepared to tell me about David's father?"

She sighed. If her relationship with Mark Harvey was going to go anywhere – and she hoped it would – he would have to know. She gave him an edited version.

"It was James Fingleton – on that same night. It was a stupid thing to do, although of course I would never wish David not here. I liked James well enough but I didn't love him. I guess the occasion and the drink blurred my judgement."

"Does Fingleton know he is the father?"

"Yes. Eventually my mother wore me down and made me tell him. He has had David for weekends from time to time. He is a real nice guy, a gentleman, but he is getting married later this year. I really don't know quite how it will progress – especially if I emigrate to South Africa."

She turned back to him clearing the worried expression from her face determined to be strong.

"But you are right, it is a perfect morning in every

other respect."

"You're telling me," he replied. "This is a really nice little golf course. Do you play golf at all?"

"No," replied Susan. "But I watch it on TV and I have thought of taking it up one day when I have more time and money."

"Have you ever been to a tournament?" he asked.

"No, just watched on telly."

"Right," said Harvey in a decisive tone, "you must come to the World Match Play at Wentworth with me this year. It is in two weeks' time and I go every year. It is much better than just watching on the box; you really get the atmosphere and Wentworth is a beautiful setting."

"OK, that's a date," said Susan enthusiastically. She thought it would be rather curmudgeonly of her to mention that the chance of them being in Wentworth in two weeks' time looked a shade problematical right at this moment.

"This place is not totally unlike Wentworth; tree-lined fairways making each hole separate. We must come and play here one day when all this is over."

She was a little amused by his enthusiasm.

They laughed again and it was a light-hearted moment of pleasure that they would both remember and cherish in the days to come. Harvey was sorely tempted to draw her closer – he knew instinctively that she would not reject him – but reality was demanding his attention.

"What happens next?" she asked.

He was silent for a few moments. He didn't know how much to tell her; in truth he didn't really know the answer to the question.

"Obviously we have got to get out of here and back to South Africa. The reality is that travelling to South Africa from Tanzania is very complicated at the best of times. The two countries are enemies and there are no flights from one to the other. The road journey involves two thousand miles over dirt roads. It crosses a number of borders of countries like Malawi, Zambia and Mozambique – all hostile to South Africa; not that well-disposed to Britain either."

"Sounds tricky."

"It gets worse. To the west is the Congo, an area larger than western Europe; we could disappear into that hell-hole for ever – probably catch Ebola into the bargain. To the north-west is Uganda ruled by the mad psychopath Idi Amin. If he gets hold of us we'll finish up in his fridge. Directly to the north is Kenya but the border with Tanzania has been shut due to an argument between the two countries over East African Airways. Anyway, it's in diametrically the wrong direction. There's no railway of any use. The problem is further compounded by the fact that we have two unwilling hostages. Were they to be discovered the Tanzanian authorities would no doubt be more favourably disposed to Havanestro and Jardine than to us."

"So what's going to happen, Mark?" asked Susan. She realized her fate was entirely in his hands. For some stupid reason that made her feel secure.

"The only real hope is somehow to reach Rhodesia. The best way I can see of doing that is to get hold of a light aircraft and fly – God only knows how. Anyway, what we will have to do first is go to see the director of the tea company. He must know that we are here by now and must be wondering what is going on. I told the doctor that Jardine and Havanestro were gold smugglers and we were taking them back to South Africa. I'm not at all sure he believed me but I will have to stick to the story." He stood back for her to go through the gate back onto the track to the hospital. "I'm just hoping that the director will be prepared to swallow it because he has to live here. The last thing he needs is to make a big issue and get the Tanzanian authorities breathing down his neck. If I make it clear that we will be gone today, I think he may just forget we were ever here. Nevertheless I should go and see him."

They were about to leave the golf course and Harvey turned to have one last look.

"Some guy must have carved this course out of virgin bush originally. That must have been a hell of an undertaking. Can you see how he has left the indigenous trees to form hazards?"

"Yes, of course," she said having not the slightest idea what he was talking about.

He smiled.

"I'm sure you do. I meant what I said you know; we will come and play golf here one day." She believed him because she wanted to.

And now the real world was waiting for them; Darnie de Villiers, to relieve him of his vigil of their two prisoners; Jardine and Havanestro, to find out what was planned for them and how they could escape. In London, Geoffrey Pritchard wanted news and in Pretoria the South African government was eager for their reappearance. The latter had now been persuaded by Pritchard that they had a genuine crisis on their hands.

Susan made breakfast with food supplied by the doctor's wife. Afterwards Harvey went with the doctor to the head office of the tea company. This was on the next ridge about four miles away.

The chief executive turned out to be a mild-mannered man in his forties. The doctor made the necessary introductions.

"I think I'd better come straight to the point and be totally frank with you," said Harvey with the air of serious honesty that he always adopted when preparing to lie through his teeth.

"Yes, I would appreciate that," responded the other

man whom Harvey learned was called Robert Wellings.

"The two people we have under arrest are members of an international gold smuggling ring. We are very close to smashing it. I am from the British CID and we have been working with the South African police in this operation. We tracked them down and gave chase and eventually they went to ground in Tanzania. After a skirmish yesterday we managed to detain them. This occurred on one of your estates, Kilimatembo. In the course of the operation one of them was bitten by what appeared to be a rabid dog. Hence we turned up at your hospital to seek treatment for him."

Harvey paused trying to read the other man's reaction but there was none worth noticing. He ploughed on.

"The situation is very delicate because we do not want to hand them over to the Tanzanian authorities. We would much prefer to get them back to England or South Africa so they may be charged and stand trial properly. I fully realize that you are in a very difficult position. You have to live and work here once we are gone. I have come merely to assure you that we will be out of your hair by tonight.

Wellings appeared thoughtful and leaning back in his chair looked straight at Harvey. "Thank you for being so frank with me, Mr Harvey," he said and Harvey realized he was dealing with a man equally able to lie as himself. Wellings had clearly seen straight through the obvious holes in the story but judged his best interests would be served by pretending to believe it.

"I do understand your position but I'm sure you will likewise understand mine. If the Tanzanian government thought this company was colluding with either Britain or particularly South Africa, we would all be in jeopardy of losing our livelihoods." He paused and without a flicker of facial expression added wryly, "The climate back in the UK is not such that there is great demand for out-of-work tea planters." He looked at his watch to signal the end of the interview was approaching. "You must forgive me but I am running a little short of time. I am expecting a plane-load of Norwegians here for a business meeting and I must get ready to go out to Ngwazi to meet them."

Harvey's stomach performed a complete loop-the-loop. The man had said he was expecting an aeroplane. Somehow he had to get hold of it – but how? He needed more information about it.

"Rather a strange place for a plane load of Norwegians to come to isn't it?" He tried not to sound too impertinent

"Not really," replied Wellings. "You see the Norwegians are starting up a wood pulping factory at a place called Sao Hill. They are keen to discuss with me details of the wages and conditions we give our labour. Neither of us wants to start a Dutch auction for labour putting both our costs up unnecessarily. So six of them are coming up in their company Cessna for talks."

Wellings had given Harvey exactly the information he wanted to such a degree that he almost felt it was deliberate… then again surely not?

"Look, Mr Wellings, I think it would be best if both of us forgot we had ever seen each other. I undertake that we will be gone by tonight and you can just get on with running your company as if nothing had ever happened. We will take our vehicles and make for the Kenyan border. I just felt it would have been unacceptable for me not to have come to make my number with you."

Wellings rose and held out his hand.

"Goodbye, Mr Harvey."

On the way back to the hospital he had a similar conversation with the doctor. He, in turn, seemed only too pleased to accept that he had never seen them. He was considerably less pleased at the request of Harvey that he should pass over the vaccine and injection equipment for the continuation of Jardine's treatment.

"Do you realize what you are dealing with?" he questioned.

"Rabies," responded Harvey. "Can't say I know a great deal about it. I've had to give injections before though – mostly morphine."

"Rabies is the most dreadful affliction imaginable. It is a virus disease transmitted to humans when the saliva of a rabid animal – usually a mad dog – enters an open wound. The virus travels along the victim's nerve fibres until it reaches the brain. This can be quite rapid or take some time – even weeks or months. When it reaches the brain the inflammation causes several terrible symptoms."

"Such as?" Harvey, like many, had only a vague idea about rabies. He could envisage that he might have to cope with it so he wanted to be as prepared as possible.

"Muscle spasms of appalling ferocity; terrible convulsions and lunatic ravings. A frequent symptom is hydrophobia; an unreasoning, hideous fear of water causes spasms of the larynx when the victim tries to drink; an obsessive fear that he will drown in his own saliva; brings on spitting fits of terrifying proportions. Believe me, Mr Harvey, I have been in medical practice in the tropics for twenty years and I have seen some terrible things. Rabies is the worst – truly shocking."

Something occurred to Harvey.

"Have you ever seen Ebola?" he asked.

The doctor was visibly taken aback.

"How do you know about Ebola?" he shot back. "It has only been around a short time. Knowledge about it is very much confined to medical circles."

"I read somewhere that it had spread from the Congo." Harvey sounded vague.

"That is the generally held view. In fact I was working in Sudan last year and I am convinced I saw it there. It isn't as violent as rabies but it is an appalling disease. If ever it gets out into society in general it will kill in hundreds – maybe thousands."

Harvey did not pursue it any further.

Eventually, the doctor acceded to Harvey's request. He consented to provide the vaccine and injection equipment for Jardine. He loaned de Villiers and Evans a hospital Land Rover and some petrol in five-gallon drums so they could go out to Kilimatembo and collect the vehicles.

Harvey worried solidly for the hour and a half they were gone. He worried that he had sent them into a trap. The people remaining at Kongwa would no doubt have tried to locate where Jardine and Juanita had gone. Kilimatembo was a pretty long shot admittedly, but sometimes fate played some nasty tricks.

It was getting on for 11.30 by the time they reappeared.

Harvey called them all together in the guest room to outline his plan. Jardine and Juanita were still securely tied to their beds in the other room.

"Alright, here's the plan, such as it is," he began. "There is a plane-load of Norwegians arriving in a six-seater Cessna light aircraft at a place called Ngwazi. We just have to get there and appropriate that plane and fly it out as far towards Rhodesia as we can. Simple to say, but not so simple to do." He turned to Dennis Evans.

"Do you know where this place Ngwazi is?" he asked.

"Yes, it's about fifteen miles to the south of here and will take about half an hour to drive there."

"Is there anywhere there where we can hide out and assess the situation regarding how we get hold of the aircraft?"

Evans thought for a moment.

"Not really," he replied. "It is much flatter out there and far more open country. Also, we need to be careful that we don't get there too soon and run into Wellings and the Norwegian party meeting up. What I suggest is that we wait until after one. By then they will all be on their way back here. Then the gin and tonic will come out before they sit down to lunch. The business meeting won't even get under way until about 2.30. They will only start back to Ngwazi at about 4.30. They will need to be back in Sao Hill before dark at 6.30ish."

"Sounds sensible," said Harvey. "What sort of set up is there out there in terms of an airport?"

"Airport is a rather grand word for it. There is an airstrip between two belts of wattle trees. The Cessna will sit on the ground at one end of the strip all afternoon with probably only one *ascari* – a watchman – to guard it. If you can fly it the plan is not impossible. Did you say it was a six-seater?"

"Yes, although I am only going on what Wellings said. Why?"

"If you would agree, I would like to come with you. It's one thing for Wellings and the doc to forget they ever saw you. However, just about every African on my estate knows I was involved. There is no way I can talk my way out of that. In truth, I am finished in Tanzania. If they get hold of me, they'll lock me up and throw away the key."

Harvey felt guilt at having involved the young man to the degree that threatened his livelihood and his life but could have done nothing else in the circumstances. Evans went on, "I thought about it a lot last night. I reckon my best bet is to try to get back to my parents in Kenya and go to ground there for as long as it takes. Kenya and Tanzania are not on such great terms with each other just now and I hope and think that would work."

Harvey had several conflicting thoughts. If he abandoned Evans here, the young man would probably get picked up by the local police and have to tell all. If he took him with them it would be an extra weight in the aircraft and would use more fuel and diminish their chances of reaching Rhodesia. However, he had no idea how much fuel was in the aircraft's tanks. He judged it would be better to prevent Evans falling into the Tanzanian authority's hands.

"OK, I agree. As long as there is room you are with us." He turned his attention to other matters. He had no idea he had just made a decision that would save all their lives. "If we have to make a forced landing short of Rhodesia we may have to trek through the bush. We will need some provisions, particularly water. Where can we get those?"

Once again it fell to Evans to answer.

"There is a company shop over at head office and some Indian *dukas* in the local settlement at Kibao. They will have what we need. I could organise it. I haven't got any money on me but they will both give me credit and the company will take it out of my salary when they fire me."

So Evans went off and returned with the necessary items plus some clothes for Susan. What she was wearing was fine for a garden party but not at all suitable for a trek through the bush. She needed jeans and a top of stronger material. Evans even produced a bra for her. He looked thoroughly embarrassed at the fact that he had had to guess her size. She merely looked amused. Where had these guys been during the swinging sixties? In the bush, she concluded. On a more mundane level he had also found her a pair of ankle-boot plimsolls, like hockey boots.

They were as ready as they would ever be.

The Cessna buzzed head office at midday and at 1 p.m. they set off for Ngwazi. They actually passed Wellings and his party returning from the airstrip but the sight of two army Land Rovers was not remarkable. By 1.30 p.m. they were parked beside a large lake.

Evans pointed to his right.

"The airstrip is over there, through that belt of wattle

trees. I suggest you just drive straight up to it. I'm pretty sure there will only be one security guy there and he won't suspect anything if a Land Rover load of Europeans turns up."

"OK," agreed Harvey. "You come with me, Dennis. Darnie, stay here with Susan and watch over our friends." He pointed at Jardine and Juanita.

Evans was wrong and right; wrong that there would be only one guard; there were two; but right that they would suspect nothing. They were in a small hut next to the airstrip cooking a couple of maize cobs over an open fire. They greeted Harvey and Evans with the friendliness that is natural to the rural African.

"*Jambo*, bwana!"

"*Jambo!*" responded Evans.

Suddenly they were both looking down the barrel of Evans's shotgun in Harvey's steady grip.

Evans quickly reassured them that they would come to no harm as he bound them up.

At the rate he was tying people up he was going to run out of rope soon, he thought.

He explained to them that they would spend a boring afternoon but would be freed when the Norwegian party returned. Mercifully the keys to the plane were with the two Africans.

Harvey turned his attention to the aircraft. It would be a squeeze but they would all fit in. He himself would fly it in the pilot's seat; Evans would be next to him as he would be the most likely to recognize landmarks while they were still in Tanzania. Susan would sit behind the pilot with Juanita next to her. Jardine and de Villiers would take the two rear seats. The provisions, such as they were, would be stored in the space behind the seats. It would be a full payload but he could do nothing about that now. They would just have to take their chance. He noticed with relief that the fuel gauges read virtually full and there was no luggage in the hold.

Evans was sent back to collect the others. Jardine and Juanita had their legs untied. It was necessary for them to be able to walk but their hands remained bound.

At a few minutes shy of 2.30 p.m. they all climbed in. Harvey spent some time familiarizing himself with the controls; then he did his pre-flight checks and started the engine. Satisfied that they were as ready as they ever would be, he pointed the Cessna down the grass airstrip. He eased back the stick and they hummed into the sky.

When the business of taking off was accomplished, Harvey levelled out at his cruising speed and set his course. De Villiers voiced the thoughts of all of them.

"Where exactly are we headed, Mark, and have we got enough fuel to get there?"

Harvey saw no point in trying to conceal the facts.

"You'll have to bear with me a bit here. I know how to fly this thing in the sense that I can take off, steer straight and land. I know the basics of navigation too. But we are in a country I have never been to before and in an aircraft that I have never flown before."

There was silence in the plane apart from the steady drone of the engine. They all knew they were embarked on a risky venture and waited for him to continue.

"I have found a handbook which is all I have to go on as far the specification of the aircraft is concerned. It seems it is a Cessna Centurion 210, reasonably new. I can only find its range expressed in nautical miles. Bottom line I reckon we can make approximately a thousand kilometres before we need to panic. The fuel gauge is reading nearly full."

He gave them time to digest that and then continued.

"My plan is to make for the most northerly part of Rhodesia."

He passed a map back to the others.

"If you look on the map you will see a place called

Zumbo which is actually in Mozambique but right on the border of Zambia and Rhodesia. The northern most place in Rhodesia is Kanyemba and that's ideally where we want to get to. I reckon it is around twelve hundred kilometres south of Mufindi. According to my estimates, we might just make it. It could depend on how hard the wind blows."

"Can we get there before it gets dark?" asked de Villiers.

"We will be just about on the limit of daylight and fuel when we get there. I'm afraid I cannot be more specific than that."

The others digested this in silence. It was obvious that they were flying almost entirely on guesswork and by the seat of Harvey's pants. Whilst it didn't seem the safest way to travel, they were along for the ride, like it or not.

"To keep the chance of getting lost to a minimum, my plan is to fly down a route following the main road to Mbeya; then over the corner of the borders of Tanzania, Malawi and Zambia, into Zambia where I aim to pick up the Luangwa River and follow it down to Zumbo."

Still no one said anything until finally de Villiers spoke.

"Well, good luck with that, mate. We'll keep our eyes skinned."

And that's what they did – almost. As the afternoon wore on they crossed into Zambia. Despite their fear that the Zambian air force would have something to say about it, no one troubled them. They picked up the Luangwa River after some false starts which cost them precious fuel and then pushed on. They skirted the Luangwa National Park to the east and eventually flew over the north-western border of Mozambique. Their hopes rose with every kilometre covered. Although they had no idea where they would land in Rhodesia or what sort of reception they would get, it would be certainly be much less hostile than in Zambia or Mozambique.

It was over the north-west tip of Mozambique that their luck ran out. If Harvey had been a more experienced pilot and had been more familiar with the Cessna, he might have been able to extract a little extra mileage out of it by playing with the throttle and pitch controls. All conjecture went straight out of the window, however, the moment the Cessna coughed. It was just a momentary cough, possibly caused by sediment in the tank being drawn into the engine, but it was enough to make up Harvey's mind. A forced landing under power would be scary enough; without power it would be impossible to control for someone so inexperienced. He estimated they could not be much more than thirty or forty kilometres from the Rhodesian border. Surely they could get lucky and make it on foot.

He eased back the throttle, lowered the landing gear and started to descend. From the aircraft the ground looked relatively easy to land on. As they got closer to it they realized that what looked like a nice level piece of ground was in fact covered in elephant grass about twelve feet high. The ground was also dotted with dangerous looking bumps and bushes. However, they had no option. Harvey selected an area that looked clearer than most of obstructions and gingerly nosed the aircraft downwards.

As they dropped into the grass several things happened at once. The plane bumped violently and with a rending crash the undercarriage collapsed. The port wing caught an anthill and the plane slewed round and went slithering on sideways. To Harvey's consternation it seemed to be gathering pace rather than losing it. For some bizarre reason he found himself remembering an occasion when he was ten years old. He had been out on his bicycle on a wet Sunday afternoon. Whizzing in through the front gate of his parents' house he cycled furiously up the garden path and shot round the back of the house. Jamming on the bike's brakes he was shattered to find the brake did not grip on the wet rim of the wheel. Like the aircraft now, the darn thing seemed to accelerate. With a cacophony of breaking glass he went straight into his father's greenhouse.

He wished he was in his father's greenhouse now. Incredibly he was sitting in the middle of Africa with complete silence all around him. There was a ticking noise in the cabin of the plane but otherwise not a sound. He tested his arms and legs and found he had survived intact. Amazingly, so had all the others. Although the aircraft had crash-landed, it had been going relatively slowly and the grass had cushioned the landing to some degree.

"Everyone OK?" he asked.

One by one they confirmed that they were basically alright. Some bumps and bruises but no one had suffered any broken bones or serious injury. His instructor, Ted Shaeffer, back at Biggin Hill was going to hear about this.

They scrambled out of the stricken Cessna. Their one idea was to put as much distance as they could between themselves and the aircraft. They were only too aware that it could burst into flames at any moment. They were also aware that, as they were in Mozambique, their landing could have been noticed by a patrol. The first place the Frelimo would go to look for survivors would be the plane.

They collapsed, panting, in some bushes two hundred metres from the crash site. Harvey spread out the map he had salvaged from the aircraft and outlined their predicament.

"If you look here you can see three places marked. Zumbue to the north-west, Zumbo to the south-west and Fingoe to the north-east. We are approximately in the middle of that triangle. We are between thirty and fifty kilometres from the Rhodesian border and we will have to cross the Zambesi to get there. We have two unwilling prisoners and one gun with four cartridges left. We could run into a Frelimo patrol and would have no chance of fighting them off. I'm sorry, but that is the reality. Anybody want to say anything?"

"What has happened to the stuff for my injections?" asked Jardine.

"In the aircraft and chances of finding it are remote, I'm afraid," responded Harvey.

"You'll just have to take your chances until we reach civilization."

De Villiers rose and started to return to the Cessna. As no explosion had taken place he decided it was worth the risk to get some provisions.

"I'll see what I can salvage," he said.

He was gone only a few minutes and the others sat with their private thoughts. Dennis Evans thought about the country he had just left. He loved Tanzania and was truly sorry that he would not be able to return to it. Susan Bennett thought about her son, David, wondering how he was and when she would see him again. Mark Harvey thought about the journey that lay ahead and how he was going to keep them all going. Juanita and Jardine thought about how they might be able to use the coming trek through the bush to make an escape.

De Villiers returned with some bread, a little water but nothing for Neil Jardine's injections.

"Any questions?" asked Harvey.

There were none. They all knew the position. There was nothing to be done but get to their feet and start walking south.

They set off in the late afternoon, Harvey leading; Susan with him; Evans next; then Jardine and Juanita. De Villiers brought up the rear with the gun. It was a strange party and strange fortune that had thrown them together.

Darkness falls very quickly in central Africa. At one moment it is light and within twenty to thirty minutes it is dark. So when darkness came, they stopped. They had only travelled about six kilometres but the hours of darkness are the hunting hours in Africa – no place for those inexperienced in bush craft to be wandering about.

Harvey and de Villiers took it in turns to stand guard over Jardine and Juanita. The others supposedly slept. In fact no one slept soundly. They were all glad when daylight returned.

Tuesday 20th September 1977

They shared out a little of the rations and moved on. It was slow going. The bush was thick and they had to move quietly for fear of attracting the attention of any passing patrols. They were also very conscious that they were in an area supposedly teeming with game. Whilst that may have been exciting in normal times, the one thing Harvey did not want was to run into a herd of elephants. Evans could have told him that buffalo were more likely to be dangerous, but there was no point in raising anxieties unnecessarily. He kept the information to himself.

Finally they reached the Zambezi. It had been hard going. Harvey and de Villiers were fit; Jardine and Juanita also; Evans was young and fit from his outdoor life and more accustomed than the others to the African bush. That left Susan. Not many jobs are as hard on the legs and feet as working in a department store day-in and day-out. Her feet were not too painful, but she was not used to sustained exercise outdoors. She was suffering. The one thing keeping her going was the presence of another woman. As long as Juanita Havanestro was still walking there was no way on God's earth that Susan Bennett would admit defeat.

They had set off at dawn and now they were meeting the real heat of the day. There are few places hotter than the Zambezi valley in the early afternoon. Having reached the great river Harvey decided they had earned a rest.

Gratefully they all sank down in a glade under some trees. He also needed thc break to work out how to proceed. The Zambezi looked considerably wider than he had imagined, by some hundred metres or so. Evans had warned him that it was home to numerous hippos and crocodiles. There was also a Zambesi shark but Evans seemed to think they did not come this far upstream. Harvey hoped he was right. How on earth was he going to get them across?

Their conversation regarding the inhabitants of the Zambesi petered out and they rested. They were roused by the sound of vehicles approaching from the east. They took refuge in a clump of bushes about a hundred metres back from the river. De Villiers left his two prisoners in no doubt as to what would happen to them if they as much as breathed too loudly.

The vehicles turned out to be two fairly old and battered Land Rovers. They were making heavy weather of the rutted terrain, their gearboxes in low-ratio four-wheel drive. They came grinding up the valley and to Harvey's dismay came to a halt at the edge of the river some hundred metres away. Six men clambered out of each vehicle. From their arms and camouflage uniforms, it was clear that they were a Frelimo patrol.

They started fanning out in some sort of training exercise. Mercifully they went away from the party huddled in bushes and only one of them stayed behind with the Land Rovers. After some ten minutes he lit a cigarette and sat down on the front bumper of the lead vehicle.

During that time Dennis Evans came up with an idea.

"Last year I was on safari with some friends in the Ruaha game reserve," he explained. "And there are a heck of a lot of thorns down there. As a precaution I took a number of extra inner tubes in the van."

Harvey winced at the idea of Evans blundering into the

heart of the African bush in a clapped out Ford Anglia van; bloody lunatics, these tea planters, he thought.

"While we were down there," Evans continued oblivious to Harvey's inner thoughts, "some elephants came down to the opposite bank of the river. In order to get across we struck upon the idea of using the inflated inner tubes as lifebelts and floating. It worked very well. I don't see why you couldn't make a serviceable floating raft from all the inner tubes in the tyres of those two Land Rovers."

Harvey and de Villiers both looked incredulous at first. After some more conversation they came to the realization that this was indeed about their only chance.

"One problem," said Harvey. "That guard is armed."

"Leave him to me," said de Villiers and silently slipped away through the bushes.

The young soldier never heard a thing and before he could utter a sound, de Villiers had him trussed up with some twine he had found in the back of the first Land Rover. It had taken only five minutes but they were five precious minutes. Harvey was surprised that the tough young Afrikaner had not just killed the man. They spoke of it afterwards and de Villiers explained. "You know, Mark, I decided after Steve Biko that I would not take any more lives unless it was absolutely unavoidable. I'm on the opposite side to Biko but what happened to him was wrong. Sooner or later it has to stop. What does it say in the Bible? They have sown the wind and they shall reap the whirlwind. That's us, man."

Harvey was a little taken aback to hear an agent of BOSS quoting the Bible. Darnie was clearly more troubled by the death of Steve Biko than he had realized. It was strange, he mused, that a passionate belief in apartheid could exist side by side with an equal belief in Christianity. But it did.

De Villiers and Evans worked feverishly to get the wheels off the Land Rovers. In all there were ten tubes including the spares. They found a foot pump in the tool box under the passenger seat. They worked like men possessed to re-inflate the inner tubes. They had no way of knowing how long the patrol would be before it returned to the Land Rovers. If they got back before Harvey's party had crossed the Zambesi, it would not be a training exercise any longer. They all knew that.

At last the tubes were all inflated and tied together with the remainder of the twine from the first Land Rover. Harvey had found a tarpaulin in the second Land Rover and they lashed this over the tubes to provide a slightly more stable platform. They had a raft. Not a very stable one, not a safe one, not crocodile-proof and in no way hippo-proof; above all certainly not bullet-proof. Nevertheless a raft that would float, a raft with which they were about to take on the mighty Zambesi.

They dragged it to the bank. Jardine and Juanita were placed in the bow where the others could at least see them. That would help frustrate any ideas they might have of escape or sabotage. It had become impractical for them to remain bound. Their legs had already been freed in order to allow them to walk through the bush but their hands were still tied behind their backs. This would now make it virtually impossible for them to retain the necessary balance on the unstable raft. Reluctantly Harvey cut them free.

The chance that they would try to make a run for it was ever present. So far they had calculated they were better off in the group than trying to escape. Harvey was only too well aware that situation would not continue indefinitely. Both he and de Villiers watched them like hawks.

De Villiers, who had equipped himself with the AK-47 belonging to the bound Frelimo soldier, was in the middle with Evans while Susan and Harvey were at the rear. The craft was fully loaded and cumbersome. It took them some minutes of noisy splashing to get it out from the bank. Painfully slowly they managed to move it towards the middle of the river. The current was surprisingly sluggish. Harvey thought that this might be just a perception brought about by their need to put distance between themselves and the bank. De Villiers, however, volunteered the information that Kariba Dam to the west and Cahora Bassa to the east had significantly slowed the once swiftly-flowing river.

Slowly the makeshift craft drifted out into mid-stream. They had reached just short of halfway when Evans saw them.

"Hippo," he said pointing over the starboard side.

"Are they dangerous?" asked Harvey.

"Depends; sometimes they just ignore you but at other times they can be very cantankerous. I read somewhere that they kill more people than either lions or elephants."

"Thanks for that reassuring news," replied Harvey.

The tension mounted as the raft drifted ever closer to the gaggle of eyes and ears. They were plainly visible now, like a convention of snorkels. Whether they had young with them or whether they were just annoyed at having their aquatic siesta disrupted was never discovered. What was discovered very quickly was they were making straight for the raft. Quite suddenly, with a noise like a hot water tank boiling, one of the animals rose out of the water. It seemed like a submarine had surfaced right under the bow of the flimsy raft. Juanita found herself staring into a mouth the size of a small garage.

She was saved by Jardine's lightning reactions. He kicked the animal straight on the snout with the superhuman strength born of terror. It made no impression on the hippopotamus other than to deflect its attack from Juanita's leg to the front of the boat. The great mouth clamped shut over the front nearside inner tube. As the two teeth ripped into the rubber, air came gushing out. The hippo backed off, momentarily startled by the noise of the escaping air. Then it charged and this time it really meant business.

Several things seemed to happen simultaneously. Juanita was already off-balance from the deflation of the tube underneath her. She went head-first into the river with a scream. Jardine leapt forward to try to save her but he was too late. All he achieved was to nearly upend the already unstable craft. Before anyone could move to help him he went into the river too. De Villiers, meanwhile, with remarkable presence of mind, grabbed the gun and fired two shots into the animal's head. The wounded leviathan wheeled shaking its head in pain and came at the craft once more. As it did so de Villiers raised the AK-47 again and fired into the animal. It slewed off course, wallowing in its death throes.

The current of the river and the disturbance caused by the encounter had moved the craft some thirty metres away from the struggling Juanita and Jardine. As both parties were wondering what to do, their minds were made up for them. A second hippo came between them. Self-preservation took hold and those on the raft started paddling furiously. They gradually moved towards the opposite bank and away from the new threat. Meanwhile the two swimmers struck out with equal urgency for the bank from whence they had come. De Villiers had to use the AK-47 twice more before the hippos decided enough was enough. By this time the boat and the swimmers were upwards of a hundred metres apart. Normally de Villiers could have picked off two people at that distance easily but he was standing on a very unstable base. The two heads were bobbing up and down as they desperately struggled to shore. Both of them realized the danger and both of them ducked their head under the water as much as possible. Reluctantly de Villiers lowered the gun. There was no point in wasting ammunition and drawing attention to themselves unless he could be certain of a hit. The patrol was bound to have heard the shots and wondered what they were. Harvey could only hope the size of the Zambezi would deter them from crossing to investigate further.

They turned their attention to paddling the raft. Despite the damage, it was now unburdened of around three hundred pounds. They made faster and safer progress. They scrambled ashore on the south side of the Zambesi. Harvey estimated they had about thirty kilometres to go to the Rhodesian border. He was uncomfortably aware that if Jardine or Juanita had made it to the other side, they would alert the Frelimo patrol at once.

Harvey looked at his depleted team. De Villiers was still in good shape. He was tough that one. Evans was holding up remarkably well. He was young and strong but he lacked the stamina and determination of the older men. More importantly he lacked their training and fitness. But it was Susan that Harvey was worried about. She was running on sheer guts. They still had thirty kilometres of hard terrain to go. Her bare arms were badly scratched.

"How are you feeling?" he asked her.

"I'm fine; don't worry about me. Let's get going."

With that they set off.

They made surprisingly good progress for a while. After an hour and a half Harvey estimated they had covered about five kilometres. It was becoming obvious that, despite her protestations, Susan could be driven no further that day. It would be better to get some rest and try and cover the remainder of the journey tomorrow.

Their rations were now very low. They still had water but food was in short supply. Harvey was not prepared to shoot an animal for meat for fear of broadcasting their position. De Villiers eventually solved the problem by pointing out some fig trees. None of them relished the fruit or the thought of the effect it might have on them tomorrow but they needed food. At least it kept their stomachs satisfied for the moment and allowed them to concentrate on other things.

As night fell those other things turned out to be lion. The African bush at night is full of a million sounds; the screeching of crickets, the chattering of hyenas, the menacing rasping cough of the leopard and the reverberating rumble of the elephant's stomach. But one sound above all chills the blood of man. It is necessary to hear the roar of a lion in the African night just once to know why he is called the king of beasts. There is an awesome authority in the sound that says to man that, no matter who rules by day, there is only one ruler of the dark continent by night.

The noise started quietly, not unlike that of a large dog heaving a sigh as it settles in front of the fire. Slowly it grew louder and stronger until it was a full-blooded roar. Susan looked to Harvey, real fear clutching at her throat. The lion roared again. It reverberated through them both; the very ground seemed to be vibrating. He could feel her trembling and knew it was not just the wild animal that was the cause. For six years he had been faithful to the memory of Kate. But he was a man and he could feel Susan's body pressing against him. Kate had gone – he accepted that; but she had never left his mind. He was torn between a memory and the reality of a woman beside him. He hesitated in turmoil. The lion roared again. It was probably three hundred metres away but sounded much closer. It broke the tension. The moment had passed. He moved away from her not knowing whether he was sorry or relieved.

In the end the lion did not kill them nor even threaten them. It saved their lives. The two patrols tracking them worked their way through the night. But they kept a respectful distance from the mighty cat. And they all lived to see the sight that has few equals anywhere on the planet – the African dawn.

Chapter Fourteen

London – Wednesday 21st September 1977

The telephone on Geoffrey Pritchard's desk burst into life interrupting his train of thought about events in Africa.

"Pritchard." He sounded curt. He was starting a headache.

"Gordon Peters here."

"Morning, Gordon. What can I do for you?"

"A strange development. Stuart Holder's wife, Marianna, has walked into Plymouth police station and confessed to killing a man by running him over."

"When did this happen?"

"Just this morning."

"No, I meant when did the incident take place?"

"June 1969. She says Jardine knows about it and is using it as blackmail to make Holder work for him. She says that Holder would never voluntarily do what he is doing; that she wants him to know that she has given herself up so that he can turn himself in."

"Where does she think he is?"

"She doesn't know but assumes it is somewhere in South Africa."

"I need to speak to her; can you keep her for a few hours while I get down there?"

"Will do."

Pritchard put the phone down and sat for a few

minutes thinking through this new development. If only he could get some news as to what the hell was happening with Harvey and de Villiers, he might make some progress. In the meantime all he could do was wait. He would drive down to Plymouth straight away to see what else he could get out of Mrs Holder.

"Lesley! Have we got any aspirin in this place? I've got to drive to Plymouth and I have a headache coming on."

"Are you alright?" Lesley was solicitous.

"Yes, I'll survive. I need less paperwork and more exercise. Maybe I should take up golf; what do you think?"

"No. One golf nut is enough in this office. How about bungee jumping?"

"Careful, you're not indispensable you know."

As he left he smiled at her. He knew that, actually, she was.

Chapter Fifteen

Mozambique – Tuesday 20th September 1977

Neither Neil Jardine nor Juanita Havanestro had any clear recollection of how they managed to swim back across the Zambezi. They were so shocked by their sudden jettison into the water that their actions were purely instinctive. They were both competent swimmers but it was a daunting task to reach the bank from where they had set out. They made progress only slowly.

The hippos were a major concern although they seemed more interested in the raft than in the two individual swimmers. In truth, that most deadly of all river killers, crocodile, was their greatest fear. There was also the very real threat of de Villiers shooting at them. It became apparent after a little while that he had given up that idea. Consequently they abandoned the practice of ducking under the water every two or three strokes and concentrated on just getting to the bank.

Juanita was the first to tire. The Zambesi is an immense river. The vast scale of its surroundings tends to make it seem smaller than it is. To swim across it is to learn its true size and power. But the Cuban girl was tough and possessed of an indomitable will. Somehow she drove herself on. Jardine too was feeling the pressure but his superior physical strength helped him cope with less distress.

At long last they lay panting on dry land. As they fought to regain their strength they were both thinking about their new situation and wondering how much they could afford to trust each other.

"We are in enough trouble as it is at the moment without fighting each other." Jardine put their thoughts into words. "So I suggest we sink our present differences and focus on getting back to civilization; otherwise we might just as well kill each other now and be done with it."

Juanita looked at him and wondered how she had brought herself to be his lover. It must have been the sea and the moonlight and the tropical night she supposed. Up to now she had always been the one in charge. She realized, however, that out here in the crushing heat and primeval savagery of the Zambesi valley, it was the survival of the fittest. Strong as she was, she recognized that Jardine, the native of Africa and the male of the species was stronger. She would have to manage the situation carefully.

"Agreed," she replied. "Let's see if we can raise that patrol."

And so a truce was declared between them; an uneasy and fragile truce. Neither would hesitate to break it when the right moment came.

Their clothes were already drying on them as they set off towards the Land Rovers. They found the young guard where de Villiers had left him. He was still bound. They freed him as he no longer represented a threat to them. They sat down to await the return of the patrol.

The shooting at the river seemed to have caused much less interest than they had expected; at first there was no sign of the patrol returning. Eventually they came trudging out of the bush. Communication was not easy as there was no common language among them. However, with a mixture of Spanish and Portuguese plus some vigorous sign language they managed. Juanita knew Richard Masingi's name and was able to make them understand that she wished to speak to him. Once she had been understood they were motioned into the Land Rover. There was a substantial delay while spare wheels were found and sent out to the stricken vehicles which were still as de Villiers and Evans had left them, wheel-less. Eventually the new tyres were fitted. They set off eastwards.

Although the Land Rover had been standing in shade it was still unbearably hot inside. The journey was made worse by the fact that the canvas hood was ripped at the back. Where there should have been a Perspex window there was just a gaping hole. It acted like a vacuum cleaner sucking in great choking clouds of dust. There was also a number of empty jerry cans which had been loaded to provide back-up fuel. Every yard of progress was accompanied by a cacophony of grinding metal.

The nightmare lasted for an hour until they reached base. Base was no more than a heavily disguised hole in a suffocating *donga*, a large ditch. Jardine found himself marvelling at the privations men seemed prepared to accept in order to wage war. Powerful radio equipment was concealed at this hideout and within ten minutes they had raised Chimoio.

When Masingi learned from Juanita that there was a South African and a British agent working together in Mozambique, he was more than interested in her story. He made arrangements to rendezvous with them that evening. The chagrin it would cause his rival in the Zimbabwe African People's Union (ZAPU), Joseph Ngaya, if he, Masingi, was able to capture them and parade them in front of the world's press would be a rare delight. He decided immediately to take personal command of the situation. Within twenty minutes of hearing the news he left Chimoio by helicopter.

Five minutes after he had gone, one of his most trusted lieutenants slipped away into the bush to a hidden radio transmitter and Ngaya learned of the situation.

Ngaya was a very different man to Masingi. He was far less single-minded and much more interested in the comforts of the Western world. There was no way he was about to start crawling around the bush in the middle of Africa. He dispatched the only man from his most easterly camp that he really trusted to take charge of the mission. He sent Stephen Olangwe. The instruction was to find and capture Harvey and de Villiers if he could; above all, he must stop Richard Masingi from doing so. The trust placed in Olangwe was soundly based. Ngaya did not delude himself that Olangwe had any great loyalty to the ZAPU cause but he knew he would hunt down Masingi if it was the last thing he ever did. Masingi's ZANU men had plundered the village where Olangwe came from. They had raped his wife and two daughters.

The two units converged on the south bank of the Zambesi late that evening and struck out towards the Rhodesian border. Tracking four people in that vast impenetrable jungle of scrub was no easy task. In fact they came remarkably close. A wandering male lion roaring threateningly in the night caused them to veer away; otherwise they may have come closer still. When dawn came the two units were some five miles apart with Harvey's group more or less in the middle of them.

Wednesday 21st September 1977

De Villiers was beginning to behave in a somewhat jumpy manner. Harvey noticed and was puzzled. He assessed the South African to be as tough as they come and not a man to be frightened by shadows.

"You OK, Darnie?" he asked.

"Ya – fine."

"Sure? You seem a little distracted."

De Villiers motioned to Harvey to step away from the others so they could talk without being overheard.

"I reckon we are either in or very near Rhodesia now, don't you?" he said.

"Yes," replied Harvey. "Right on the border is my guess."

"You are worried about Frelimo and ZANLA or ZIPRA groups tracking us down?"

"Yes, of course."

"Mark, you want to start worrying about something far more dangerous."

"What's that?"

"The Rhodesian Selous Scouts. Do you know what the Selous Scouts are?"

"I've heard of them – a sort of Rhodesian SAS."

"Those guys are tough, really tough, man. I knew one in SA a couple of years ago."

"So?"

"I don't think you are understanding me. To even get into the Scouts is harder than hard. Their training base is at Wafa Wafa at Lake Kariba. When they arrive for their training they find nothing at the base. No one greets them. No one tells them anything. There's no food. The idea is to starve and exhaust them and see how they cope. If they survive this initiation – only about twenty-five per cent do – they are then put through a training course that would kill bloody Superman stone dead. When they relent and give them some food it is rotten animals. This guy I knew had to do a hundred-kilometre march with thirty kilos of rocks on his back. The bastards even painted the rocks red so the recruits couldn't dump them and refill at the end. After he had got through that they sent him to a camp where he was taught to behave like a guerrilla – no shaving – hence their nickname of 'Armpits with Eyeballs'. The point is, Mark, if they think we are the enemy… not good news. I'm telling you, Frelimo and ZANLA are bloody kindergarten beside these guys."

"Thanks for that, Darnie. I needed a bit of good news." Harvey could see the South African was genuinely concerned. Dropping the ironical tone he said, "Seriously, man, thank you. I hadn't thought about danger from that angle but you are right. We must be super alert."

The climax came at around 2 p.m. Harvey did not know when they crossed into Rhodesia, but he was sure that they must have done so by now. Not that anything changed at all. The African bush seemed impervious to man's artificial borders. Also they were still at great risk of being attacked, not only by terrorists, but now, Harvey realized, by the Rhodesian forces themselves.

Harvey and de Villiers were tired but fully operational. Evans was still holding up remarkably well but Susan was in a bad way. She was scratched all over her arms; a night disturbed by the wandering lion had done little to revive her. She was running on empty and Harvey knew she could not hold out for much longer.

For some time Evans had been vaguely conscious of the call of an emerald-spotted wood dove. It is a somewhat mournful sound starting with a few fairly high-pitched notes with quite an extended interval between them; then gradually a decreasing interval and a descending pitch giving it its characteristic melancholy effect. It is a sound inseparable from the heat of the African day. Evans had grown up with it in his Kenyan childhood. It was a sound he knew so well that he hardly noticed it any more. But something deep down in his subconscious must have been listening and suddenly alerted him. He realized that the call was changing. The change was almost imperceptible but it was there. The first few high notes were not quite right. There had been more of them than usual, but gradually the number was decreasing with each call. He brought his exhausted mind to bear and counted the high notes that began each call. There were eight, then seven, then six. With each call the number was decreasing by one. Now it was five, then four, then three…

"Look out! Get down! Take cover!" he screamed, startling the others. But they could tell he was deadly serious.

Harvey grabbed Susan and dragged her down with him behind a fallen tree trunk. De Villiers dived behind a thicket of bushes. Evans went to ground behind a tree. For a few moments there was silence; an unnatural silence as if Africa was suddenly holding its breath. Then with a shattering cacophony, a hail of machine-gun bullets thudded in to the tree trunk in front of Harvey. Then silence again. The emerald-spotted wood dove was nowhere to be heard. Then the crackling of a twig ahead of them; de Villiers did not hesitate; this was life or death; the AK coughed twice. An African fell out of a bush sprawling in a heap on the track some forty-five paces ahead of them. The track exploded hurling his body thirty feet into the air in a disintegrating shower of flesh. Susan realized that the land mine had been meant for them.

A machine-gun began to chatter. De Villiers had moved immediately after his original firing. The AK coughed twice again. The machine-gun fell silent and two men leapt out of the grass to one side of them. A gun, but not fired by de Villiers this time, fired twice and they both fell instantly dead; then the sound of crashing through the bush all around them. Harvey tensed for action. Then he realized, with an overwhelming feeling of relief, that the noise was receding. The men were running away.

His relief was short-lived; there was no mistaking the feeling of hard steel on the back of his neck. Harvey was a trained man used to hand to hand combat but he had not heard his assailant. Whoever it was, he thought, knew his job supremely well and was clearly not to be messed with.

He raised his hands.

"Git up viry, viry slowly; the girl too." Harvey was never so happy to hear the Rhodesian accent. They had been apprehended by a patrol of Selous Scouts. The leader looked somewhat nonplussed at finding three white men and a girl in a ragged state in the depth of the African bush.

"I don't know who the heck you are or what you are doing out here but you don't look like part of Mugabe's shower to me. I am taking you to headquarters in Salisbury."

The young man pointed eastwards. "We have transport just a mile away over that ridge. We must go very carefully as this is dangerous country and we did not get them all by a long chalk."

They had just reached the Scouts' vehicles when they heard shooting.

"What's that?" asked Harvey stopping mid-stride.

"Relax, man," replied the Rhodesian. "That is brother Olangwe and comrade Masingi settling a little quarrel between themselves."

They climbed into the army truck and turned towards Salisbury.

They arrived in the early evening and were taken straight to the Rhodesian security services headquarters. Harvey was allowed to contact Pritchard. That worthy was so glad to hear from his subordinate that he immediately tore him off a strip for not making contact sooner.

"Where the hell have you been? Stopped off for a golfing mini-break I suppose."

"No, sir; been on a walking safari actually and seen plenty of game too – you should get out more."

One thing Harvey was able to establish for Susan was that David was safe. Susan's mother had come from Kent to look after him. David was worried and upset by his mother's disappearance but otherwise had not been harmed in any way. Later that evening they enjoyed the luxury of a bath, some supper and blissful sleep.

Chapter Sixteen

Mozambique – Wednesday 21st September to 1st October 1977

Richard Masingi was in trouble. The ambush he had prepared for Harvey's group had gone wrong from the start. The extraordinary awareness of Dennis Evans had saved them from walking straight into the mined pathway. Thereafter de Villiers had proved a more formidable adversary than they had expected. To cap it all the materialization of the Selous Scouts found them totally off-guard. They suffered several casualties. By the time Masingi's force had regrouped, it had been tracked down by Stephen Olangwe's patrol. They were cornered in a shallow glade. Masingi lost his entire unit apart from himself, Jardine and Juanita. They escaped as they had not been directly involved in the fighting.

Masingi and Juanita had stayed together. They took stock of their situation. Jardine had vanished into the bush during the fighting. There was nothing they could do about that. To start to try to track a lone individual in that sort of country was totally out of the question. Neither of them were trained for it. Jardine was. If it came to a showdown in the African bush between them and Jardine they would almost certainly finish up dead. They decided their priority was to somehow get back to Chimoio.

Soon the Land Rover, that they still had, ran out of

petrol stranding them. They had almost five hundred kilometres to cover to get back to Chimoio. At times they were able to get help from the local Africans who gave them food and lifts. Finally, a full week later, on the evening of Wednesday 28th September they walked back into Chimoio Camp.

The next morning Juanita Havanestro woke early despite her exhaustion from several days in the Mozambique bush. She had a mission to accomplish and regardless of the setbacks, she was still resolved to do just that – or die in the endeavour. She still did not know where Stuart Holder was or whether he was any longer important. What she had construed from her limited conversations with Jardine was that he had secreted the three canisters in various locations in South Africa. He was the only person who knew where those locations were and he was not about to part with that information for nothing.

However, on arrival at Chimoio the matter was taken out of her hands. She received instructions to be acted upon straightaway. She was to fly to England on an important mission. She left on Saturday evening, 1st October.

Chapter Seventeen

Salisbury, Rhodesia – Thursday 22nd September 1977

It took Harvey a good half-day to extricate himself from the clutches of the Rhodesian security forces. In the end the intervention of a mightily-relieved Geoffrey Pritchard proved decisive. It was not until well into the afternoon that Harvey, Darnie de Villiers and Susan Bennett were airborne to Johannesburg.

They said goodbye to Dennis Evans. He had decided to stay and rebuild his life in Rhodesia. He knew that he had become involved in something with international implications. To return to Tanzania was impractical. He had dropped his original idea of returning to his parents in Kenya. He felt it could easily compromise them. He had taken an immediate liking to Rhodesia. If he could manage to get work on a farm he thought that might well be the most practical answer. Harvey was grateful to the young tea planter. His local knowledge and astuteness had been of great value but the time had come for the parting of the ways.

Pritchard had managed to get an overnight flight from Heathrow. They all met in the arrivals terminal at Jan Smuts airport in Johannesburg. Their first priority was to find Stuart Holder. Pritchard brought Harvey up to date with the conversation he had had with Peters regarding Marianna Holder turning herself in.

"Apparently Holder's wife had run over and killed a man when she, Holder and Jardine had all been at Kent University. They had been returning from Ramsgate to Canterbury and it seems Marianna had been stoned. Marianna and Holder married shortly after that. He is known to be devoted to his wife and Jardine used that to blackmail him."

Pritchard had been to see her as planned, but really learned very little more of substance. She explained the circumstances of the car accident which had killed Fred Bostock. The police had already checked that and found it to be true. Bostock had been run over in June 1969 in a fatal hit-and-run incident. No one had ever been arrested or charged. Hitherto the case had remained unsolved.

Harvey in turn brought Pritchard up to date with what had happened to him since they were last in contact. The incident at Kilimatembo where Jardine was attacked by the rabid dog was of particular relevance. That had enabled Harvey to force Jardine to give him the information he sought as to the whereabouts of Holder. Jardine had implied that the supplies of EV77 were with Holder. Harvey was less convinced that it was the whole truth. Nevertheless it was a starting point.

Jardine had claimed that Holder's living quarters were in a flat in Johannesburg. For work he was using a defunct area of the South African Breweries complex as a laboratory.

"Do you know where exactly?" asked Pritchard.

"Darnie says he knows the place but that it might be easier to catch up with Holder in his flat. Also, I'm not keen to go anywhere near a laboratory with Ebola in it if I don't have to."

"Yes, fair enough," agreed Pritchard. "Whereabouts is his flat?"

"On Jan Smuts Avenue at Braamfontein Ridge."

Harvey decided it was time to repay Pritchard for his

endless banter about golf. Innocently and with not a flicker of expression on his face he said, "You no doubt know that it is a fascinating place for hydrologers. When it rains, it is said that eventually half the rainfall finishes up in the Atlantic Ocean and half in the Indian Ocean."

"What the hell are you talking about?" demanded Pritchard testily.

"Quite true isn't it, Darnie?" Harvey turned to de Villiers

"Whoa… don't get me involved in this, man – let's just go find the flat."

They moved to get into the estate car that was to take them to Van Ruyen's office. The journey passed with Harvey filling in the details of the trek through Africa. As they were alighting from the vehicle Pritchard paused mid-stride. He turned to Harvey, a stern look on his face.

"Just a small point, Mark."

"Yes, Chief."

"Its hydrologists not hydrologers."

Harvey smiled inwardly. The old bastard had won again!

The plan was agreed that Harvey and de Villiers would go and try to find Holder. Pritchard would remain with Van Ruyen and await news. Meanwhile arrangements were made for Susan to fly home to be reunited with David. Pritchard noticed that she seemed to be in a turmoil at leaving. He imagined she would simply be relieved to be going home to her son. Clearly that was the case. But additionally she seemed actually quite upset to be going.

'It's that darn Harvey again,' he thought to himself. 'My own PA goes all doe-eyed when he appears; he should stick to golf.'

Braamfontein Ridge was known to Darnie de Villiers in as far as it was a suburb that he had been through once or twice. He was more familiar with Empire Road than Jan

Smuts Avenue. They were the two main thoroughfares. They found the place relatively easily. The flat turned out to be in a tower block. The two men split up, de Villiers remaining at ground level while Harvey took the lift to the ninth floor where number 909 was situated.

There did not appear to be any guard or surveillance that Harvey could detect. Holder must be wondering where Jardine had got to. Harvey thought that he could easily have done a runner, although how far he would have got was uncertain. Harvey still had no idea how much Jardine's masters were aware of Holder's exact location – or to what degree Jardine was working on his own. He also had no idea that Jardine at that moment was still fighting his way back to South Africa. He was worried that the South African might have somehow got back to Johannesburg and could turn up at any moment.

Seeing nothing to stop him he approached the door of 909 and rang the bell. There was no reply. He rang again three or four times and still no reply. Now evening, Harvey felt that Holder should have been back from work. He rang the bell at 908. A young woman he judged to be in her mid-twenties came to the door.

"I'm looking for the gentleman who lives at 909, but there is no reply. I'm wondering if you have seen him around recently."

"I'm afraid not; he hasn't lived there very long and has kept himself very much to himself. In the last few days I haven't seen him at all."

"OK thanks, I'll just push a note under his door."

The girl hesitated for a moment assessing Harvey. She liked what she saw. It was a long time since a tall, dark, handsome stranger had knocked on her door.

"My dad is the caretaker here and is away at the moment. He has left the keys with me and I could let you in if you wanted to leave a note in the flat."

"That would be terrific; I'd be really grateful." He gave

her his most winning smile.

"Just a moment." She disappeared back into her flat. She reappeared a few moments later with a large bunch of keys. Harvey noticed she had changed her slippers for a pair of high heels and lipstick had been applied.

They approached the door of 909 and the girl started to unlock the door.

"Just a moment," said Harvey placing his hand on her arm.

"What's the matter?" she asked.

Harvey had realized what they were going to find in Holder's flat. Standing close to the door he had recognized an odour with which he was only too familiar. He had been vaguely aware of it before but had not consciously placed it.

"I think you'd better let me go in there first," he said and before she knew what had happened he had pushed the door open, quickly stepped inside and shut the door in her face.

"Hey wait a minute!" she cried trying to push her way in but he held her back.

He opened the door a crack.

"What's your name?" he asked her.

"Charlene," she answered. "Why?"

"Well look, Charlene, I want you to do something for me. There is something not very nice in here. Please will you go downstairs where you will find a man standing at the entrance. His name is Darnie and he is a police officer. Tell him that Mark needs him to come up to number 909 immediately. Will you do that for me please, Charlene?"

Something in Harvey's voice convinced the girl that he should be obeyed. She did as he asked. De Villiers was there within a few minutes. Charlene was told to go back into her own flat and stay there until they came out of 909 and spoke to her again.

Stuart Holder was lying on the floor. How long he had

been dead neither of them could tell. There did not appear to have been any sort of struggle and there was no blood on him. They assumed he had taken some sort of poison. Harvey was only too aware that he had been working with EV77. He wondered if there had been some sort of accident. Neither he nor de Villiers had suffered any reaction so he could only hope that the flat was not contaminated in any way.

"Let's get out of here," said Harvey. "We need to get back to Pritchard and Van Ruyen and decide how we are going to play this."

He rang the bell at 908 again and Charlene appeared looking very worried.

"What's going on?" she asked, fearful that she would get into trouble with her father for letting Harvey in.

"Charlene, there has been a nasty accident in that flat. Are there any keys other than the ones you used to let me in?"

"No."

"I'm going to lock that flat up. I'm afraid you are going to have to come with us. When is your father due back?"

"Not till Sunday night. He has gone on a long weekend fishing in the Berg."

"Is there anybody else in the flat with you?"

"No; I live here on my own and my dad has the flat at the entrance on the ground floor."

The girl was very uncertain about closing up her flat and going with Harvey and de Villiers, but in truth they gave her no choice. She was sensible enough to know that she was looking at a death, possibly murder. It wasn't the time to start getting difficult. De Villiers drove and in less than an hour they were back in Van Ruyen's office.

Harvey brought Pritchard and Van Ruyen up to speed on what had transpired at Holder's flat. Neither of them looked very surprised and the reason for that was immediately forthcoming.

"Mark, there has been a development at this end as well. Holder apparently wrote what amounts to a suicide note and posted it air mail to Gordon Peters at Boughton. He actually received it yesterday and has been in touch to reveal its contents to us. I have it transcribed here."

He held out a couple of sheets of A4 paper. Harvey took them and started to read.

Dear Mr Peters

You may be surprised to hear from me but I do not know another way to get this message safely out of South Africa and into the hands of those who need to see it.

Two weeks ago I was approached by Neil Jardine whom I knew at Kent University. His alleged purpose was to get me to fly to South Africa and analyse a blood sample. This had been obtained by his organization which is essentially in opposition to the apartheid government. My wife is a black Jamaican and I am strongly against apartheid. The task did not seem to me to be either too difficult or too immoral. I agreed to do it. I was able to confirm that the sample contained the virus Ebola.

I was then instructed to concentrate this into a solution capable of infecting a potential victim with Ebola. This was not our original agreement but he threatened me in such a way that I felt I had no option but to comply. I regret I am not prepared to divulge the nature of that threat.

Rather unimaginatively he called this solution EV77 – Ebola Virus 1977. The facilities provided here are excellent and given the original virus the work was not especially difficult. I emphasize, Mr Peters, that nothing at all has been removed from Boughton. I have worked purely from the infected blood sample provided here.

I now realize that I have made the greatest mistake of my life. Analysing a blood sample is one thing. Developing a deadly substance for dissemination is quite another. I cannot go through with this despite the threat held over me by Jardine.

Jardine has not been in evidence for a few days and I have taken advantage of that to destroy all the remaining supplies of the so-called

EV77 in production here. At the last time I saw Jardine I handed over to him three separate flasks. They are in aerosol canisters somewhat like those used for shaving gel but stronger, larger and with a robust outer packaging. For some reason he was very insistent that I should provide him with three.

Jardine either does not understand the properties of EV77 or seeks to provoke alarm. He talks of filling a tanker and touring the white suburbs spraying it around. This is fanciful nonsense. Ebola is only transmitted by bodily fluids – saliva, sweat, urine, semen, etc. It is not airborne. Although work has been going on to attempt to combine the virus with other agents like myxomatosis this has not been achieved. Nevertheless, there is no doubt that the agent in its present form, although crude, is a highly toxic substance. It may well have the scope to infect a number of people if they actually ingest it or have enough of it sprayed directly onto their skin. Once an infection has got started it would be easily transmitted from person to person. Ebola usually develops after just a few days. We estimate it is fatal in most cases but not invariably so.

For the above reason this agent could be absolutely deadly if used by a terrorist organization on a civilian population. Ebola has only recently been discovered. It might take hold and infect many hundreds of people before anyone realized what it was or how it was being spread.

I realize that my life is completely ruined; that of my wife also. I am in total despair and feel I have no hope of ever remedying that situation. I cannot continue here and I cannot face returning to the UK. I have reached the end of the road. There is nowhere else to turn. By the time this is read I will have taken the only honourable course of action left to me.

It is an irony that being someone who has worked with the most deadly substances, my death will be caused by the two most mundane drugs in existence – alcohol and paracetamol.

Please tell my wife that I am sorry. I have let her down; I have put her in an intolerable position. But I have always loved her and I always will.

Stuart Holder

Harvey silently handed the note over to de Villiers for him to read.

"What now?" he asked looking at Pritchard.

"Well, I have had a little time to think about this. I've come to the conclusion that the best thing to do at present is nothing."

"How do you work that out?" enquired Harvey, taken aback.

"I think we have been barking up the wrong tree; this operation is not and never has been aimed at toppling the apartheid regime. The Soviets know that is unrealistic just as much as we do. Their method has always been to go about it piecemeal. They have got their way in Angola and Mozambique and their next realistic goal is for Rhodesia to become Zimbabwe. So far that has not gone so easily. Once we renounced the use of force our influence became very limited. Yes, we've put sanctions on them but they have survived those for years already and are not about collapse. Unless…"

"Go on."

"Well, who does Ian Smith depend on? Not the Americans, nor the British; but of course the South Africans. We can huff and puff all we like but in the end it is Mr Vorster who matters to Mr Smith. With the backing of Vorster, Smith can continue; without that backing he is staring down the barrel of a gun and will collapse in months."

Harvey finished for him.

"So you reckon the plan is to threaten South Africa in some way to make them withhold support from Rhodesia and, bingo, we have Zimbabwe."

"I don't know that I would have put it exactly like that, Mark, but, yes, basically I think that could be their plan. That being the case sooner or later the threat to use this EV77 will materialize."

"Why do you think they need three canisters of the

stuff?" mused Harvey.

"I don't know the answer to that yet. I dare say it will become clear soon enough. In the meantime I have agreed with Mr Van Ruyen that Darnie and a team will set about trying to track down the canisters while you and I return to London. We have plenty of other things to be getting on with anyway."

As Geoffrey Pritchard and Mark Harvey flew out of Johannesburg the next evening, on their way home, Harvey looked down at the terrain below. It had been his first real taste of Africa. It had been tough, stressful and exhausting. He had loved it. He thought of the vast emptiness of Kongwa, the oasis of Mufindi, the merciless heat of the Zambezi valley, the thrill of that awesome lion. The drug which is Africa had begun to infect his being. He would never be free of it again.

SIPOLILO
SALISBURY
RHODESIA
BULAWAYO
BOTSWANA
THE MATOPOS
NATIONAL PARK
SOUTH AFRICA

Chapter Eighteen

Rhodesia, Wednesday – 21st September to Saturday 24th

Neil Jardine had resolved to get back to South Africa on his own. He had no illusions about Juanita Havanestro or Richard Masingi. They were both as treacherous as each other. The only remaining card in his hand was his knowledge of the whereabouts of the three canisters containing the virus. Once they had beaten that out of him they would simply dispose of him. He had to get away and negotiate from a distance if he was to have any hope of coming out of this alive.

Whilst he was no friend of Rhodesia he was white. No one in that country would find it remarkable for a white man to be driving a car. He knew also that Masingi and Juanita would slip back into Mozambique. They would be much safer there. They would make for Chimoio. They would not want to follow him deeper into Rhodesia.

The first night he spent under the stars. Other than a noisy warthog the wildlife left him alone. On the next morning he came upon a tobacco farm. Knowing there would be vehicles there he crept up from the bush side and settled himself behind a large acacia tree. He would watch and see what transpired. When the moment came he would steal a vehicle and be gone.

The day wore on with no sign of activity. The heat became oppressive. Jardine had eaten nothing since lunchtime the day before. He decided the time had come for action. He eased himself from his hideout and started to walk away from the farm. If there was a farm there must be a road nearby. In less than twenty minutes he came upon a farm track. He assumed it would lead out to a larger road. He estimated that he must be about fifty kilometres inside Rhodesia by now. He needed wheels.

He started to walk along the track when a sight he could not believe met his eyes – a Volkswagen Beetle standing beside the track with the driver's door open and the engine running. He thought the gods must be smiling on him. Had he known the area better he would have known it was not an exceptional sight. The farmer had seen something of which he disapproved and had leapt out of the car to admonish the unfortunate African responsible.

Jardine did not hesitate. He was into the car in a flash and driving south as fast as the Beetle would go. He realized that the farmer would be after him in no time; more than likely in a more powerful car. Shortly he came upon a township. He learned from the signage that it was called Sipolilo.

The main street contained a number of shops. Cars were randomly parked outside them. He abandoned the VW. He walked along the parked vehicles until he found one open. He was just about to leap in when a large Rhodesian Ridgeback dog inside caused him to change his mind rapidly. In the end he saw a woman loading groceries into a Peugeot 404 station wagon. He waited until she had nearly finished; he needed the provisions. Then he struck. Pushing her powerfully aside, he grabbed the keys from her. He was into the car and away before she could recover.

He learned, again from the signage, that Salisbury was

a hundred and fifty kilometres to the south. That is where he made for. His idea was to change vehicles there. That proved relatively easy and by mid-afternoon he was on the road. He had managed to appropriate a Mercedes taxi standing at a rank. The driver had been further down the line of cars talking to a colleague. He had decided that he would fare better trying to cross out of Rhodesia if he went into Botswana rather than South Africa. The border was less well protected. Consequently he pointed the car to Bulawayo.

By nightfall he had made the Matopos National Park. All he knew about the place was that the tomb of Cecil Rhodes, after whom Rhodesia was named, was there – in a place called Malindidzimu – translated to 'world's view'. He had no time for sightseeing and Rhodes was not one of his favourite historical figures. He pressed on.

As he neared the border he stopped and ate from the groceries which he had kept from the Peugeot when changing cars in Salisbury. Then he abandoned the Mercedes; it was very low on fuel and he had no money to buy more. In any case he had decided he would stand a better chance of crossing the border on foot at night. This turned out to be a far more tiring exercise than he had envisaged. It took him the best part of the night and it was 3.30 a.m. before he was certain he was in Botswana. He slept.

He woke with the dawn and started the search for transport. He was looking for a parked car when he heard a large lorry approaching. It turned out to be a petrol tanker. He risked thumbing a lift. It was with a mixture of relief and apprehension that he approached the cab. It was a friendly African only too pleased of company on his long trip. He was taking fuel to South Africa.

During the journey south Jardine managed to get the man's confidence. He told him of his work in opposing the apartheid government. The African agreed to hide him in the lorry to take him over the border into South Africa. This was not so easy in a tanker as a normal truck. However, there was a bunk above the cab and Jardine was in luck. The border guards were not interested in it. In the early hours of Saturday 24th September Neil Jardine was back in his native South Africa making for the country club at Vereeniging.

Chapter Nineteen

Surrey, England – Wednesday 5th October 1977

Susan Bennett fell in love with Wentworth from the start. She thought of that morning six thousand miles away in Tanzania when they had stood on another golf course. They had promised themselves this day. At the time it seemed highly unlikely they would make it; but here they were at the World Match Play Championship – just as Harvey had promised her.

She asked if they could follow the match between Gary Player and Manuel Pinero as Player was the only competitor she had heard of. They followed the match hole by hole, pausing on the right-hand side of the fourth fairway to look back up the sweeping lawns of one of the most beautiful gardens she had ever seen. When they reached the eighth hole Susan, in company with most people, stayed by the tee while Harvey walked on down the fairway and over a little wooden bridge to the side of the green. She rejoined him as the match came back up the ninth fairway which ran directly counter to the eighth.

The match finished at the thirteenth green in the afternoon and as they walked back to the car Harvey asked her if she had enjoyed it.

"Yes, it was a lovely day," she responded enthusiastically.

"Would you like to come again tomorrow?"

"Yes, I'd love to."

"OK then. Let's get here early. We can get the car into a little place I know on the right-hand side of the seventeenth fairway. It saves walking miles to the main car parks. If we arrive early and look after the attendant, he will let us in."

"Sounds great." And so it was agreed.

Since his return from South Africa time had dragged for Mark. He felt restless and frustrated by his enforced inactivity. His mind was still full of the inconclusive events in South Africa. Pritchard had sensed the unease in his subordinate and left him to come round in his own time. He knew that Harvey always saved a few days leave each year to be able to attend the golf tournament at Wentworth in October. He packed him off telling him to report back on Monday 10th October in a better frame of mind.

They repeated their programme the next day and followed a fascinating match between the Open Champion Tom Watson and the young Spanish swashbuckler, Severiano Ballesteros. As they came down the seventeenth fairway Susan stopped off at the car to prepare the picnic lunch she had brought. Harvey walked on with the match to the eighteenth hole.

They had another good day and decided to come again on the Friday. The young Spaniard had defeated the Open Champion and was due to face the American Ray Floyd. Harvey told Susan that it could be a tough battle as Floyd was a doughty competitor. For her part she was just enjoying the occasion – particularly being in a tension-free environment with the man she now knew she loved. She didn't feel totally confident that Harvey felt as strongly but at least they were here together.

They followed that match to the seventeenth the next morning and as the game left the green Susan walked back to the car to prepare the picnic. The matches were over thirty-six holes so this came as a half-time break. Harvey went on up the eighteenth. Both players hit good drives but it was the second shot from Ballesteros that set the match alight – a crashing wood into the heart of the green.

It was at that moment that Wentworth 1977 ended for Mark Harvey.

"What the hell are you doing here?" he exclaimed.

"I've come to talk to you," answered Juanita Havanestro. "This seems about the only place to get you without your girlfriend tagging along."

"What do you want?" he asked incensed at having his great day interrupted.

"Let us walk across to the main complex while we talk."

There are few places more private than a deserted golf course and there were no players or spectators as they crossed the fairway on the first hole.

"I've come to tell you what you have to do to reclaim the EV77 canisters."

"Go on then but don't expect too much." His eyes were bleak and hard. "There's only so much mileage in a flask of EV77."

"Which is why we have three, Mr Harvey. We require three things to happen. First, South Africa must cease support for Rhodesia. We are confident that it is only a matter of time before Mr Vorster agrees to this. He knows very well that one-man one-vote will come to Zimbabwe. He will not risk a catastrophic epidemic in Johannesburg to postpone the inevitable."

"I'm not so sure you are right there," countered Harvey. "The Afrikaners are a very stubborn people and they will not take kindly to being threatened."

"EV77 in the hands of the Black Liberation Front will focus his mind," said Juanita dismissively. She looked at Harvey. "But I did not come here to talk about Mr

Vorster. I came to talk about the United Kingdom."

"So?" prompted Harvey.

"When Mr Smith concedes one-man one-vote he will have to reach an agreement with some faction of the Zimbabwe Africans. His obvious choice will be to try to come up with the much talked of 'internal settlement' involving Muzurewa and any other puppets ready to join."

"Yes, nothing new there." Harvey was curt.

"When Mr Smith reaches such an agreement he will turn to the United Kingdom for ratification. If you give your approval, America will do so also. If both the UK and USA ratify the agreement sanctions will be lifted. Elections will take place which the puppet Muzurewa will win. Zimbabwe will become just another capitalist country like Kenya – but richer." The Cuban girl's eyes glinted with fanaticism. "But that does not suit us at all, Mr Harvey. The United Kingdom will not support the internal settlement or any other settlement that does not include the agreement of both Robert Mugabe and Joshua Nkomo which we now call the Patriotic Front."

Harvey was outraged. His voice barely above a whisper but full of such menace that she was visibly shaken.

"Are you daring to stand on British soil and tell me that if Britain does not toe the Soviet line on Rhodesia you will attempt to unleash an Ebola epidemic on one of our cities?"

"Oh come, Mr Harvey, let's remain professional and unemotional. Of course I am not saying that. The only outcome of that would be war. You know that we fight on different battlefields now. What I am saying is that it would be better for all of us if we could reach an agreement on this."

"And if we don't?" he said.

"Well if your government decides to be perverse then we could not guarantee that a canister of EV77 would not find its way into the hands of Colonel Gaddafi. I believe he has good relations with the IRA. Think about it carefully, Mr Harvey."

Harvey was indeed thinking about it and beginning to understand a lot of things very quickly. Their plan was beginning to unfold. The IRA in possession of a Soviet weapon supplied directly by the Soviet Union would not be in any way acceptable. It would risk almost certain war with NATO countries. But a British biological weapon – made in breach of the 1972 agreement – supplied to the IRA by Colonel Gaddafi would not implicate the Soviet Union. It would impale the United Kingdom on the horns of a particularly uncomfortable dilemma. Harvey now saw why Jardine had been at such pains to claim that the EV77 substance was British. Also, despite Peters' repeated assurances, Harvey was still not convinced that Boughton was as innocent as he claimed. In his private view the Cold War was a dirty business and Britain did not maintain influence by being the only one playing by the rules.

"What is the third canister for?" he demanded of Juanita.

"Please, Mr Harvey, let us keep to the point. I have contacted you here to preserve as much privacy as possible. The fewer people that are involved the better. I have brought you to this place so that you may make a telephone call to your superiors." She gestured towards the bank of public telephones provided adjacent to the practice putting green and first tee. "I suggest you call Mr Pritchard and advise him that you need to speak to him urgently. He could then meet you behind the eighth green this afternoon. I have noticed that you walk on down to that green while Miss Bennett remains behind. At the back of the eighth green is a road suitable for a car which separates the East course from the West one. He can then go back to his superiors and put our demands to them. I will contact you in forty-eight hours to hear the answer."

Harvey looked at the girl in disbelief.

"You can't really imagine you are going to get any answer, let alone the answer you want in forty-eight hours, do you?"

"Yes, I do," she said. She walked away to a car that had appeared on the road leading away from the first tee.

He called Pritchard from one of the public telephones. They arranged to meet as Juanita had suggested. He jogged back to Susan.

"You've been gone ages," she greeted him.

"Yes, I went on up to the gents and there was a hell of a queue. I'm famished, let's eat."

In the afternoon they followed the normal pattern and Pritchard just managed to make the rendezvous behind the eighth green in time. Quickly Harvey put him in the picture concerning Juanita's demands. The same question arose in his mind as had done so in Harvey's earlier.

"I wonder what the third canister is for?"

"So do I," answered Harvey. "I asked her but of course she refused to tell me."

Pritchard stared into the distance and then turned to Harvey.

"When she contacts you tell her that she will get an answer by the end of this month and no sooner. They will wait because they know they are pressing their luck. There is only so much one canister of EV77 can get them. They also know that nothing will happen in Rhodesia before that anyway."

Pritchard looked directly into Mark Harvey's eyes.

"You have till the end of the month, Mark. I don't care how you do it but you must retrieve all three canisters by that time. This whole bloody thing is getting out of control. It's gone past the point where it really matters who produced this EV77. Until we get those flasks back, they are calling the tune. Whatever help you need, ask me, but you must not fail… understood?"

"Yes, sir – perfectly."

Pritchard turned away to walk back to his car and then turned to face Harvey.

"Oh and Mark…"

"Yes."

"Enjoy the rest of the golf match."

Some hope, thought Harvey as he walked back to rejoin Susan.

It took Raymond Floyd until the thirty-fifth hole of the match to defeat the young Spaniard. By that time Harvey and Susan were well on the way back to London. Harvey's mind was no longer on golf. As he dropped Susan at her flat he said to her, "I don't think tomorrow would be such a good idea. With only one match of any interest going on the crowds get very trying. Anyway the weather forecast is not good."

Susan sensed that something had come up to do with the South African issue. She agreed without question. As he got back into his car and drove away she suddenly felt very alone. She had just realized that she might never see him again.

Chapter Twenty

London – Sunday 9th October 1977

Harvey spent the Saturday making plans for returning to South Africa. He booked himself on the Sunday evening flight to Johannesburg. His preparations were interrupted by a telephone call from Pritchard demanding his presence the next morning in the London office.

He found the chief looking at his most forbidding. In the office with him was Russell Friedland, the most senior BOSS official in London.

"Good morning, Mark; you know Russell Friedland, don't you?"

"Yes indeed, we have met," replied Harvey.

"I want you to listen to him; I think we now know the full plans that Havanestro is charged to communicate – including what the third canister is for."

Harvey looked at Friedland. He was a short, dark-haired man with hard, grey eyes. Harvey thought he would not like to be interrogated by this man in a lonely cell. Friedland began to speak in the clipped accent of the Transvaal. "I had a visit this morning from my opposite number in Mossad."

"How has the Israeli Secret Service got involved in this?" asked Harvey.

"Very directly." Friedland looked in a measured way at the two Englishmen as if trying to assess whether they were competent to be trusted with what he was going to tell them.

Then he went on, "Israel and South Africa have developed a degree of military cooperation which is beneficial to both parties." He walked to the window and stared down at the traffic; sparse on a Sunday morning.

"It really got started in 1967. You may remember that the Six Day War in that year was started by a pre-emptive strike by Israel. At that time they had a substantial amount of French military equipment. France immediately cut off the supply of spare parts. South Africa also had significant amounts of French armour. We quietly came to Israel's aid in sending the spare parts and replacement equipment needed."

Friedland paused for effect. He clearly thought he was imparting momentous news. In fact Pritchard was well aware of that cooperation.

Friedland continued.

"South Africa has helped Israel in other ways too. For some time Israeli tanks have been manufactured in a specially processed steel which provides a much greater protection against anti-tank weapons than conventional steel. In Britain you have a similar thing which you call Chobham armour. The point is that the Israeli process demands a particular type of steel which only three countries in the world can supply. Of the three, South Africa is the only one that will actually supply it to Israel."

Friedland was warming to his topic now and Harvey was wondering why he had not suspected Israeli/South African cooperation before. When it was explained it seemed so obvious.

"There is another important way in which we are useful to Israel. I know that you have seen their nuclear facility in the Negev Desert. Nuclear weapons require uranium, Mr Harvey. Where do you think Israel can get that? Perhaps from the country that has over a quarter of the total known world deposits – South Africa."

"OK, I get the picture but what does South Africa get out of this?" replied Harvey.

"Very straightforward really; Israel gets access to South Africa's raw materials and South Africa gets access to Israel's technological know-how. South Africa has one of the most advanced nuclear programmes in the world, courtesy of Israeli technology."

Friedland was obviously proud of the power that this gave his country. He continued, "In addition to that, our pilots train with and share secrets with the Israeli air force. You will recall the spectacular Israeli mission to free the hostages at Entebbe in Uganda last July. South African intelligence was critical to Israel in mounting that operation. They could not have done it without us. But, Mr Harvey, there is one thing above all others that we are getting out of this partnership."

Once again he paused to emphasize the gravity of what he was about to say.

"We are concerned about getting involved in the sort of bush war Rhodesia is facing now. We have a massive land frontier to defend. The one thing we need to know is when and where that is breached – and we need to know it immediately it happens. As we sit here, Israeli technicians are building an electronic wall with electronic sensors around the entire perimeter of our country. It is a gargantuan task but it is progressing well. At least it *was* progressing well – but a problem has arisen."

"What's that?" obliged Harvey.

"Miss Havanestro has told the Israelis that unless they cease with immediate effect all work on the project, it is likely that a canister of EV77 will find its way into the hands of the Palestine Liberation Front."

Silence descended on the room as the three men pondered the implications of this development.

Pritchard spoke. "So there you have it, Mark, the

Soviet plan which they have codenamed 'Project Capricorn'. Canister one for South Africa to cease support for Rhodesia. Canister two for the United Kingdom to withhold support from any settlement that does not include the Patriotic Front. Canister three for Israel to cease its technological help to South Africa in its nuclear programme and in defending its borders. In all three cases, not a direct threat but the implication that the virus will find its way into the hands of a terrorist organization fanatically opposed to that regime. Pretty bloody deadly, isn't it?"

"It certainly is," responded Harvey. He was still marvelling at the concept of an electrified wall around a country the size of South Africa… An Electric Curtain… The Iron Curtain was a political and ideological barrier, but apart from the Berlin Wall, not a physical thing. This was the same idea brought to a physical, or at least electronic, reality. "What is the next move?"

Pritchard took the initiative back.

"Two things – firstly we decide, with Pretoria and Tel Aviv, our response to this political blackmail. Secondly we track down and recover by any means the three canisters. I'll do the first – you do the second."

"How do you think the political angle will be played?" mused Harvey.

"Pretty quietly, I imagine," replied Pritchard. "Sooner or later, probably sooner, Rhodesia will have to come to the negotiating table. I don't imagine Britain will be very keen on any settlement that doesn't include the Patriotic Front. Israel will probably take its technicians quietly out of South Africa."

Harvey looked horrified.

"So are you saying Havanestro and her masters have won?" he asked in disbelief.

"What I'm saying, Mark," responded Pritchard testily, "is that as long as they have the EV77 and the world believes it is a British weapon, we are fighting a rear-guard action. The brutal fact is that they might well win if we don't get that bloody stuff back. So may I suggest you stop concerning yourself with my problem and start addressing your own. Once we have got all the damn virus back inside Boughton, whether or not it is ours, you might find us a little more ready to administer the smack of firm government."

Harvey could not remember seeing the older man so rattled before. He accepted the rebuke without further comment.

Pritchard spoke again. "How do you see yourself setting about the task?" he enquired in a more conciliatory tone.

"Only one thing I can do," replied Harvey. "I'll go back to South Africa and get BOSS to pressure Pretoria to agree to round up every suspect; anybody with any known sympathy for the Black Liberation movement and any record of political involvement; interview them one by one until somebody cracks and puts us on the scent. Not very original or imaginative but I hope it's effective and that's what matters now."

Later that evening Mark Harvey flew out of Heathrow for Johannesburg. The final act had begun.

Chapter Twenty-One

Johannesburg – Monday 10th October 1977

Darnie de Villiers was at Johannesburg's Jan Smuts airport to meet Harvey. As they drove back into town they went through the case together. It was important that they both shared all they knew. Obviously they had a joint interest in solving the case. Also they worked in a dangerous business. It was always possible one of them might be left on his own.

"So where are we?" said Harvey, half to de Villiers and half to himself. "We'd better take Holder's note as being true. At least there is not an endless supply of EV77 floating around all over the place – just three flasks; but that's enough to cause a hell of a lot of mayhem."

"Yeah," replied de Villiers. "We know that Jardine took the stuff from Holder and hid it somewhere, but we don't know where. We have to assume Havanestro and whoever she represents, presumably the Soviets in some form, have now learned from Jardine where they are. Where that leaves Jardine we don't know and don't much care – other than if we can get hold of him we might yet get it out of him."

Harvey was silent for a few moments, then spoke.

"I can't see any other way of proceeding apart from rounding up every known Black Liberation sympathizer. We have to hope that sooner or later we come across one who knows something and can be persuaded to part with it. Not very subtle but can you think of a better plan?"

"Unfortunately not," replied de Villiers. "The government won't like it. As soon as we do it, the outside world will come crashing down on our heads. We like to keep below the radar as much as possible. The longer we can avoid trade sanctions, the better able we will be placed to cope when they come."

"Do you mean when they come or if they come?" queried Harvey. "Surely you hope to avoid them."

"Oh they'll come alright, Mark; maybe not this year or even next but they'll come. The West, particularly Britain, is too economically weak at the moment but as soon as your economy picks up… We have no illusions; South Africa is on her own. Nobody is going to help us. Our policy is to buy time to arm and prepare for the struggle."

"Can't you do something to avert that? Can't you liberalize a little? What about this guy Nelson Mandela you've got locked up on Robben Island. A lot of people seem to think you should let him out."

"You must be bloody joking, man. If we let that troublemaker out there will be a bloodbath. No, the truth is that the faster we give way the faster we will be driven into the Antarctic Ocean."

"Maybe not," countered Harvey. "Maybe you can negotiate with him."

"Why would he negotiate with us?" said de Villiers. "What frame of mind is he going to be in after being locked up for half his lifetime? He would have to be Jesus Christ himself to come out and turn the other cheek."

There was silence in the car apart from the growl of the three-litre Cortina engine. Harvey had never had reason to think deeply about the South African dilemma. He felt instinctively that apartheid must be wrong and that some sort of compromise should be reached. Now he was being confronted with the reality of how a South African saw it. He didn't assess de Villiers as inherently a fascist or even an out and out racist; just a young man fashioned by having been born into a system that sought to preserve the white man's place in South Africa.

De Villiers summed it up. "I don't like a lot of what goes on here, Mark, but what else can we do if we want to survive?"

"Anyway, whatever the rights and wrongs, let's deal with reality," said Harvey, bringing himself back to the job in hand. "If your government doesn't want an international outcry, how are we going to play it?"

"There is a further complication," added de Villiers. "There is a general election in a few weeks and the National Party won't want to go to the nation in the middle of an outcry about our brutality at the United Nations."

"On the other hand they won't want to have an election in the aftermath of a catastrophe," countered Harvey.

"Of course, and for that reason, we expect to get clearance for the round-up quite soon," said de Villiers

Their conversation was brought to an end by their arrival at Van Ruyen's office.

Chapter Twenty-Two

Vereeniging, Transvaal, South Africa

Time was running out for Neil Jardine. Juanita Havanestro had returned to Chimoio resolved to track him down and demand the canisters from him. She had threatened three world powers with the possibility that she would let a canister fall into the hands of a terrorist organization at war with them. As things stood she didn't even have one canister. Action was required, and fast.

She assessed the best chance of finding Jardine would be through the Zandukwes. It was unlikely that he would show up at his recruitment agency but it was more than likely that he would be in hiding somewhere around Vereeniging. It was also highly probable that he would have made contact with either Mary or Johannes, or both.

On Tuesday 11th October she entered South Africa through Swaziland. Her eyes were hard with ruthless determination as she sat in the back of the yellow Chev speeding her to Johannesburg. The two men in the front knew of her but had not had dealings with her before. They hoped they would be allowed to go home to Russia when this was over.

She was in possession of Johannes Zandukwe's home address. He was part of the organization for which she worked and there was no great problem in ascertaining it. However, it would draw unwelcome attention to her if she drove into Sharpeville with two white men. She also had his work address and ultimately was able to contact him that way. It took her until Wednesday to finally meet him face to face.

Johannes Zandukwe undertook to get Mary to try to get in touch with Jardine. He felt he would be more likely to respond to her than anyone else. In the event it took Mary the rest of the week to track him down. She decided to lie in wait in their glade by the river on the Saturday evening. She just had a feeling that he might go there. She was right.

Jardine had not really known how to proceed since his return. He wanted to contact Oscar Tembi. His original instructions had been to advise Tembi of the whereabouts of the three canisters. He did not know exactly what Tembi planned to do with them but reasoned that if he got to Tembi now he might yet come out of this OK. He did not know to what extent Tembi knew of Juanita. He presumed he must know Masingi but there was often no love lost between the various factions of freedom fighters. If he contacted Tembi he could tell him that this was the first opportunity he had to pass on the information. Indeed that was absolutely true. Furthermore he had not been instructed to tell Juanita or Masingi and therefore his absconding from Rhodesia could be portrayed as perfectly reasonable. That's what he told himself.

He had no direct way of contacting Tembi. The obvious way was through Johannes Zandukwe. In turn the way to him was through Mary. He decided to be at the glade every evening for a week. It might just work. On Saturday 15th October it did.

"Hello, master," said Mary. She was intent on seducing him. Her plan was to soften him up so that he would agree to a further assignation. She would not tell him that she planned to bring her father and Juanita to that meeting.

Jardine was relieved to see her. He was beginning to get very worried about his situation. Juanita and Masingi would have mobilised any help possible to track him down. Furthermore, he had not as yet had the confidence to go to the medical authorities in Johannesburg to get the injections he was still in need of for the dog bite he had received at Kilimatembo. Also, he felt physically attracted to Mary.

The combination of all those emotions made him easy meat for her.

"I have been missing you and just hoped you might be here on a Saturday evening."

As she spoke she started to unbutton her blouse.

"Does your father know you are here?" He realized it was a pointless question. She was bound to answer no whether he did or not.

"No he doesn't," she replied. "I'm sorry about that time he caught us together. I should have known he would spy on me. Tonight he is with friends in the township. We are alone." She had continued to undress as she spoke and Jardine was aflame. He prevaricated no further. He took her with a desperation that she had not felt in him before.

When it was over she did not rise immediately and leave. She stayed and talked. She sensed that he was a worried man and felt she could use that to get him to confide in her. At first the talk was the usual inconsequential nothings that follow sex. Jardine was shocked to discover that something had been stirred in him that he had not known was there; something that was a relation to what he had felt for Mary's little sister, Sara, all those years ago.

"You seem unhappy, Neil." Unusually she used his first name to foster the intimacy.

"Not unhappy; just a bit weighed down at work." He

sought to deflect her.

"What's been happening to you?" she asked.

"Oh this and that," he parried vaguely.

Time to get to the point, he thought.

"Have you or your father been in touch with Oscar Tembi recently?" He made it sound as casual as he could.

"I haven't but my father deals with him fairly regularly; why?"

"I haven't seen him for some time and would just like to catch up."

"I could ask my father for you if you like."

"Yes that would be very helpful, Mary."

"Let's meet back here on Monday evening," she said. "That will give me time to make the contact and if Tembi is in Johannesburg he might even come himself."

"Monday evening then; here."

And so it was agreed.

Jardine spent Sunday keeping out of sight. His parents knew he was back but no one else did and he just kept a low profile at the club. Eventually the wait was over and he was on his way to the glade on Monday evening.

Mary came first. She was friendly but did not attempt to seduce him this time. She explained that Oscar Tembi was on his way.

He wasn't. Johannes Zandukwe and Juanita Havanestro were.

"Good evening, Neil." Juanita's voice was icy cold. Jardine could see the gun glinting in her right hand. "Time for some straight talking. You will tell me now where the three canisters are. The location of the canisters… NOW!"

Jardine had been thinking fast since the moment she appeared. His first thought had been to wonder whether Mary had known what was going to happen or whether she had been betrayed also. First things first – he must get the gun off Havanestro. He was stronger than her but she was tough and very quick. If he lunged and missed she would be merciless.

With the speed of a striking cobra he was on her. Zandukwe was taken completely by surprise at the speed and venom of his attack. Juanita and Jardine went down in a heap of flailing arms and legs. Jardine may have prevailed if it had been just him and Juanita but Zandukwe recovered in time to strike him with sickening force on the back of the head with a small rock he had picked up. Simultaneously there was a shot followed by a roar from Jardine. He had been hit in the top of the left arm.

Nevertheless he fought on but the outcome was inevitable now.

"Tell me, Jardine, you fool; tell me now or I will shoot you in both knees."

Jardine was in pain and dazed from the blow from Zandukwe but sufficiently operational to recognize the time had come to give some ground.

"Take that bloody gun out of my face and let me up. I can do better than tell you. I will give you a canister."

He was permitted to rise and staggered over to a tree.

"There," he said pointing at a patch of bare earth under the tree. "If you look in the bushes–" he gestured towards a thicket, "–you will probably find a spade."

Juanita did not move. The gun remained pointed at Jardine's knees with deadly precision.

"Look," she ordered Zandukwe. There was no doubt who was in charge.

Zandukwe did as he was ordered. In less than five minutes he returned with a spade and started digging. A further ten minutes and he picked up the canister from the hole.

"Where are the other two?"

"My orders are to tell Oscar Tembi, not you." Jardine desperately tried to stall.

"Don't mess me around, you prick!" A shot rang out and the earth by Jardine's right foot spurted up.

"Bloody hell, Juanita; that missed by inches."

"What do you think this is? A game of chicken? Grow up, Neil. You are finished. Tell me."

"They are both in Cape Town," he lied. "I did not have time to separate them and there was one here and two in Cape Town."

"Where in Cape Town?" she demanded.

"On Table Mountain." He explained the location in detail. He reasoned that she would go there. When she only found one she would be back after him. But by that time he would have thought of some way of using the remaining one to save his skin.

"For your sake you'd better be right." She turned to Zandukwe.

"Bring it. We will go back to your place."

They left and Jardine was alone with Mary.

"Give me a hand. I need to get this wound patched up."

Mary tore a length of material from her cotton skirt. She dipped it in the river and cleaned his wound as best she could. It was just a flesh wound but he didn't want it going septic. She finished by binding the material around the wound. The bleeding appeared to have stopped. She looked into his eyes.

"I really didn't know that was going to happen; they told me Oscar Tembi was coming."

"Yeah sure," responded Jardine. He didn't know whether to believe her or not.

"Was that the truth?" she asked. "Are they really both on Table Mountain?"

Whether it was the aftermath of the tension-laden event he never knew. Maybe he just wanted her to know that he had not been totally humiliated. Before he realized what he was saying he blurted out, "Do your bloody worst. There is only one canister there. I still have the third one."

"Where?"

He made his mind up about her; she was in it – right up to her magnificent tits.

"Are you completely mad? Do you really think I am going to tell you when you have double-crossed me at every turn?"

And the strange relationship that had brought them together was over. She turned to go after her father and Juanita. As she made her way across the rocks in the river he thought of Sara coming the other way all those years ago. It tore at his heart. He felt very alone. He would never see Mary again.

Chapter Twenty-Three

Johannesburg, South Africa – Wednesday 19th October 1977

Just nine days after Harvey's return, the South African security forces carried out a series of raids. They arrested sixty people, banned two newspapers and proscribed eighteen organizations.

One of the sixty people was someone known to BOSS as having played a significant part in the Soweto uprising of 1976, a certain Johannes Zandukwe. All morning de Villiers and Harvey were involved in the systematic questioning of all the detainees. With Afrikaner thoroughness they started the interrogation in alphabetical order. They were not to know that the man they sought had a surname beginning with 'Z'.

At 11 a.m. Mary Zandukwe walked into Sharpeville police station. At midday there was a telephone call to Van Ruyen from Sharpeville and at 12.15 Harvey and de Villiers were called to his office.

"I fancy we may be on to something," he explained. "One of the guys we picked up this morning is apparently a chap called Zandukwe. We know he was involved in the Soweto riots last year. He has a daughter who is at Sharpeville police station saying she knows where Neil Jardine has hidden something very important. She will part with that information in exchange for the freedom of her father. She will not say another word to anybody there until she gets an assurance from my office that her father will be released if she tells us what she knows. Of course I will not negotiate with her but I am having her brought here so that we can get this information out of her. You two might care to join me when I see her."

At 2.30 p.m. Harvey and de Villiers followed Van Ruyen into the basement of his office building to a small very plain room with two chairs either side of a table. On one of the chairs sat a young black African woman. She looked sullen but did not appear to have been harmed at all. It was the first time Harvey had seen Mary Zandukwe. She made a fine figure. She sat upright with her head held back. Her demeanour exuded defiance. She was at a hopeless disadvantage, but she was not about to capitulate easily.

Van Ruyen began.

"Have you heard of the Bureau of State Security?" he asked.

Fear flickered in the girl's eyes. She had heard of BOSS and there was no need for her to reply.

"I am part of that organization and in charge of today's detentions. It is therefore in my power to release your father or keep him locked up indefinitely. So, if you have something to say we are the people to say it to and now is the time to say it."

The girl cleared her throat nervously and shifted uneasily on her chair. Her eyes were on Van Ruyen unflinchingly. The set of her mouth was determined. She was wary but she was not cowed.

"My name is Mary Zandukwe," she began, "and this morning the security services arrested my father. Whatever the reason, they will do the same things to him. If he knows anything that is useful, they will beat it out of him. If he doesn't know anything, he will make something up just to stop the pain. So I have come. I know about my father's affairs and I will tell you what I know, if you will let him go."

"He will not be very pleased about that will he, Mary?" interjected de Villiers.

"What does it matter? They will torture him until he tells them what I can tell you anyway. I am just trying to get it over more quickly and with less suffering for him."

"Well, what do you know that you think is important?" Van Ruyen was becoming aggressive.

"First will you release my father?"

Van Ruyen's eyes narrowed. He was not accustomed to defiance from a black girl and he did not like it one little bit. He controlled his anger.

"We will see about that when you tell us what you know," he parried.

The girl's spark of defiance seemed to die for a moment. She realized how entrenched was Van Ruyen's hostility towards her and began to despair of achieving anything but her own detention.

"I don't know what it is you want to know from him but if you will tell me that I will cooperate with you."

"You will bloody cooperate anyway, young woman," Van Ruyen's voice was full of menace. "If you know something spit it out now."

Harvey realized this was going nowhere. The antagonism between the two was so entrenched that despite the fact that they both wanted to talk to each other, their hearts and minds were programmed in such a way that killed any such communication before it could begin.

"I would like to talk to Miss Zandukwe on my own, if you will agree," Harvey said to Van Ruyen. His tone was as conciliatory as he could make it. He knew how much the South African would resent his interference.

Van Ruyen looked at him sharply and it took no expertise to read his mind – 'jumped up little do-gooding squirt; thinks he knows how to deal with these people better than me who has lived here all my life.' But he knew how much importance his government attached to this exercise. His orders had been to give Harvey any possible help short of endangering the security of the state. In truth he could see no valid reason for assuming that allowing Harvey to speak to the girl on his own would endanger the security of the state.

"Alright by me," he said impassively and together with de Villiers he left the room.

When the two South Africans had gone Harvey turned to the girl.

"I will do a deal with you, Mary. I am not from BOSS. I am not even South African. I am British and I have no interest in your father's politics. As you may know, my country opposes apartheid and so do I. While I do not have the direct power to have your father released I can, because of the present situation, bring very heavy pressure to bear. I will tell you what we need to find out. If you then tell me all you know you have my word that I will do everything I can to have you and your father released."

The girl looked at him with a cold, hostile stare. If he expected her to leap into his arms because he had spoken nicely to her, he was going to be disappointed.

"OK," she said at length showing no expression.

"Listen, Mary, and listen well; I am trying to find three flasks like aerosol cans about the size of a large coffee thermos. I think you may know the ones I mean?"

"I know them." Mary was still deadpan.

"They have gone missing and it is very important that we find them."

"Important for who?" she asked. "What is in them?"

"I'm afraid I can't tell you that," replied Harvey. "All I can tell you is that they contain a highly dangerous substance that could kill many people if it is released."

"A sort of poison gas?" she asked.

"Yes if you like," he responded.

There was silence in the room. Harvey so nearly tried to fill it with further explanation. Somehow he managed to remember what Pritchard had taught him. *Let them feel obliged to fill the silence; not you. Then they will probably tell you something they didn't mean you to know.* For all the banter between them he greatly respected Pritch and had discovered that the older man was nearly always right.

Harvey felt that Mary must know something, otherwise she would merely have asked him to continue. Her silence meant she was trying to decide how to gain the most advantage from what she knew. In spite of the situation Harvey found himself admiring the young woman. Everything was stacked against her but she had the spirit to fight even so.

"I know where they are," she said simply.

"Where?" shot back Harvey.

"I want the BOSS chief back so he will guarantee to release my father if I tell him."

Harvey recalled Van Ruyen and de Villiers. He explained the situation. He extracted a reluctant pledge from the former to release Mary and her father if her information turned out to be correct.

And then she told them about the showdown in the glade at Vereeniging; that Juanita had taken one of the flasks. She told them that Jardine had lied to them about two canisters being on Table Mountain. There was only one there. She did not know where the third one was but Jardine had mentioned to her many years ago that he had a small property in Natal; somewhere with a name like Shifveld Reach. Maybe he had gone there to hide and recuperate from his wound.

"Alright, Mary," said Harvey when the girl had finished. "You have told us what we wanted to know and now you are going to have to trust me. We shall try to recover the flasks. If your information turns out to be true, we will release you and your father. If things are not as you say, we will need to speak with you some more. I want you to think very carefully; is there anything at all you know that you think may help us find the containers quickly and safely?"

The girl was silent.

"Alright, you will be held here for the time being and you will not be harmed."

Mary watched them as they left. She had no option but to trust them and there was no point in arguing. She watched Van Ruyen and de Villiers go with a look of resigned sullenness darkening her fine features; a look that said in eloquent silence to the group of white men as they left: *Today, my friends, you sow the wind. Tomorrow, you will surely reap the whirlwind.*

Chapter Twenty-Four

Cape Town, South Africa – Saturday 22nd October 1977

Darnie de Villiers never failed to be moved by the spectacular beauty of Cape Town. There cannot be a more beautiful city anywhere, he thought. The majestic Cape scenery, the white beaches and the meeting of the two mighty oceans. He looked up at the dominating presence of Table Mountain and turned to Peter Rowan beside him in the car.

"OK, let's get up there," he said simply.

Peter Rowan was a local Cape Town agent. While de Villiers had been to Cape Town a number of times, he was really a Transvaal man. To have someone along who knew the local terrain should prove useful.

They drove slowly up the winding road to the cable car station. They left their vehicle in the parking area outside the building that contained the ticket office and the lower station. They made a strange sight, each with a hefty spade; but there were few people around at that hour. They bought tickets and climbed aboard the cable car. It began to be hauled slowly upwards on its wire.

This was the first time de Villiers had been in the new updated cable car. It had been brought into service in 1974. The two of them were alone in the cabin with the attendant.

"Lovely day," said de Villiers.

"Ya sure," replied the attendant. "Big trouble last night though."

"Oh, what was that?"

"Last trip down some guys had been on a stag party at the top. One of them is getting married today. They got stroppy and started trashing the cabin."

"Pretty stupid thing to do wasn't it?"

"Ya and bloody dangerous. We had to come in early to clean it up."

"Seems OK now."

"Ya; only thing needing further repair is the radio connection."

"What does that mean?"

"Not a lot; we have radio connection to the upper and lower station in case of any problem arising. It's out of action at the moment."

"Well let's hope we don't get a problem," said de Villiers.

Beneath them Cape Town was spread out. To the north-west he could make out the shape of the island lying at the mouth of the bay, Robben Island. He recalled his conversation with Harvey and thought of Nelson Mandela incarcerated there. They would have to let Mandela out one day, he supposed. What would happen then God only knew. Better not to think about it. He had a job to do.

They disembarked from the cable car at the upper station and made their way to the area that Mary Zandukwe had explained in detail. Rowan pinpointed the spot quite quickly. It was the sort of place that courting couples might come for a picnic but there was nobody there on this day. They set to work straight away. Rowan did not know exactly what was in the container they sought; only that it was important that de Villiers recovered it and took it back to Johannesburg as quickly as possible. He began to dig with vigour.

"Hey, Peter, go steady, man; this container must not be damaged in any circumstances."

"What's in it?" asked Rowan looking up and pausing in his dig.

"Never mind; just dig, but dig carefully."

They worked on in silence digging outwards from a central point they had identified from Mary's description. After a while Rowan slowed and said, "I think I have it, Darnie."

They gingerly scraped the earth from the object they had found.

"Yes, that's it alright," said de Villiers. "Thank God we got here first."

But they had not. The two men that had got there first had sat in silence, unseen, while the two South Africans did their work. They had come up on a number of days but had been unable to find the spot. They had not properly understood the directions given to them by Juanita. They were in a dilemma. They could not just shoot de Villiers and Rowan in case the canister was damaged in the process. They knew enough about its contents to know it was lethal if the substance inside was released.

Their problem was solved by the preoccupation of de Villiers and Rowan on their find. The two men were bent over the hole peering at the object they had found, reluctant to take hold of it. Eventually de Villiers picked it up and as they both straightened up, they were felled from behind. One of the assailants snatched the canister from the falling de Villiers's grasp and they both set off for the cable car station at a run.

It was a few minutes before de Villiers came round. He had sustained a blow that would have put an older or less fit man out of action for much longer; but his toughness went with the job. Quickly he worked on Rowan to bring him round as well. They both cursed themselves for their carelessness. De Villiers additionally cursed himself for his obstinacy in coming up without full support. The obvious course had been a full-scale police operation to avoid this very occurrence but de Villiers had been worried that such a large operation would get out of control. There was no love lost between BOSS and the uniformed police. He had decided to go it alone with Rowan. Now he had blown it. He would have to get the police to help anyway. He was mad with himself.

"Quick, they must have gone to the cable car station!" he shouted. They set off as fast as their condition allowed. With any luck there would not be a car going down yet and they would catch up with the two men at the station. But lady luck was not with him. The cable car had just started on the downward journey. The two men must be inside it. Rowan was familiar with the layout and was into the upper station in a flash.

By communicating with the lower station they managed to get the cable car stopped about a third of the way down.

De Villiers used the telephone in the upper station to phone through to police headquarters in Cape Town. He needed to have the lower station sealed off and the area around it cleared. It was a relatively short call as even senior policemen did not argue the toss with BOSS.

It was then that de Villiers recalled the conversation with the attendant on the way up.

"Is that the car with the vandalised radio?" he asked. "Has the radio connection been restored?"

"Sorry no; we are still working on it."

"So how the hell are we going to communicate with those guys?" De Villiers looked at Rowan.

"I don't know," answered Rowan. "I guess we better just get down to the bottom so that when the car is finally brought down we can be there to arrest our men."

De Villiers looked again to Rowan for help. "How do we do that without the cableway in use?"

"I hope you are fit," responded Rowan. "Because we are going to have to run down on foot. It's possible but it is not easy and time is not on our side."

"You can say that again; I don't know how much those guys know about what is in that flask. We have to set up some mode of communication before they get agitated enough to do something foolish."

"Follow me," said Rowan and set off at a jog. He shouted over his shoulder as they moved as fast as the terrain would allow.

"The most direct way is via the Platteklip Gorge. I've never gone down it but I have come up it a couple of times, so I know the way. The first time I came up with the family and it took two and a half hours, the second time on my own and it was just on the hour. I guess it should take about three quarters of an hour or so to get down this way."

They reached the lower station to find George Deacon, Divisional Commissioner of Police for the Western Cape, waiting for them. He had only conceded command of this operation after coming under heavy pressure from Pretoria. He had ordered his men to alert him the moment anything seemed to have gone wrong. He did not know what was in the container. He suspected it was plutonium. He took his responsibility for the safety of Cape Town very seriously.

"Good morning, Mr de Villiers; I believe you have run into some trouble. My orders are to give you all possible assistance. I must tell you that before I can do that I need to know the details of this case. What is in this container that is so important?"

De Villiers ignored the question.

"Have you been able to establish how many people are in the cable car?" he asked.

"Yes, there are ten in the car coming down and just four in the one going up… But I won't be diverted, what is in the container?"

De Villiers decided this was not the time to parry words. He needed the Commissioner onside.

"The canister contains a very powerful biological agent. It has the capability, depending on where it is released, to infect thousands of people in the most horrible way. It is a virus you may never have heard of – Ebola. Believe me, you don't want to take any chances at all with this bug. Obviously it will infect more people if released in a densely-populated area. I have had the cable car stopped because it is in a relatively remote position. Even if they throw it out it should not be a problem unless someone is unlucky enough to be close to where it breaks open. But if we bring them down and they discover a way of releasing the contents it will almost certainly contaminate someone. It only has to infect one person and you could have an epidemic." He hoped he had got the point across.

"I see," responded the Commissioner. "Thank you for being direct with me – you have my full cooperation; what can I do to help?"

"Is there any way of communicating with that cable car?"

"No, I'm afraid there is not. The radio connection is out. We may get it back. Problem is, it is the weekend and they won't get on to it until Monday."

"You referred to a car going up. Is there more than one stopped?" asked de Villiers.

"Of course; they are counter-weighted; as one goes up one comes down."

"So the four people in the car going up are stranded as well?"

"Yes. It's lucky there are only four; normally there would be far more and it could get very unpleasant."

"That's just bloody *lekker*!" exclaimed de Villiers sarcastically. "I hope they don't have any pressing engagements."

Ever since the cableway had been brought to a halt, de Villiers had been thinking about how they would communicate with the men inside. Now the time had come for him to voice the only solution he had been able to think of.

"I am going to have to be lowered onto that cable car from a helicopter," he said.

"Don't be ridiculous; all that will achieve is your early death and I will still have the problem." The Commissioner was dismissive.

"No, sir, it is going to have to be done. It's vital that we establish communication with the car as soon as possible. Unless you can get the radio connection working there is no other way, is there? Can you think of one? I'd be really grateful if you could."

There was no response and de Villiers continued.

"We can start the cableway rolling again and have an armed response unit at the lower station. But they would just use the other seven passengers as hostages to barter for their own safe passage. They will probably do that anyway, but as long as they are swinging around two thousand feet in the air we will at least have a bit more going for us in negotiation."

There did not seem very much more to say and just after 2 p.m. de Villiers was airborne in a South African Navy helicopter from the Simonstown naval airbase. He had trained with the army and had jumped from aircraft before but he had never been winched down, as he had seen done in air-sea rescue operations. Ruefully, he thought, there was a first time for everything.

They gained height quickly and were soon hovering over the stranded cable car. It had completed only about a third of its journey down and was, as de Villiers had said, around two thousand feet above ground. It sat stationary, swinging slightly in the afternoon heat. The helicopter seemed to be hovering an inordinately high distance above the cable car. De Villiers decided the pilot's perspective was doubtless a good deal superior to his.

They strapped him into his harness and he sat at the open door with his feet dangling over the edge. To think this was his idea in the first place! He must have a death wish, he decided. And then he was out in space swinging quite sickeningly from side to side beneath the hovering helicopter. He hung there with absolutely nothing between him and the Cape far below. Behind him and to his left, the sea stretched to the horizon, a brilliant blue. Far below the dark green of the land with the cream-coloured scratches that were roads and away over to his left Lion's Head. He concentrated on not getting the wire that held him twisted, otherwise he would have to spin to untwist it.

Slowly but remorselessly the gap between himself and the helicopter widened. He could see the cable car drifting slowly up to meet him. He was still swinging through a considerable arc. Getting on to the top of that car which itself was swinging slightly was going to be a nightmare. The cable from which the car hung was a further hazard.

For eight minutes that seemed like eight hours he just hung in space while the forces of gravity and inertia were allowed to come into play. Gradually the arc through which he was swinging became less. When he estimated that there was a fighting chance that he would not be cut in half if he struck the cable, he signalled to the winch man to let him down.

He struck the cable with a force that knocked every last breath of air out of his lungs. Somehow he found the strength to cling on. Then they edged him slowly down towards the car. When he reached a point over one end of the cab, he paused to summon his composure. This was the most hazardous part of the operation. If he missed his foothold he would fall from the cable car roof. Although his harness should save him, he was not at all sure whether the weight of his fall and sudden stop would be enough to destabilise the helicopter and even bring it down. He would go falling into space and then inevitably back, smashing right into the side of the cable car. Even if they managed to winch him up to avoid the car he would be sliced in half by the cable above.

He looked at the red roof of the cab below him. It shone in the sunlight and against it the olive green framework from which it hung showed up clearly. The frame rose from the roof of the cab to the cable in two converging struts which met under the pulleys from which the whole edifice was suspended on the cable. A strengthening strut, running horizontally mid-way up the converging arms, gave the frame the appearance of the letter 'A'. Down the vertical stroke of the 'A' ran a ladder. Looking down he counted the rungs of the ladder. There were eight. He decided to go for the second from the top. Steadying himself with his back to the cable he signalled for them to let him down. Somehow his feet found the ladder and he grabbed a black square-shaped bar on the apex of the 'A'. He had made it. His legs were quivering with the tension and reaction as he clambered slowly down the ladder.

He took from his pocket the card on which he had written in capitals:

I HAVE NO GUN. I WILL OPEN THE ROOF HATCH A FEW INCHES TO ALLOW US TO SPEAK.

He lay down flat on the roof and then, with his stomach churning at the thought of what he was going to do, he reached down over the side of the cab. He held the note in his right hand while he clung to the framework of the cab with his left. He had attached it to a stone to prevent it being blown away; he threw it through the open side onto the floor of the cabin.

He had been shown how to undo the maintenance hatch in the roof and he set to work. After a few minutes he had the hatch open just a crack but enough for what he needed. He shouted through the hatch.

"Listen carefully! This cable car has been stopped because there are two men in it who are wanted by the police. They have with them a canister containing a dangerous substance. This car will not be moved until that canister is handed over to me. If you wish to hand it up now, well and good." He paused but knew he would get no response and continued. "Otherwise, signal by waving some white clothing when you are ready to do so. The car is under constant surveillance and we will see your signal. Your position is hopeless. The sooner you give up, the sooner you will be allowed down."

There was silence apart from the soft moaning of the wind then a voice shouted back, "You listen. You know what in this. You get car go again. Else I throw. Many people die." The English was fractured but the meaning clear.

De Villiers responded. "That will not help you. I repeat, this cable car will not move until you surrender. I repeat, your position is hopeless and you should give up now."

There was no reply and warily de Villiers got to his feet. The sight of Cape Town spread out beneath his feet churned his stomach. All he was thinking about as they winched him up was that he would probably have to go through it all again.

Half an hour later he was back with Rowan and the Commissioner.

"How did it go?" asked Deacon.

"No progress at present. I told them their position was hopeless and the sooner they gave up the better for everyone."

"What was the response?"

"A raspberry."

"So what now?" Deacon was sounding impatient.

"Now, nothing," replied de Villiers. "Just let them sweat for a bit. I have been in touch with a British guy, Geoffrey Pritchard, who is a big shot in their anti-terrorism set-up. He was in charge at a siege in a place called Balcombe Street in London recently. He was also closely involved with one at a Spaghetti House hold-up in Knightsbridge. The Dutch people brought him in as an advisor during a train siege they had there not long ago. He says you just have to keep everything as low key as possible and sit it out. It seems to work, but it is hell on the nerves. Almost everyone wants to take some sort of action but that's not the modern thinking."

George Deacon was not the sort of man to be impressed with 'modern thinking' but kept that to himself.

"OK, Mr de Villiers. I shall return to my headquarters and you can get me immediately if you need me. In the meantime, good luck with your theory."

De Villiers settled down to sit it out.

Chapter Twenty-Five

Natal – Sunday 23rd October 1977

Harvey drove along the coast road north of Durban. It had taken the rest of the week to hack through the jungle of bureaucracy that went with apartheid. Eventually Van Ruyen had come in on Friday morning saying he had enjoyed a 'eureka' moment the previous night. Shifveld Reach was, he reckoned, a resort north of Durban called Sheffield Beach. Further searching unearthed the fact that Jardine actually owned a small property there.

Harvey swung the car to the right off the main road and towards the sea. It took him some time driving around winding tracks, but in the end he had the place marked. It was a holiday villa overlooking Sheffield Beach. It had spacious sloping lawns. It was the ideal setting for sipping ice-cold Castle lager in the evening while gazing out across the Indian Ocean… if only.

He parked the car half a mile inland and approached the villa on foot as inconspicuously as possible. He could have driven up with the horn blaring. There was no one there. Jardine had flown. There was nothing to do but to return to Durban for the night and then back to Johannesburg to await developments.

The developments came sooner than he had anticipated. Under the windscreen wiper of his hire car was a white envelope. Harvey opened it and read.

To Mark Harvey

I thought you would find me. Although I had kept the chalet a secret I assumed the great Mark Harvey would ferret it out. A lot has happened in recent weeks but circumstances are not materially altered by those events.

I am still prepared to reach an accommodation with you. That being the case, I suggest you come to room number 1814 in the Elangeni Hotel in Durban at 6 p.m. tomorrow night. I stress that you must come alone. Remember I still have the EV77.

Neil Jardine

Harvey sat in the car thinking over the situation. He knew that whoever had slipped the envelope under the windscreen wiper would be long gone by now. The only practical course was to meet Jardine as suggested and play it from there. It seemed clear that Jardine was still prepared to part with the EV77 if a deal could be done. His best option would be to go and try to do such a deal. He noted that Jardine said he had *the* EV77. He presumed therefore that the third canister was wherever Juanita had taken it – Chimoio probably.

He drove pensively back to Durban and spent the afternoon checking with de Villiers on developments in Cape Town. Later he tried, without success, to rest in his hotel room.

Chapter Twenty-Six

Cape Town – Sunday 23rd October 1977

Darnie de Villiers had not conducted a siege before. As he had explained to George Deacon, he knew the theory and had taken good advice. The reality was a very different thing. He was a worried man. His plan had been to leave the cable car hanging there all night and then make another attempt to speak to them at dawn. He would also take some water with him. There were other people in the car besides the two who had been sent by Havanestro. He assumed from the accent of the one who spoke that he was Russian; probably they both were. He didn't want a raging thirst driving the Russians to do something desperate.

A gaggle of newsmen had gathered at the lower station. Apparently a relative of one of the people held in the cable car had reported them missing. To bring the cable car to a halt on a Saturday afternoon had become news all over Cape Town. At first it was assumed to be a running fault. As time wore on it began to take on a greater significance. A substantial police presence caused additional curiosity. However, apartheid South Africa was not a place to argue with the police and the small crowd was held well back. Television coverage was primitive compared to the American and British models.

Darkness fell. To see the lights of Cape Town from the

cableway at night is a breathtaking sight. The beauty of the panorama was somewhat lost on those imprisoned in a cable car hanging two thousand feet in the air. The two Russians sat hunched against one end of the cable car. The other seven passengers were sitting on the floor in the centre. The attendant was at the opposite end. At first there had been very little conversation; the majority assumed it was an engineering problem that had brought the cab to a halt. There were a British couple in their mid-twenties, a family of Germans – mother, father, teenage boy and ten-year-old daughter, a South African man in his late twenties and the same attendant who had taken de Villiers and Rowan up in the morning.

After a while the German man had asked the attendant if this was a normal occurrence.

He was told that it was unusual but not unknown. They had all become progressively more restive. Being stranded two thousand feet in the air with no explanation about when the car would move again began to get to them. The little German girl began to cry.

Their concern turned to fear when they heard the helicopter and de Villiers threw his note in through the side of the car. Then they realized they were in a siege situation. The conversation between de Villiers and the Russians did not require any interpretation. They knew they were in for the long haul. The two females began to get very concerned about the lack of any toilet facilities on board.

The night wore on and de Villiers and Rowan each tried to get some sleep while the other remained on watch. The worst time was between 2.30 a.m. and 4.30 a.m. when the circadian rhythm brought a physical and mental low. De Villiers was depressed and pessimistic. But then the sun started to rise over the Indian Ocean to the east. The time had come to take action. Now the moment was at hand he remembered the sickening lurching feeling in his stomach as he swung in the air trying to get a foothold on the cable car.

He made it on to the roof in the same way as before. This time he opened the hatch wide enough to lower the two-litre container of water he had brought with him for those in the cab. Conditions were deteriorating. The stench of human excreta came up to meet him as he opened the hatch. De Villiers could see that the two women and the children were very upset. The three men were trying to look tough but were at a loss to know what to do. The German father was more concerned about his wife and children than anything else. The British back-packer was trying to look as if he was comforting his girlfriend. In reality she was made of sterner stuff than he was. If anyone was going to attempt to overpower the Russians it was going to be her and the young South African.

"Thought any more about coming down?" he shouted.

The moaning of the wind was his only answer.

"I'll come again at dusk."

The sun rose and beat down mercilessly on the stranded cab. De Villiers had arranged for water to be sent up to the other car which was also still stranded. That was not quite such a hazardous undertaking as it was at a much lower altitude and there was no danger from the occupants. Nevertheless it was an extremely unpleasant experience for them just hanging there, not knowing why or for how long. The heat in both cabs was uncomfortable although the open sides allowed some air through. Still there was no sign of surrender.

Police Commissioner Deacon had appointed a police spokesman to deal with the ever growing media interest. Fortunately he was well chosen. He hit the right balance between uncompromising toughness tempered with concern for the innocent captives.

De Villiers went up again at dusk taking with him more

fluid. He was limited in what else he could provide. He wanted to give food to the innocent captives. The reality was that any food would be commandeered by the Russians.

It was a beautiful sunset, the sun an orange blaze over the Atlantic Ocean to the west.

"Surely you're ready to quit now," he shouted through the hatch.

Only the wind answered him and suddenly de Villiers was concerned. The wind was answering him a little too strongly for comfort. The wind is a very capricious lady at the Cape and a storm can be whipped up in no time. His eyes swept the bay and his fear was confirmed. There were white horses dancing on the waves as far as he could see.

"There is a storm brewing. I advise you strongly to quit. It will be very unpleasant up here tonight."

He did not expect a reply but suddenly someone was shouting back to him.

"Take car down – have aeroplane – fly Mozambique – we not open bottle – take people – let go in Mozambique."

De Villiers brought to mind everything he had been advised to do; play for time to lower their expectations and resistance. The wind was beginning to howl menacingly and was whipping at his feet. The helicopter pilot was signalling for him to be winched back up without delay.

"No deal." His voice was harsh. "This cable car goes nowhere until you give up the canister." He slammed the hatch down and signalled the chopper to winch him up.

He got away none too soon. The wind began to toss the cable car around like a dog shaking a rat. All night long it blew. De Villiers could only guess at what sort of a nightmare it must have been inside those cabs. They must have been sick with the constant motion. The fear that the cab would be blown clean off the cable must have terrified them. But he could do nothing. Even if he had wanted to there was no way to move those cable cars in that wind. By morning he felt their resistance must crack; no one could stand that sort of battering for any length of time. It was the sort of night to admit defeat.

But they didn't. They swung there all the next morning. Matters were becoming very difficult to handle on the ground. Now it was not just the South African media that was alerted. An American television crew had arrived and was very much less inclined to accept the bland assurances of the police spokesman. They pressed hard for more information. There were women and children in that cable car and they would be in a bad way by now. The children in particular were a concern. If someone died up there this would become global news.

De Villiers was beginning to seriously doubt the strategy. They had rigged up a telephone connection and he decided to ring Van Ruyen.

"Yes, Darnie; how's it going?"

"Nothing at all at present. I'm getting worried about the other people in the car. There are women and children in there. I am dead worried about anything happening to them."

"Courage, my friend." Van Ruyen was completely matter-of-fact. "If we lose a couple of them that will be better than an Ebola epidemic in Cape Town." He sounded as if he was discussing losing a couple of branches in order to prune a rose bush. "Stick it out."

With that he rang off.

De Villiers now knew he was going to be left to carry the can if anything went wrong.

He was a worried man. Then Rowan suddenly shouted.

"Look! The window! A white cloth! They're quitting!"

De Villiers was bound into his harness and once more flown up above the cable car. He was lowered onto the roof of the cab. He opened the hatch just a little way, wary lest a trap was being set.

"Are you ready to hand over the canister now?" he shouted.

There was a slight pause and then a voice came back to him from inside the cab. "I give to you."

It seemed that the surrender was complete but de Villiers was still suspicious. He lay full length on his stomach and reached down through the hatch. The man below meekly handed up the flask.

Whether it was sheer relief that caused his lapse in concentration de Villiers could never say. What he could remember later was simply that he tripped. He was standing on the red roof of the car and just by his left ankle was a cross-member of the green frame. As he stood up he stepped backwards and with a thump, a clatter and some desperate scrabbling he went over the side of the cable car and down into space.

A million things seemed to go through his mind. Above all he must not let go of the canister. He fell about twenty feet before the slack in the rope was taken up. With a jar that just about severed every sinew in his body, it snapped taut. Unbeknown to him the helicopter pilot was fighting for all their lives to keep the aircraft from being totally destabilized. Then he was swinging out into space; swinging in an arc of death. On the return journey he would quite probably smash into the cable car. His only hope was that the helicopter winch man would see his plight and somehow manage to winch him up in time.

But there was no way they could winch him up far enough in the seconds available. He also knew that there was no way he could hold onto the canister if he did hit the cable car. The consequences for dropping it were too appalling to contemplate. In those few seconds he acted simply on instinct. He lobbed the canister in a desperate lunge. Mercifully he saw it go through the open side and back into the cabin.

That was the last de Villiers saw of it as he swung back towards the cab. He could see as he approached it that they had not winched him up. They had left him as he was, judging that he had enough rope to pass under the car. The rope cracked against the side of the cab and then de Villiers felt as if a giant hand was ripping his every bone and muscle apart. He spun a few times but gradually the spinning and swinging slowed and stopped. Amazingly he was still attached to the harness.

He was still alive.

He did not know where the canister had fallen, but assumed it was somewhere inside the cabin and they would have to start from scratch again. He tugged on the rope and slowly they started to winch him up. Only his lightning reactions saved him. As his head reached the level of the cable car roof he saw with horror that a man was lying full length on the roof, arm raised, gun in hand ready to strike. Obviously the man had seen de Villiers fall and had seized the chance to regain the initiative. If he could use the canister by threatening to throw it he might be able to take de Villiers by surprise. He might then get himself into the harness and force the helicopter at gunpoint to fly him away from Cape Town. It was a totally impracticable idea, born of desperation and it was never going to succeed.

De Villiers jack-knifed himself sideways and then leapt for the roof of the cable car. The two men went down in a sprawling mass of flailing legs and arms, striking at each other in sheer desperation. De Villiers saw the other man get away from him and clamber over the green frame and on to the ladder leading up to the cable. He lunged after him and in moments they were on the ladder grappling with each other. The terrifying void yawned wide below them as they fought for their lives. The end was sudden. The man without a harness slipped and lost his footing.

With a piercing scream of terror he went over the side off the cable car and fell to his death.

De Villiers clung to the ladder sweating and trembling. The second Russian had had enough. He was clearly shattered by what had happened to his comrade. He passed the canister up through the hatch without another word.

Regaining his composure de Villiers noticed that the wind had sprung up again. He was not being winched up; nor was the helicopter hovering. It was flying out over Cape Town Bay taking him on the end of a rope, at one hundred plus miles per hour.

After all he had been through he did not think that anything could make him feel ill again. He was wrong. The sensation of flying out over the sea dangling on the end of a rope was terrifying and nauseating. And then he understood what they were doing. The wind was blowing almost directly from the west. They were flying due east out over the Indian Ocean. If out of sheer exhaustion or loss of consciousness he dropped the canister it would fall into the sea. The deadly virus would be blown eastwards away from Cape Town out into the ocean. The next landfall would be western Australia, thousands of miles away. By that time it would have dispersed.

At length they slowed. They winched him up still clinging desperately to the canister. Presently they landed at Simonstown.

The two cable cars were returned to the stations. The passengers were freed and the remaining Russian taken into custody.

The Cape Town cableway siege was over.

Chapter Twenty-Seven

Durban, South Africa 6 p.m. – Monday 24th October 1977

Mark Harvey stepped out of the lift on the eighteenth floor of the Elangeni Hotel. It was a modern building, a sky-scraper in a slight crescent shape. Harvey had learned from his research that room 1814 was at the front of the building, overlooking the beach and sea. It had a private bathroom and a balcony. He turned right and walked down a long corridor. He passed two men and then he reached room 1814.

He knocked on the door and stood back to one side. The door was opened and Neil Jardine ushered him into the room. The door clicked shut, locked, behind him. There was to be no easy escape that way.

"Well, we meet again, Mr Harvey."

"Indeed we do," replied Harvey. "I see you survived the Zambezi crocodiles."

"Yes I did, somewhat fortunate. I was sure one of us would get taken, but in the end we made it." As he spoke Jardine wiped some excess saliva from his mouth.

The two men faced each other across the small hotel room sparring until the business started in earnest.

"What can I get you to drink?"

Jardine tried to sound calm but Harvey noticed he looked more agitated than he had seen him before.

Perhaps the situation was getting to him.

"A Castle would be good."

The Castle was poured and the atmosphere changed.

"Right, Mr Harvey, let's talk business. I have the EV77 and you want it. I am prepared to let you have it for a price. That price is one million US dollars in a Swiss bank account. I will give you the number. You will also cooperate with me in a convincing staging of my death so that I may disappear to live happily ever after with my million dollars." Jardine rubbed his arm as he spoke.

Harvey played for time.

"Have you decided where to disappear to?"

"Yes I have, but needless to say I am not about to tell you or anybody else." Jardine's neck muscles were standing out rigid. Harvey thought the man was definitely getting very jumpy. "Suffice it to say that my ideals are not all a pile of ashes. I would still like to see the evil of apartheid destroyed. I just don't think that murdering thousands of innocent people in a fruitless attempt to start a revolution is the best way. The best way is quite different and that is my affair and mine alone." Jardine yawned. "Sorry, I'm not sleeping so well at present."

At that point Jardine's dream went sour on him. The two men whom Harvey had passed in the corridor were suddenly not outside the door any more. Harvey assumed they must have got hold of a key to the door. Whether that was the case or not one thing was certain. They were very much in the room with Harvey and Jardine. The older of the two men spoke in perfect English but with a Russian accent. Meanwhile the younger covered them with a very steadily held handgun.

"You will hand over the canister to me now."

"What the hell are you talking about?" blustered Jardine. He must have known he was finished but he would not go down without a fight.

"I'm talking about treason," came the reply, quiet but

deadly. “Betrayal of all the people in our movement and betrayal of all that we have worked for. It was necessary for us to go through with this meeting and listen to your conversation in order to be completely sure.”

He gestured in the general direction of the light fitting. Harvey supposed he was inferring that there was a listening device fitted there.

“Now you are condemned out of your own mouth. You will surrender the canister or we will kill both of you now and take it.”

There was silence in the room. Then, suddenly, Jardine was in action. The next few seconds seem to take place in slow motion to Harvey. There was the ‘phut’ of a silenced gun being fired and a fight of quite devastating ferocity ensued. Jardine fought with a fury that shocked even Harvey who thought he had witnessed most things. Jardine lunged into the younger man with the gun, who let out a cry of agony as his right arm snapped. The gun went spinning across the room and in a flash Harvey was on it.

A savage blow to the back of the neck of the younger man put an end to his participation in the proceedings, possibly to his life. Meanwhile Jardine had the older man pinned to the floor throttling the life out of him in a titanic struggle. It was over quite quickly and as the man died, Jardine rested for just a moment. A moment too long. Harvey struck him with the butt of the gun hard enough to kill most men. Jardine was dazed and rendered prostrate but he was tougher than Harvey could believe. He did not die.

Harvey ransacked the room in desperation looking for the canister of EV77. He found it in the most obvious place – the drinks fridge. He cursed himself for not thinking of it sooner. He turned. Unbelievably Jardine had recovered enough to stand. He was propped against the wall with an evil-looking knife in his hand – his eyes glittering as if he had a fever.

Harvey could not risk a fight. The flask must not be damaged. The chance of getting past Jardine, even in the latter's weakened state, was non-existent. Instinct took over. He stepped swiftly out of the room onto the balcony. Before he had time to let common sense kick in, he lobbed the canister onto the balcony directly below on the seventeenth floor. Refusing to look down at the sickening drop beneath him he went over the balcony like a cat. He could see that Jardine was recovering and starting to lurch across the room towards him. Somehow he had to drop into the balcony of the room below. As he dangled there it seemed to him inevitable that he would fall to his death. He had only seconds before Jardine reached the balcony and kicked away his hands from their hold on the balcony wall. He knew if that happened he would fall outwards and miss the balcony below.

In desperation his eyes swept the building. There was only one way. He did not stop to consider that it was madness. He worked his way desperately to the corner of the balcony where there was a pillar standing proud of the wall. It was smooth stone but it was all there was. He clung to it for dear life. His ankles were grazed, his legs and knees were grazed, his arms were grazed; even his chin was grazed, but in two or three terrifying seconds he landed in an untidy heap in the balcony of room 1714. He was alive. The canister was intact. He had been terrified it would break open when it landed. It seemed that the well-developed sense of self preservation of the scientist who designed it – Stuart Holder – had taken into consideration that one day some idiot might drop it.

He had no time to lose. Heaving himself up he pushed open the door into room 1714 and barged through. A young woman sat at the dressing table applying her make-up preparing for the evening ahead. It flashed through Harvey's mind that had he been James Bond the girl would have been naked. She was fully dressed. 'Can't win them all Harvey,' he said to himself. He was through the room and out into the corridor before she could move.

He ran along the corridor to the lift and pressed the call button. The lift arrived. Slowly, slowly the doors hissed open. But time was against him. Jardine had run down the stairs and was hurtling along the corridor. Harvey could see that if he got into the lift he would not be able to get the doors closed before Jardine got there. He took off down the stairs. Jardine hesitated. The lift would get him down far more quickly than Harvey could run down the stairs; but he would surely lose the Englishman who would dart onto one of the floors and escape to another staircase. Jardine set off after Harvey.

Both men were reeling by the time they reached the ground floor. Harvey felt as if he had been running down those stairs all his life. He went out through the lobby entrance. Luckily there was an open door beside the revolving door. He went straight through it and out into some gardens. He did not know where he was going; only that he must put distance between himself and Jardine. He was relying on the crack on the head that the South African had received to slow him down. Incredibly it was not doing so. As they reached the promenade between the main road and the sea he realized with disbelief that Jardine was actually gaining on him.

In desperation Harvey turned towards the sea. He was an adequate runner but clearly no match for Jardine. All those hours Harvey had spent in the pool at Manchester Grammar School being coached to represent them in the freestyle events were about to pay off. He could not believe Jardine would match him in the water. It wasn't much of a plan, but it was all he could think of in the circumstances. He would run to the water, throw the canister out to sea and swim after it and keep repeating the exercise until he was well clear of Jardine – always supposing the damn thing didn't sink. As it was supposed to be a spray Harvey assumed it would be under pressure and therefore would float. What a mess! The safety of thousands reduced to a swimming match between two men.

They went into the water with Jardine not more than ten metres behind Harvey. The flask flew into the air and about thirty metres out to sea. Harvey thrashed after it in an all-out crawl. He reached it and snatched a look behind him to see how close Jardine was. What he saw would stay with him for the rest of his life.

Jardine was knee-deep in the water standing stock-still with a look of utter terror on his face. Then quite suddenly with a howling shriek of anguish he leapt vertically into the air. As he came down he started thrashing the water in a frenzy of total insanity, clearly petrified that the water was attacking him. Gradually his maniacal activity worked him out of the water. With a terrified look at the sea behind him he began to run in a random lurching gait around the beach letting out insane, screaming, yelps of terror as he did so.

It was the manner of his gait that brought Harvey to an understanding of what was happening. The way he moved had something about it that reminded Harvey of the dog he had seen in the moonlight at Kilimatembo. With a sick horror he realized that Jardine was rabid. Now it became clear why the wretched man had appeared to have an excess of saliva, why he had been rubbing his arm where the bite had occurred, why he was so agitated and feverish, why he had not been sleeping – all symptoms of the imminent onset of full rabies. Most likely the stress of extreme activity had caused the untreated virus to reach his brain and the terrified man was reduced to a raving lunatic in dread of the water in front of him. Flecks of foam were gathering around his mouth as he took off towards the road.

Neil Jardine had not had much luck in his life. It began

with the trauma of Sharpeville. It progressed to the drug culture of university in 1960s Britain. It culminated in the consuming rottenness of Soviet conspiracy with its necessary bedfellows, violence and suppression. He never really stood a chance. But now the gods relented and did him one last favour. As he ran across the road there was no way the petrol tanker could stop. Neil Jardine died instantly.

Harvey found himself shuddering uncontrollably. He set the canister down and sat on a breakwater to compose himself. Then he picked up the flask and pushed his way through the gathering crowd.

"Just call the police," he said wearily.

MOZAMBIQUE
SALISBURY
UMTALI
CHIMOIO
RHODESIA
BEIRA

Chapter Twenty-Eight

Salisbury, Rhodesia – Wednesday 23rd November 1977

At 6 a.m. six Dakotas, each carrying twenty-four paratroopers, took off from New Sarum air force base in Salisbury, Rhodesia. In the first of them was Mark Harvey. He was paired with a Rhodesian SAS captain who was the only person who knew why Harvey was there.

"Who's flying this old bucket?" shouted Harvey jokingly. "Is he any good?"

"You bet – Bob d'Hotman – Flight Lieutenant – if anybody can get you there he will."

"We didn't expect so much low cloud, did we?"

"No – our boys have managed to hack into the Intelsat satellite weather transmissions to Europe which gives us a cloud map at ten every morning – but yesterday's forecast did not lead us to expect this today."

At 7.41 a.m. 'Operation Dingo' began. Afretair was a cargo airline run by Jack Malloch, a World War Two pilot. He had flown Spitfires. His flight commander had been Ian Smith. He now supplied a Douglas DC-8 which flew over Chimoio Camp in western Mozambique, fifty miles east of the Rhodesian border. Chimoio was Robert Mugabe's base for the bush war being waged against the Smith regime. The four jet engines created a deafening roar as the aircraft went into maximum climb mode. The purpose was to distract Mugabe's troops at early morning muster and to cover the sound of the approaching attack aircraft. Having realized that it was not a danger to them they were lulled into a false sense of security, little knowing what was to come.

Four minutes later three Hawker Hunters dived out of the sky to attack the sprawling complex that was Chimoio. Their armament had been changed due to the unexpectedly low cloud. They dropped Frantan bombs – locally designed napalm canisters. No sooner had the Hunters gone than four Canberra jet bombers took their place dropping their formidable load of 'Alpha' bombs. These were bouncing bombs that were primed to explode at low level thereby increasing their effectiveness as an anti-personnel weapon. Each Canberra carried three hundred of these deadly bombs. Chimoio Camp was devastated. What was not totally destroyed was ablaze.

The Dakotas were next. At 7.50 Harvey jumped from five hundred feet – a low altitude in order to minimize the time spent descending. Sniper fire from the ground was a very real danger. The sky was full of other paratroopers. The ground was a mass of humanity running in all directions.

Harvey saw his partner, the SAS captain, coming under fire from the ground. Drawing his gun, the captain returned fire. Distracted by the action he omitted to take the correct landing position and was lucky not to break his ankles and knees. But he was as tough as they come. He dived into a ditch and was returning fire within moments of his uncomfortable landing.

Harvey was just feeling relieved that he had not been hit by sniper fire when his parachute snagged a mopane tree. He was brought to a halt so suddenly that he was temporarily winded. He hit the quick release mechanism and crouched down behind the tree to recover. He made straight for Chaminuka Camp Complex C. British

Intelligence had established that Robert Mugabe stayed there when he was at the camp and that Juanita Havanestro was expected to be there at present.

He began his search. The carnage around him was shocking. He had seen nothing like it before. He had seen terrorist outrages. This was not a terrorist outrage. This was all-out war.

Harvey never saw her but she saw him. Dressed in her usual bright colours Juanita felt she was bound to be seen. Desperately she rolled in the earth to discolour her clothes. Then she tried to get out of the complex. At one point she lay prone among some corpses covering herself in blood. A Rhodesian soldier kicked her body to check whether she was alive. She gave no reaction at all and he passed on. She managed to get out of the camp. She hid in the surrounding wooded country. She never knew what happened to the canister of EV77 which she had brought from Johannesburg. It was three days before she managed to get out of Chimoio and down to Beira. From there she was able to return eventually to Kongwa in Tanzania to await further instructions.

The day wore on. Harvey had come under fire a number of times and had to take evasive action which interrupted his search. He took cover in a building within the Chaminuka complex.

Salisbury and Mike Yardley seemed a long way away. By coincidence he had known Yardley in London before Yardley had been posted to Rhodesia.

"How's our man in Salisbury?" he had asked when they met three days ago.

"Keeping pretty busy actually."

"How's the war going?"

"Not much change; Smithy could probably last another three or four years if he has to."

"Will he have to?"

"I don't know; there seems to be quite a lot of activity on the diplomatic front. It is pretty common knowledge that he will try to resuscitate the internal settlement deal with Muzurewa."

Harvey nodded – then he said, "Mike, I am going to have to take you into my confidence. What I am about to tell you has been sanctioned by the British, South African and Rhodesian authorities. Considering all three are working in entirely different directions with entirely different political priorities, you will appreciate that when they all actually agree on something, it must be pretty vital."

"Sure," replied Yardley; a puzzled look on his face.

"Rhodesia is about to mount a major operation codenamed 'Operation Dingo' against Mugabe's stronghold at Chimoio in Mozambique. Ian Smith was not keen on the idea originally – a number of reasons – it's a pretty high risk operation, he could lose most of his air force and he will bring down the condemnation of the world and his wife on Rhodesia."

"So why is he doing it?" Yardley had been surprised.

"Two reasons – first he has finally had it with the Anglo American plan. UK has lately become adamant that no settlement will be sanctioned that does not include the so-called Patriotic Front. So Smith has decided to go for the internal settlement with Muzurewa. To give it the best chance of success he wants to knock Mugabe out of the equation for the time being. He sees him as a more serious threat than Nkomo. Mugabe is based at Chimoio. He is very much the main man although he is not the military commander there; that's a guy called Tongagara. Smith hopes to put the whole complex out of action."

"You said there were two reasons?"

"Yes; and this is where it gets sensitive – and why I am involved. As you know Britain has a microbiological research centre on Dartmoor. Recently a top scientist there was forcibly kidnapped and brought to South Africa. He has been instrumental in developing a substance codenamed EV77. This is a toxic biological weapon based on a recently discovered virus. Ultimately there were three canisters of the stuff produced. One of them fell into the hands of a Cuban woman called Juanita Havanestro. She is working with the Black Liberation Front in South Africa. We have tracked her down to Chimoio. We simply have to get that canister containing the virus back. If the contents are ever released it could cause a horrendous epidemic."

Yardley spoke, half to himself, "So that's why Smith has changed his mind. He was in favour of a different action codenamed 'Operation Virile' to blow up some bridges in Mozambique. Just two days ago he suddenly did a volte-face and sanctioned 'Operation Dingo'. I see why now."

"My personal mission," Harvey had told Yardley, "is to make for Chaminuka Camp on the south-eastern border of the Chimoio complex. We suspect that Havanestro is there. We believe that she will not have let the virus canister out of her control. I have to go in, find it and bring it out."

As he sat, now in Chaminuka Camp, Harvey could well remember the look of incredulity on Yardley's face. Yardley had been silent for a while.

"Well good luck with that, Mark. Rather you than me."

'Too true, matey,' thought Harvey. He had been in some pretty awful holes in his life. None worse than this accursed place. Suddenly his thought process changed. He saw Susan Bennett striding down the fairway at Wentworth – but it wasn't Susan. Her hair was dark and her eyes were blue. God almighty it was Kate. He shook his head and got up. EV77 or no EV77 he was going to survive and get out of this hell hole.

Reluctantly he gave up the search at 5 p.m. There had been no sign of Havanestro and no sign of the canister of EV77. Mugabe was not in the camp either. How Harvey had not got himself killed he didn't know. But he was still alive. He was flown back with other paratroopers to Grand Reef, a forward base just west of Umtali.

Harvey learned that nobody knew precisely how many of Mugabe's troops had been in the camp or how many were killed in Operation Dingo. The most frequently given estimate put their casualties at three thousand killed and five thousand fled, injured. Incredibly eight thousand of the nine thousand in the complex had been either killed or put to flight. The Rhodesians suffered two fatalities and twelve wounded.

Back in Salisbury Mike Yardley was in triumphant mood.

"Well I guess Smithy has really knocked the shit out of Mugabe this time."

"Yes," replied Harvey soberly. "But the carnage was horrific. I have a nasty feeling, Mike, the Rhodesian whites will pay a heavy price for this in the long run."

On the next day, Thursday 24th November 1977, Ian Smith announced that he was ready to yield to majority rule in Rhodesia.

Chapter Twenty-Nine

Rye Golf Course, Sussex, England – Saturday 3rd December 1977

Tony Joy was in trouble. The eighteenth hole at Rye Golf Club runs along a saddle-back with a large dip on the left and thick gorse on the right. A somewhat weary slice and he was deep in the gorse. At sixty-one years of age he no longer had the strength to do anything but chip out sideways. He and his partner had needed a four to save the match with their two opponents. With Joy's partner in the dip, things were not promising. They failed. The good-natured banter lasted into the dressing room until the steward came to tell Joy he was wanted on the telephone.

His playing partners looked at each other knowing that they would be drinking as a threesome this evening. Tony Joy was a Queen's Messenger and in that capacity was sent all over the world at short notice. This time he learned the destination was Salisbury, Rhodesia.

He took the evening British Airways flight to Johannesburg. Next morning he boarded a South African Airways flight to Salisbury. Mike Yardley was there to meet him and handed him a large Manila envelope. Joy flew back to Johannesburg. The next day he returned on the British Airways flight to London.

At 9.30 a.m. on Tuesday 6th December he was in Geoffrey Pritchard's office. He handed him the envelope.

Pritchard opened it and sat staring at the contents for some time. Then he picked up the telephone and called Gordon Peters.

That night Peters and Stuart Holder's successor, now the top microbiologist in Boughton, flew out of the UK to Salisbury. They returned five days later and reported their findings.

Pritchard knew all now. He sought an appointment with the head of MI6.

It was a crisp December morning when Pritchard eventually sent for Mark Harvey.

"Come in, Mark, take a seat."

There was a large Manila envelope on his desk and he pushed it towards the younger man.

"Take a look at these," he said. After a pause he continued, "I should warn you they are not very pleasant."

Harvey looked sharply at Pritchard. What was the matter with the old man? he wondered. After all they had been through and seen together in Northern Ireland he could not imagine there was anything much worse to see.

But there was and suddenly he was looking at it. He was looking at a photograph of a scene that was more sickening, more horrifying and more appalling than anything he had ever seen before. In his heart he knew exactly what it was. It was Chimoio; of that he was certain. As he looked at the photographs a dreadful certainty gripped him. There were a seemingly endless number of African corpses just sprawled where they has died. There were a few others who could possibly still be alive. The whole scene was horrendous.

A low whistle escaped from his mouth.

"What the hell are these?" he asked knowing only too well exactly what they were.

Geoffrey Pritchard gathered himself.

"They are photographs taken by the Rhodesian

security forces; photographs of a civilian encampment quite close to the military camp of Richard Masingi at Chimoio. Ever since the November raid there have been rumours of some sort of civilian massacre together with vague reports of thousands dying of disease. These photographs are the evidence upon which the Rhodesian forces could be accused of an appalling atrocity."

"But these people did not die by Rhodesian bombs or guns," interjected Harvey.

"No, Mark; you and I know that. It has taken a little time and research to ascertain the actual cause of death but I can tell you now, without any doubt at all, that these people died and are still dying of the Ebola virus.

"What exactly happened?" asked Harvey.

"We don't know for certain. Both sides blame the other. ZANLA claim it was biological warfare waged by the Rhodesians. The Rhodesians are adamant that it was Richard Masingi. They claim that the Rhodesian strike on Chimoio was a killer blow for him. He thought he was finished; perhaps it was a last despairing attempt to halt the Rhodesians; perhaps he just wanted to take some of them with him; perhaps he did not truly understand the terrible nature of the weapon at his disposal or maybe he wanted to make the Rhodesians appear guilty of an appalling crime… On the other hand, maybe a Rhodesian soldier found it and released it. Maybe it just got damaged in the chaos of battle. I doubt that we shall ever know the truth."

There was silence in the room while the two men thought their private thoughts.

"How many died?" asked Harvey.

"Again we can't be certain but it is going to be thousands. They are in the midst of a full-blown Ebola epidemic. The problem was compounded by the fact no one there knew what was happening. They thought it was malaria. By the time someone realized it was something worse, hundreds had been infected."

"How can it have spread so fast?" asked Harvey.

"As you may know, it is part of their custom to wash the dead. Apparently that is the most certain way of catching it. An infected corpse is highly toxic. They have been dying in their hundreds."

Pritchard paused, his face deeply creased with concern.

"We know what happened; the Rhodesians know; probably the Soviets know. Everyone is so appalled by the implications that it is being swept under the carpet with utter finality. As we speak the bodies are being buried in several mass graves. Apart from the notion that there was some sort of civilian massacre and an outbreak of disease, the world's press knows nothing more. That is how it will remain."

There was no more to be said or done. Harvey got to his feet.

"Sit down, Mark." Pritchard's voice had a softer tone than normal. "I see you've put in for that leave we owe you over Christmas. Would you mind telling me what your plans are."

Harvey was immediately alert. Pritchard wasn't just going through the motions of an interested boss. His question had an ulterior motive.

"I am planning to go back to Tanzania for some golf. Susan Bennett is joining me – why?"

"Mark, you may want to cancel that."

There was silence as Harvey waited for elaboration. He was puzzled by the way Pritchard had expressed himself. The chief wasn't given to issuing orders by saying 'you may want to…' Harvey did not know what to expect. The one thing he was not expecting was what Pritchard said next.

"We have learned where Kate is. She's being held in Afghanistan."

Harvey was stunned. He should feel exhilarated.

Maybe that would come later. Now he just felt numb.

Pritchard was continuing, "You may know that West Pakistan regarded the loss of East Pakistan in 1971 as a humiliation. Prime Minister Zulfikar Ali Bhutto decreed in January 1972 that Pakistan should develop nuclear weapons. Kate was left there with the intention that she get as close to the operation as possible to keep MI6 informed on progress. It seems she got a bit too close and was captured. We lost all contact and that is where it stood until last week."

"What happened then?" asked Harvey.

"I don't know how much you know about Afghanistan. The country had a revolution in 1973 when Sardar Mohammad Daoud Khan took advantage of the absence of the king to abolish the monarchy and appoint himself president and prime minister. Earlier this year he brought in a new constitution but there is still considerable unrest. In July MI6 sent one of their people to report on what was really going on there. Our interest has been sharpened by the fact that the Soviets are getting involved; it is thought possible they will actually mount an invasion in the foreseeable future. Anyway, this man has discovered that a female British agent is being held in Helmand Province. The description fits Kate. We are satisfied it is her. How she got from Pakistan to neighbouring Afghanistan and why they are holding her we don't know."

Pritchard looked up from his desk.

"Mark, to be quite straight with you she may not be in a very good state. She has been in captivity for at least five years – perhaps much of it in solitary. We need to get her back to the UK. It will be a very hazardous assignment and it will require a top operative. MI6 want to second you from my team and send you. However, because of your previous relationship with her this is not an order; you do have a choice."

Harvey met Pritchard's eyes. "When do I leave?" he asked.

Chapter Thirty

Kongwa, Tanzania – Monday 12th December 1977

Kongwa was parched. There had not been a drop of rain since the end of the wet season in June. Now, at last, merciful release seemed to be on its way. The thunder had started in late November, rumbling ominously far away to the south over the plains of Zambia. Juanita Havanestro had become accustomed to the sound in the far distance gradually growing closer and hardly noticed it any longer. Today she had noticed it. She had noticed it because quite suddenly it had stopped. In its place had come an awesome silence that prickled the nape of her neck and covered her skin in goosebumps. She felt as if her hair was standing on end. By chance she caught sight of her reflection in the wing mirror of the Land Rover. She could not believe her eyes. Her hair *was* standing on end. And then she understood what the silence portended.

Sweeping up from the arid plains of southern Tanzania it came, roaring over the escarpment up to the highlands; bursting irresistibly right into the cracked, parched earth of central Tanzania. In the silence she heard, far away to the south, a rushing, hissing sound. Kongwa darkened to an eerie half-light. And then she could see it rampaging across the scrub towards her, bending the crippled thorn trees almost to the ground. Suddenly the silence had gone and in its place came the hissing she had heard in the distance transformed into a roar right on top of her. But first came the scent of it – the scent of blessed rain on earth dying of thirst; then it hit her drenching her to the skin in seconds.

The rains had broken and with them the invisible tension of the last few weeks was broken for her also. She had not realized what a slave man and woman are to the climate in which they live. She felt reborn. The frustration of failure was swept away and drowned in the deluge. She stood and let it cleanse her. Then she climbed into the Land Rover that was to take her to Dar es Salaam on the first leg of her journey to her new posting.

Her South African mission was over. It had not been completely successful. Harvey and de Villiers had thwarted her plans. The worst atrocity was being visited now upon innocent Africans, not on the authors of apartheid. However, one thing had been learned: apartheid South Africa would never be subjugated while the Shah of Iran ruled the world's third largest oil-producing country on the planet.

Juanita had never been to Iran. Major demonstrations were planned for January. She had been briefed on a man named Ayatollah Ruhollah Khomeini. She must not fail this time.

Epilogue

Pretoria 5 p.m. – 31st December 2013

It was his last day at work. For the past twenty years he had been part of the unit guarding the most famous and revered leader in the world. Now it was over. Nelson Mandela was dead. The old man had managed what everyone thought was impossible. He had overseen the transition of South Africa from apartheid to democracy – without bloodshed. He had been buried just over two weeks ago.

There had been difficult moments in recent years. Nelson Mandela was not without enemies. Attempts had been made by extremists to return South Africa to apartheid.

The man now clearing his desk took satisfaction from the thirty-five-year jail sentence passed just two months previously on Mike du Toit, the ringleader of a white supremacist group. They had been bent on killing Mandela but he had helped to foil the plot.

Now as he gathered his few belongings together he felt the satisfaction of a job well done. 'Madiba' had not been killed by a knife or a gun; he had died of old age.

His office had always been sparse; he was not a man for clutter. It had not taken long to clear it. His secretary had been very subdued when the time had come to say goodbye. She had shed a few tears.

But now he was completely alone. He had always said that he would stay in post until Mandela died. His allegiance to the old man was total; he regarded him as the greatest human being he had ever met. He smiled wryly when he recalled telling that British agent that Mandela was just a troublemaker. The old man was gone now and had no more need of his protection. He would watch some rugby and take that fishing trip to Malindi in Kenya that he had always promised himself.

He took one last look round the room and picked up the nameplate from the desk. He would not need that any more. Anybody who needed to know already knew the name of Darnie de Villiers.

The End

Author's note

This novel is a work of fiction. None of the main characters existed and they are not based on any real people.

However, the book is set against actual events and accurate dates.

Lothar Neethling existed. He arrived in South Africa as mentioned and held the position detailed. The transport of a blood sample from the Congo to South Africa, however, is fiction.

Project Coast was real but truly got into its stride in 1979 under PW Botha's personal physician, Wouter Basson.

The events surrounding the discovery of the Ebola virus are described accurately. The fact that it was suspected to have existed in Sudan also has been documented.

The date of Steve Biko's arrest and death is accurate.

The floods of 1975 in the Vereeniging area did occur.

The Soweto uprising in 1976 happened.

The letter from Cyrus Vance to Mr Botha in August 1977 is a copy of that held in the Woodrow Wilson International Center For Scholars.

The burning down of the Britannia Bridge took place on the date described and in the circumstances detailed although, of course, Bennett, Jardine and Fingleton played no part.

The crackdown by the South African authorities on 19th October 1977 happened.

Operation Dingo is a matter of history. Clearly ZANLA on the one hand and the Rhodesian Defence Force on the other have sharply differing perspectives. I referred extensively to *Operation Dingo* by J.R.T. Wood published by Helion & Company Limited, Birmingham, England and 30° South Publishers (Pty) Ltd., Pinetown, South Africa.

Ian Smith finally accepted the concept of majority rule in Rhodesia on the date given.

There were reports of widespread disease in the Chimoio area immediately following Operation Dingo. "Those who survived and returned to the camp discovered there was no food. If they found it, it was poisoned. We lost a good number of survivors to food poisoning." (Oppah Muchinguri, ZANU (PF)'s Secretary for Women Affairs.)

The dead were buried in mass graves.

Acknowledgements

The idea of writing this book seemed straightforward. The reality has been very different. I am greatly indebted to a number of people.

A few years ago I took what I imagined was a fair copy to Diana Cambridge at The Sherborne Literary Festival. Over the next few weeks and months she gently brought me to the realisation that considerable further work was required. Her input was invaluable.

I thank my faithful readers, Charles Sime (who valiantly read two different versions), Peter Jennings and David Joby. Also David's sister-in-law Noëlle Joby who, as a microbiologist, gave important advice. I stress that any remaining inaccuracies regarding microbiology are entirely my own and not hers.

I have to thank my stepdaughter Jayne who, when asking me what I wanted for Christmas did not flinch at the answer *Germs.* The book with that title by Judith Miller, Stephen Engelberg and William Broad published by Touchstone, New York, was very helpful.

I am grateful to Laura Deal of The Woodrow Wilson International Center For Scholars, who confirmed permission for me to use the letter from Cyrus Vance reproduced in the book.

I thank Simon Goodway who provided the diagrams of Africa that help keep track of where the action takes place.

I thank Jane Dixon-Smith who provided the design for the cover with speed and professionalism.

I particularly thank Helen Baggott who helped me get the book into a state where it could be published. Her patience and help in that and in subsequently guiding me through the publication process was indispensable.

Finally I thank my wife Pat who read various drafts and provided unflagging support and encouragement. That is important when the fifth re-write is not going so well.

Printed in Great Britain
by Amazon